Halfelfin

Book One of *"The Tales of Albion Trilogy"*

Other Works by R.J. Pommarane

The Tales of Albion Trilogy
"Halfelfin"
"Fae"
"Daemonic"

Short Story Collections
"Darkness in the Art"

Poetry Collections
"The Body Chaotic"

Halfelfin

Book One of *"The Tales of Albion Trilogy"*

R.J. Pommarane

Cover Art and Illustrations by
Heather Lewis

Sunfyre Books, LLC

First Printing: 2014

ISBN: 978-0-9903709-3-2 (paperback), 978-0-9903709-4-9 (eBook)

Sunfyre Books, LLC
PO Box 12024
Portland, OR 97212
www.sunfyrebooks.com

Cover Art: Copyright © 2014 by Heather Lewis
Author Website: www.rjpommarane.com

This one is for my Kevin:
I love you more than you will ever know.

Acknowledgments

First I would like to show my appreciation towards all the authors who have inspired me over the years: J.R.R. Tolkien, Lewis Carroll, J.K. Rowling, George R.R. Martin, C.S. Lewis, Terry Brooks, Jim Butcher, and H.G. Wells, just to name a few. I want to thank MP Brew, CEO of Sunfyre Books, for all his monetary and moral support as well as all those who helped with the editorial process. Many thanks to my cover artist, Heather Lewis, and my friend, Randi Mikels, for helping bring me and Heather together. Thank you to my sister, Tara, my nephews, Gabe and Tyson, and my niece, Ehko, for all the love you bring into my life. Most of all, I want to thank my mother for always encouraging me to dream and showing me the true meaning of unconditional love.

Table of Contents

Prologue
"Raanon Speaks"

"The wheel of time turns ever onward as war finds its way back into the heart of Albion."

"The long years of Albion began when the other Old Gods and I came from the Void to quiet the tumults of the living world and bring enlightenment to the burgeoning ranks of mankind. We raised the Great Pyramid on the island of Mu and watched as men flocked to our presence, building the Ancient City of Lemuria as their ancestral home. There were but a few faithful men. The vast majority remained in distant lands, in their warring tribes. No matter how we tried, we couldn't tame the violence in their hearts. Eventually they brought war to our doorstep. We were faced with a choice: fight against mankind, or leave behind the living world. We chose the latter and ascended forever into the Otherworld, but not before sending out a call into the wide universe, asking another race of beings to come and try their hand at bringing peace to the chaotic nature of man."

"Elfkind fared better than we did in befriending men. They raised the Eternal City of Atlantis with the Palace of Silver Light at its heart and took great care to earn the trust of mankind. Elfkind introduced their less evolved peers to the powers of magic, by way of the Art. A short line of Elfin Empresses ruled the four corners of Albion with benevolence and understanding but, even as they made their sacred code the law of the land, darkness crept into the living world in the form of a fallen god. Earlier, just before the arrival of Elfkind, the goddess, Tsira, descended into Albion and murdered the One God, Theis, absorbing the strength of his spirit into a ruby amulet that enhanced her magic exponentially. Tsira was punished and the amulet taken, finding its way into the hands of an even greater threat."

"Ragnar, God of the Twilight, had long kept secret his sycophantic desires for power and pleasure. When the Amulet of the One God fell into his hands, it gave him the opportunity for which he'd been waiting. Armed with the amulet, he descended into the living world with a vengeance and brought terrible war to Elfkind. In a desperate attempt to defeat him, the Elfin Empress Saavika Thirdborn sacrificed her earthly body to join her soul with her tiara, forever after known as the Autumn Crown. The crown of Elfkind was taken up by Saavika Thirdborn's daughter, the Lady Eanora, the Last Elfin Empress. But the war sewed the seed of discontent in the hearts of men and soon open revolts threatened the peace of Albion again."

"The men who rebelled against the Last Elfin Empress were led by a great wizard called Theron Kalenti. Theron used a form of spirit-magic to gather together the fallen souls of all his peers and fuse them to his enchanted ring, the Ring of a Hundred Souls, before going forth in open war against Elfkind. His forces stormed the Eternal City and surrounded the Palace of Silver Light. Theron Kalenti took the Last Elfin Empress hostage and forced her to relinquish the Autumn Crown. With the combined might of the Autumn Crown and Ring of a Hundred Souls, Theron cast a powerful incantation which caused Elfkind to vanish from Albion in near totality. Only three of the Elfkind remained, for they weren't present in the living world at the precise moment that Theron spoke his spell. These were the Lady Leanida, the Lady Caenara, and the Lady Rheis. Rheis went at once to the Eternal City and demanded Theron relinquish the Autumn Crown into her keeping. She succeeded in gaining control over the crown but couldn't topple the tyranny of the newly established monarch."

"The reign of the Wyt Kings was relatively short lived, considering the lengths the Kalentis went to securing their control over Atlantis. Theron Kalenti ruled peacefully for nearly twenty years but, where his determination to provide for his subjects was strong, his judge of character was his failing. He allowed his son, Eathon Kalenti, to fall in love with and marry the deadliest mortal woman ever to live in Albion, she who in time came to be known as the Witch-Queen."

"Lady Nerys Sanva started out as nothing more than an innocent noblewoman forced into a situation that drained her spirit and set her on the path to darkness. She was promised by her father to the harsh and unfeeling Lord Dernevariost when she was only a teenager before she endured years of abuse at his hands, until she had an affair with a young peasant man and unleashed the wrath of her husband. The Lord Dernevariost divorced Lady Nerys, throwing her out into the cold night with nothing, after beheading her lover in the most vicious manner possible. She swore she would have her revenge and, in time, she brought it to fruition. Once she was sure Prince Eathon was under her spell, she murdered her ex-husband, her former best friend, and the Wyt King himself, paving the way for Eathon to ascend to his throne. But Lady Nerys did not stop there. In her rage and lust for revenge, she struck down the Second Wyt King and assumed his authority, becoming the Witch-Queen and calling a terrible army of Undead to do her bidding."

"The Witch-Queen instilled fear into the hearts of every man in the living world for many years, until she was challenged by the wandering wizard, Anaximander. A terrible battle of magical might ensued, with Anaximander destroying the Ring of a Hundred Souls, feeding the Witch-Queen's power, and took her into his custody. She was deposited in the heart of the Marshland Forest where she lived out the rest of her days as a frail old hag. When it came time for her to pass away, Anaximander led her spirit into the Otherworld. While he was absent, another dark power rose to reclaim the lordship of Albion it once held."

"The Black Prince returned with such ferocity that the world was taken completely by surprise, overwhelmed by the might of his talisman, the Amulet of the One God. He devastated the Eternal City and utterly destroyed Tansapar, forever after known as the Ruined City. It seemed he would rule eternally but, even as his authority reached its apex, the wizarding clan known as the Wyt Robes journeyed to the Atland from their homes on the Isle of Ikaria to engage the Black Prince in battle. Their war was epic. The Black Prince was cast out of his body into the deepest recesses of the Void while the authority over Albion was placed tentatively in the hands of the Wyt Robes. But their reign would not last."

"The Temple of the One God, once an insignificant, foreign religion localized in the easterling isles, and Lemuria, had grown to such an extent under the leadership of their Matriarchs that their presence in the Atland was overwhelming. The Tetrarchs, or Priests, of the Temple willingly upheld the laws of the Matriarchs regardless of the political climate or repercussions. Soon the Temple was declaring open war on all practitioners of the Art, whether they worked the Light or the Darkness. The power of the Matriarchs grew, especially that of their leader, Faceless, until they were in a position to storm the Eternal City and take control of Albion. The Wyt Robes were sentenced to die at the stake but, even as they breathed their final breaths, they prophesied the coming of twin souls born of the two races, who would possess the power to destroy Faceless and bring peace to Albion forever. Faceless took the words of the Wyt Robes seriously and searched relentlessly for the twins of the prophecy. This is the story of those twins, the children of two worlds, faced with a mighty destiny as the first, the last, the only Halfelfin…"

Part One
"Apart"

"Sir Elam Orthelios and the Elfin Lady Caenara"

Chapter One
"Disassociated"

In the long years of the Eternal City at the heart of Albion, there was never a prophecy as important as that of the last Wyt Robes: Braanos, Maglos, and Nestor. As they were marched to the pyre, to be burned to death in the name of the One God, the three Wyts spoke in unison, foretelling the coming of twin souls with a power long unseen in the living world. They swore these twin souls would save Albion from the forces seeking to disrupt the natural order in their quest for absolute power. At the heart of these forces were the Divine Matriarchs, leaders of the Temple of the One God and rulers of the Eternal City. These five women had risen to power nearly overnight, waging a bloody war against the Wizarding Clans and utterly exterminating the Wyt Robes with ruthless efficiency.

The forces of light, the forces of darkness, and the forces of the One God had long been vying for supremacy at the expense of Albion. The living world had fallen into decay as violence swept through the traditionally peaceful Atlandish tribes. Plague and famine came to the Eternal City as the peasants starved and the nobility grew fat and lazy. The Tetrarchs who served as the priesthood of the One God relentlessly drove the Old Religion out of the Atland and demanded the conversion of the Atlandish people, despite their personal devotions and feelings. The One God had always been the deity of faraway Lemuria, taking hold in the Atland only within the last century. The struggle for power had brought chaos to the order and peace of Albion and each side saw the prophecy of the Wyt Robes as the means to destroy their enemies once and for all.

Unbeknownst to the outside world, the wizard, Anaximander, used a powerful talisman called the Ring of a Hundred Souls to draw the spirits of the fallen Wyt Robes inside him, fracturing his psyche and creating a hive-mind intelligence calling itself the Collective. The Collective was immediately aware of the meaning of the prophecy and went to share its revelation with the Elfin Lady Rheis, protector of the tropical kingdom of Ikaria and keeper of the Autumn Crown.

"We believe we know the meaning of the prophecy spoken on the pyre," said the Collective but he was greeted by only an apathetic stare. The Elfin Lady Rheis was unmoved by the Collective's words and instead addressed another concern that was plaguing her mind.

"You are not my friend, Anaximander," she said, "I sense seven different minds merged into one. I see Braanos, and Maglos…Nestor and the other four Wyt Robes staring out at me from your eyes but I do not see or sense Anaximander…where is he?"

"He is here," replied the Collective, *"he is sleeping. We are in control and we have need of your wisdom. We believe that you might yet bear children…twins fathered by one of the Mankind. You will give birth to the children of the prophecy."*

"Absurd," laughed Rheis, "I have never and will never take a man to my bed…it is against the laws of nature to mix the races. Besides, the prophecy spoke of twin powers rising in the east and we are in the south."

"But you are the last of the Elfkind…if the children are not born through you, who else could it be?"

"I will tell you nothing."

"I think you will…"

The Collective employed every means at his disposal to learn the truth from Rheis, while the forces of darkness and of the One God used their own methods to learn the same. Eventually, it became known that a second she-elf was still alive in Albion, living disguised as a peasant woman on the edges of the Sylveroad Woods in the east of the Atland. She was known as Caenara and she had married a man named Elam. Together they conceived twin sons and so the prophecy came to pass. The forces of light dispatched their wizards, the forces of darkness their minions, and the forces of the One God their army, all meant to converge upon the Sylveroad Woods and bring the infant twins into their keeping.

The soldiers of the One God were the first to arrive in the small village called Darendon. Elam and Caenara dwelt a fair piece from the village and had heard the commotion as the soldiers searched for the twins. Elam left their cottage to investigate and was terrified by what he saw before him. He came limping into the room, slamming the door and bolting it firm. He rushed over to his wife and infant sons crouched in the corner. The sky outside was filled with clouds, lit every few seconds by flashes of lightning and powerful claps of thunder that frightened the boys and shook the house. In the distance, there were a great many fires burning, not bonfires or brushfires, but houses and storehouses, stables and shops. The whole edge of the city was aflame and many dark figures could be seen darting from burning building to burning building brandishing swords and spears. Elam took his wife in his arms and hugged her close.

"It won't be long now," said Elam softly into his wife's ear, "you need to do exactly what I say. Save yourself, Caenara. You know I can't run with my injured leg. You have to think about the boys now."

"I won't leave without you," cried Caenara.

"You must! I'm not impervious to your powers, especially the ones you must invoke tonight, but the boys are. You must get them to safety. Take them back to Ikaria. Rheis will protect you."

Just then there came a loud pounding on the door, like someone was using a sharp axe to chop through wood, before the lock gave way and more than a dozen invaders wearing the tunics of the One God rushed into the room, brandishing their longswords, forged in the style of the Xani Barbarians. Caenara sobbed as the men advanced forward, not from fear but because she knew what she must sacrifice in order to secure the safety of her children. The twins were in small weaved baskets at Caenara's feet while Elam stood between his family and the invaders. If he had not hurt his leg in a recent riding accident, he would've drawn his sword and fought. His skill with a sword was exemplary and he may have been able to defeat the advancing warriors. The leader of the invaders, a madman called Gruun, stared into Elam's face, a sinister grin adorning his weathered face. For a few moments, they stood there, locked in an endless stare, each attempting to intimidate the other into submission. Then Gruun raised his sword and lunged forward. Despite his injury, Elam was able to dodge Gruun's attack three times before he was finally caught hard in the shoulder by his enemy's sharp blade.

"Now, Caenara," pleaded Elam, "do it now…"

"*Stop,*" screamed Caenara, not out loud but directly into the heads of the invaders and her husband. Gruun became frozen in place, paralyzed by the powerful psychic command. But the effect was only momentary and no sooner had Caenara started to move towards her husband than Gruun started to struggle against the enchantment. Her first plan, the one which would've saved her husband's life had failed and now she would have no choice but to resort to a more permanent solution.

As she stepped towards the center of the room, Caenara took on a different look, seemingly transforming from a meek and meager woman into an otherworldly being whose presence was fearsome to behold. She stood taller than any of the men and her shadow stretched out to cover every corner of the room. Her eyes became the color of molten silver and her hair brightened to a fiery red but the most notable transformation took place in her face. It became white to the point of being gaunt and contorted into a grotesque alien shape, erasing all vestiges of humanity that had been present in her only moments before. Finally, the mark of the crescent moon adorned her brow and shined with the same silvery light emanating from her eyes.

"*You come here with your swords and spears,*" said Caenara telepathically, "*bringing your violence and your hatred brandished like a righteous weapon against the innocent. You burn our homes in the name of your One God and spill our blood for mistresses who have only ever sought to deceive you. I name you the condemned...and command you to burn in the fires of your own creation, that the divine justice of Annatar strike you down and boil your flesh from your bones!!"*

As though they had been tied to a pyre above a stack of brambles, each of the invaders instantly burst into flames, screaming and flailing as they were consumed slowly by the enchanted fire. Caenara paid no attention to the invaders. Her attention was drawn to her husband, also painfully burning away. She rushed over to him and put her hands on what remained of his charred face, tears cascading down her once again human face.

"I am so sorry," she sobbed.

"You did what had to be done..."

Elam died while Caenara held his smoldering remains in her arms. After her tears had subsided, she picked up the baskets holding her sons, one in each hand, and rushed out of the cottage. There was no one alive in the fields outside the house. The invaders had retreated with their spoils of war after butchering the villagers. Caenara ran furlong towards a grove of trees in the distance which would provide her cover as she made her way towards the small longboat she kept docked in a hidden lagoon about three miles south. She was almost to the edge of the miniature forest when a bolt of crackling purple lightning struck the ground at her feet.

"Did you really think it would be that easy?" laughed a shrill voice Caenara had hoped to never hear again, a voice that terror and fear into her heart and mind.

From the nearby bushes stepped a short and stout woman shrouded in a black cloak, her rotting face indistinguishable amidst the shadows cast by her long hood. She had withered hands with long, scaly fingers and yellowed nails which twisted grotesquely into curls. Caenara dropped the baskets carrying the twins on the ground and then turned around to face her new attacker. She began to grow taller, once again transforming into her alien form, but before the process was complete the shrouded woman laughed again.

"Oh, I don't think so," she cackled and, with a flick of her wrist, she caused the shadows cast by the trees to come to life, wrapping themselves around Caenara as though they were ropes meant to tie her to the ground. She struggled against their power but she couldn't transform and was unable to access the full might of her powers.

"Oh how I have longed for this moment," sneered the woman.

"I am glad I can be of service, Idris. Now tell me, where are your sisters?" asked Caenara, "I'm sure they're nearby...you four are never apart...are they skulking in the shadows? Too afraid to come out into the light and face me?"

"We are here," echoed three voices in unison from behind where Caenara was held prisoner by the shadows. Two of the three were identical to Idris, shrouded and cloaked with deformed hands, but the third was a tall and beautiful young woman with alabaster skin and platinum hair. She could've passed for a princess in some foreign court and all those who gazed upon her became intoxicated by her looks.

"Aneira, Oryne, and Jadzia," smiled Caenara, "now that the famed Shadow-Weavers are all here, we can begin."

Suddenly there was a great burst of white light, as though someone had ignited a lantern as bright as the sun itself, blinding the Shadow-Weavers and freeing Caenara from her bonds. She instantly transformed into her Elfkind self and took flight, soaring towards Jadzia, the sister who was not covered in shrouds, and attacked her head on, knocking her to the ground before raising her hands and causing a sword to appear from nowhere. This sword was shaped like a scimitar, a blade carried by the easterlings, but it was made entirely from crystal and glowed as though the moonlight had become trapped within it. Caenara brought the blade down swiftly but Jadzia had already recovered, throwing something that seemed to be sand formed by shadows into Caenara's face. Caenara stumbled backwards, clawing at her own eyes and screaming from the intense burning sensation induced by Jadzia's 'black sand'.

Meanwhile, the source of the burst of light became apparent as a man emerged from the forest, a wizard armed with a long willow staff and dressed in the robes of the Green Order.

"Koneth atar aska'ani," echoed the voice of the wizard, as though it were thunder barreling through a ravine, "You will bow before the power of the Gods of Light, fallen sisters…"

Another burst of pure white light erupted around the Shadow-Weavers, causing them to scream in agony, for creatures of the darkness cannot endure the pure rays of light magic. The Shadow-Weavers tried to retaliate but each time they sought to use dark magic they were subdued by the wizard. Jadzia continued to fight with Caenara but even she was soon brought to submission. The wizard joined Caenara, who looked at him like an old friend reappearing after many absent years, and together they rounded on the dark sisters, intimidating them with their powerful presence.

"Is conjuring the *pure light* the only trick you can employ, wizard," spat Jadzia, her sisters standing at her heel, "we can also play such games, if that is what you wish…"

The world seemed to completely fade away as a blanket of darkness erupted from the sisters, shrouding their surroundings and depriving both Caenara and the wizard of their ability to see.

"You think me afraid of the darkness?" laughed the wizard.

"Fear was not our objective," replied Jadzia alone, "we meant only to blind you…to keep you from seeing us move…"

"No!" screamed Caenara.

The wizard made quick work of the blanket of darkness, willing it away as if it were an unpleasant smell being carried on the wind. Oryne and Idris had already vanished and Jadzia and Aneira were bent over the basket containing baby Aras. It took the wizard only seconds to realize what Caenara already knew. Arad was gone. Caenara hurtled herself at the remaining Shadow-Weavers, the air around her charging with the same fires that she had used to defeat the soldiers of the One God. For the first time that night, Jadzia looked afraid, grabbing Aneira by the arm and running off towards the woods, vanishing into the shadows as though they had stepped around a corner and out of sight. Caenara made to pursue them but the wizard placed her under a freezing enchantment, preventing her from moving and causing her to revert to her human form.

"Let me go, Tamriel," she spat viciously.

"Pursuing the Shadow-Weavers would be suicide," replied Tamriel, lifting his spell and setting Caenara free.

"That may be," cursed Caenara, "but they shall not have my son...I made a promise...take Aras to Rheis and keep him safe."

Tamriel knew what Caenara would do next and he attempted to stop her with a holding spell but she was too quick, disappearing in a puff of crimson smoke. Tamriel sighed dramatically and for the first time, his advanced age and physical infirmities became apparent. He leaned heavily on his staff as he walked over and picked up the wicker basket holding Aras. He stared lovingly at the baby sleeping gently, completely unaware of the loss of his brother and mother.

"I'm so sorry little one," he said to the baby, "it seems after only six months in this world, your life has already descended into chaos...perhaps you *will* be the one to save us."

Tamriel took Aras by way of a secret road from the burning village of Arunak, through the Sylveroad Woods, to a hidden lagoon on the edge of the Atland where a tiny sailboat was moored. He placed the baby beneath the small overhang serving as the underdeck and set sail, calling a favorable wind to carry his tiny vessel towards the island of Ikaria. The normally violent waves that prevented ships from safely navigating the expanse known as the

Southern Sea were calm and complacent as Tamriel took his precious cargo to safety. He meant to give Aras over to the care of the Elfin Lady Rheis and then return to the Atland. He had no idea that events had transpired that would alter the course of his and Aras' futures forever.

Chapter Two
"The Red Tower"

Jadzia and the Shadow-Weavers used the darkness like a highway to carry them unseen away from the Sylveroad Woods. Traveling in the shadows is much faster than walking, or even riding on the back of a horse, but the Atland is massive and their journey took many days. After the war installing the Divine Matriarchs to power and forcing the Wizarding Clans to flee from the Atland, the territories of the island had become intolerable towards the practitioners of magic. Those wizards and witches who remained stayed on the outskirts along the Wynterlande Forest where the power of the Matriarchs wasn't as strong. On the edge of the woods stood the Red Tower, a massive spire forged from red marble and sheets of gold, pointing upward like a giant finger stretched towards the heavens. Once the home of the elfin-sorceress called the Red Witch, the tower was abandoned after her demise, left to ruin in the rugged wilderness until a particularly malevolent Grey Robe named Araxim decided to claim the tower as his own.

Araxim, along with the Shadow-Weavers, was one of the Black Prince's most devoted servants. After the defeat and banishment of his master, Araxim took up residence in the Red Tower to plot a way for the Black Prince to return. Like the rest of the world, Araxim believed the halfelfin twins to be the answer. It was he that dispatched Jadzia and the Shadow-Weavers to retrieve Aras and Arad, stressing to the sisters that they must bring him both children for his plan to succeed.

The Shadow-Weavers were somewhat slow to return to the Red Tower, taking their time to spend the night beside a grove of willow trees. Jadzia was the most anxious about returning to Araxim without Aras. She, unlike her undead sisters, was susceptible to torture and could feel pain. Being immortal, she would never die from age or sickness but the point of a sword or a terrible spell would be capable of ushering her towards death and Araxim was skilled in the uses of both.

"Can't you shut that thing up?" spat Oryne, one of the undead sisters, as Arad wailed. He had been crying since they carried him away from his brother. The Shadow-Weavers were impatient and quick to suggest heinous solutions to Arad's fits but Jadzia kept a cool head.

"He's hungry," she said, "we need to find a way to feed him."

"Give him your tit," hissed Aneira, "ours will yield only dust but yours, yours may yet have some milk."

"You only bear milk in the months following childbirth and Jadzia is barren," sneered Idris.

When Jadzia made the deal with the Nameless Goddess that granted her immortality, she forfeited her ability to become pregnant. She hoped her resurrected sisters would be enough to quell the sadness present in all women without children, but she was mistaken. Her sisters were hollow and unfeeling, cold and callous. The Shadow-Weavers had become the embodiment of pure evil and, each day, Jadzia's control over them was growing weaker. She still held each of their souls alongside her own in the enchanted silver medallion hanging around her neck, but their power was becoming too strong for her to contain. Soon their souls would break free from the medallion and, if that day were ever to come, Jadzia would be left at their apathetic mercy.

"We should find a goat...I've heard goat's milk can nourish an infant in place of a mother's breast," said Jadzia.

"Anything to have some peace and quiet," replied Aneira before she and the other Shadow-Weavers vanished into the darkness, teleporting away to find dinner for the famished Arad. They were gone for nearly fifteen minutes before they reappeared with a start, a she-goat held tightly in their grip with a full teat. Jadzia emptied her water skin and gently coaxed milk from the nanny, cooing at her with gentle whispers until the water skin was overflowing. She pulled the tip of the water skin over on itself and then used a sharp pin from her hair to poke several small holes in it, forming a tiny nipple capable of feeding Arad.

When he was full, Arad went to sleep and the grove fell into silence. Jadzia nestled Arad into her bosom and covered him with her cloak as she laid down by a small fire she built to keep warm. The Shadow-Weavers kept watch as Jadzia and Arad slept, standing together in the darkness at the edge of the fire, wrapped in their shrouds, their faces obscured, except for their glowing red eyes.

"Do we really care what becomes of this brat?" asked Aneira, once she was sure Jadzia was asleep.

"Jadzia cares…and so must we," replied Oryne.

"I don't know about you two," said Idris, "but I'm getting tired of worrying about what Jadzia wants."

"Such insolence. Have you forgotten the power she holds over us?" said Oryne sharply.

"There's one thing I remember quite well," said Aneira, "and that's the power the Black Prince has over Jadzia…he nearly led her to her death once and us along with her. I say we free ourselves from her influence and return to our eternal rest."

"I agree," said Idris.

"There's only one way for us to return to our graves," said Oryne, "we would have to take Jadzia with us and I'm not willing to kill my own little sister, no matter what she's done."

"Don't you think she'd be better off?" asked Idris, "in this world, she will only ever be a puppet…serving the Black Prince and Araxim in the hopes of seeking revenge against an enemy that hasn't been seen in Albion for dozens of years. We have sat by and watched her try and try to no avail. Perhaps we should take her with us."

"We must render her powerless, for her own good," said Aneira.

"I will take no part in this," said Oryne.

"You were always my favorite sister, Oryne," said Jadzia suddenly as she sat upright, Arad still cradled in her arms. She looked from Oryne to the other Shadow-Weavers, like a stern mother glaring at a child throwing a tantrum in public.

The Shadow-Weavers drew back from Jadzia as she rose to her feet and strolled towards them.

"You think you have the strength to make me powerless?" sneered Jadzia, "I dare you to try…"

While Oryne and Aneira stared fearfully at the ground, Idris raised her hands offensively to cast the most potent curse she could muster but, before she blinked, Jadzia waved her hand and Idris fell lifeless to the ground. She looked like a corpse which had been unearthed by grave robbers, her limbs twisted in on themselves and her face planted in the dirt.

"Your turn, Aneira," smiled Jadzia but Aneira didn't attempt to attack her, staying still at Oryne's side.

"Wise decision."

Jadzia waved her hand again and Idris' corpse took a deep, raspy breath, uncurling her limbs and standing to join the other Shadow-Weavers. If their faces weren't obscured by their hoods and shrouds, Jadzia would've seen their glares. Even so, she could feel their discontented subservience.

"Now I trust I can return to my rest without any more talk from you three," said Jadzia sternly.

Jadzia laid back down by the fire and the Shadow-Weavers sat silently beside her. Arad woke up twice during the night and Jadzia fed him. He remained quiet and sleepy even as the sisters rose the next morning. The sun was especially high in the sky, making it impossible for them to reenter the shadows. They were forced to take to the dusty old western road, moving slowly through deserted villages and brackish, withered woods, towards the highlands in the northwest of the Atland. The journey took hours and they were forced to stop and rest twice more before they rose to a dark, stormy sky, allowing them to travel again through the shadows. In just a matter of hours, they emerged on a wide rocky road at the edge of the enormous Wynterlande Forest. The protection spells around the Red Tower extended outward for miles in every direction and made it impossible for the sisters to take refuge in the darkness. Luckily, the road was destitute. The local Wildermen and Gnomes avoided the tower, not from a fear of the darkness but of magic in general.

The tower stood like a tall monolith reaching towards the hazy heavens, its walls forged from bright red bricks of marble overlaid with sheets of gold bullion. It was surrounded by overgrown hedges and thorny brambles, while many of the windows were cracked or missing their glass entirely. The Wynterlande Forest loomed eerily next to the tower, casting a deep shadow across the grounds. The sun was setting behind the canopy of the trees and a dull orange glow was present in the windows of the tower's first floor. Jadzia and the Shadow-Weavers stopped at the edge of the overgrown, untended gardens as Jadzia was overtaken by fear. She had half a mind to turn around and run into the forest but, as she stood there pondering her choices, an eerie voice rose on the wind.

"Why do you hesitate, dearest?" said the voice, *"Surely you have nothing to fear from me."*

The doors leading into the tower swung open, symbolically ordering Jadzia to enter. She drew a deep breath, wrapped her arms tightly around Arad, and rushed through the brambles and hedges to the tower, disappearing inside with the Shadow-Weavers at her heels. The doors snapped shut with a loud clap before the gardens returned to silence.

The interior of the tower was unlit and desolate. There was no furniture, nothing adorning the walls, and no rugs to dull the harsh cold of the marble floors. The air was stale and filled with dust as Jadzia conjured a small orb of orange fire to light the eerie passageway in front of them. Jadzia and the Shadow-Weavers were wary as they made their way to a large hall at the heart of the tower, the only room with all its windows still intact.

Seated on a large wooden chair, by a hearth on the far wall, sat a tall, lanky man dressed in black robes. He had a full black beard that obscured his long, narrow face and asymmetrical jaw, while his head was as bald as the head of a newborn falcon. He looked like a miserably unhappy man with a permanent scowl and brown eyes glaring with cynicism and disgust.

"What took you so long?" asked Araxim without standing.

"There were complications," said Jadzia, staring down at Araxim's feet, "we were not the only ones to come for the babies."

"The Atland Enforcers?" asked Araxim.

"And Tamriel," replied Jadzia.

"They must've known we were making our move tonight," said Araxim, "but the question is how…we must have a mole somewhere in our ranks. Idris, take your sisters and root it out."

Without looking at Jadzia, the three Shadow-Weavers retreated back down the passage that had brought them to the great hall, disappearing into the silent darkness. As soon as they were alone, Araxim stood from his chair, revealing his unnatural height as he moved to tower over Jadzia.

"I only see one baby clutched to your bosom," he said coldly, "where is the other child?"

"I don't know. Tamriel drove us off before we had a chance to see…I assume the child is with him, en route to Ikaria."

"You are aware of what capturing the twins meant to our cause," said Araxim, "without both of them, we cannot hope to succeed. You have failed us, Jadzia, and failure is not acceptable."

"I have brought you one of the children," cried Jadzia, "and I will secure the other, if you just give me more time."

"I can do nothing without consulting with him first," said Araxim.

"Must you?" said Jadzia fearfully.

"You know I must. Stay here until I return."

Araxim strolled over to a where a long, faded tapestry was hanging on the wall and pulled it aside to reveal a narrow spiral staircase descending in endless darkness towards the heart of the earth. Araxim grabbed a torch from the wall and lit it with a wave of his hand before marching down the cold, stone steps. The stairs spiraled ever downward and Araxim walked for nearly an hour before he reached a landing stretching out towards a series of archways held open by massive stone pillars. Araxim chose the center archway, which led him to a small chamber with riverstone walls and a tall antique mirror standing alone in the otherwise vacant room. The torch in Araxim's hand flickered and went out as an eerie cold wind swept by him.

"Master, are you here?" Araxim asked the darkness.

Araxim was answered by silence. The darkness crept in around him like mice searching for food and he felt his breathing constrict. Then the mirror began to glow with a dull gray hue that cast a twilight shadow across the small stone chamber. As the light grew sharper, the silhouette of a monstrous manly face appeared in the glass, its red eyes burning like the torch extinguished just moments before. Araxim bowed his head as the face grew larger and more terrifying.

"You come seeking my advice," said the face in the mirror, *"As is always the case, you are completely incapable of performing even the minutest of duties without my constant supervision. What do you have to tell me, my son?"*

"Jadzia and the Shadow-Weavers have failed us, master," cried Araxim meekly.

"If they have failed me then so have you," said the Black Prince.

"We have one child with us here but the other one has eluded us. How should I punish Jadzia? Tell me what to do…"

"Stop whining, Araxim, it doesn't suit you. We only need one child. The other must be destroyed no matter the cost. Do I make myself clear?"

"I hear you, master, but how? The child is with Tamriel, no doubt already passed the borders of Ikaria and beyond our reach."

"The walls of Ikaria have begun to crumble...it is only a matter of time before they collapse altogether."

"And then we will make our move," said Araxim, "brilliant, master, brilliant...and what of Jadzia?"

"As punishment for her failure, Jadzia will serve as guardian to the baby she even now holds close to her chest. She will raise him away from here, in a secluded place of your choosing...she must raise him as a Grey Robe and teach him the ways of the darkness in the Art. She may take her cursed sisters with her, though none but you must know where she has taken the boy. When the time is right, we will destroy the other child and I will be reborn."

"I live to serve you, master," said Araxim with a dramatic bow.

"Yes, my son...you do."

Chapter Three
"The Green City"

As Tamriel docked his small boat in the Bay of Aranos, on the southern shores of Ikaria, he felt a chill pierce him to the bone, as though he had stepped naked from a warm house into a winter snowstorm. The normal warm reassurances of returning home was replaced by concern when no one came from the houses at the edge of the nearby village to greet him. There were no lanterns lit on the road and an eerie silence had settled in over the hills in the distance. He looked intently at his willow staff for a moment before stamping it on the ground. The earth shook slightly as he spoke a spell that echoed across the waters of the bay like a foghorn guiding ships through a storm to safe harbor.

"Theodor hyd ir wal dyrwyn...Oda yedrith a adeilad."

Tamriel expected the wave of energy generated by his spell to rebound against the island's defenses with an explosion like fireworks. Instead, his spell continued onward into the village and beyond, until it dissipated near the Jade Road. The spells of protection that had stood around Ikaria for centuries were gone. Tamriel rushed down the dock and through the village, setting out down the unlit Jade Road. Normally, the village would've been alive with laughter and merrymaking. The townspeople usually gathered to eat their evening meal communally and afterwards, a band would strike up music and the people would imbibe spirits and dance. That night, there was not a soul to be found. The houses were locked up and dark and the marketplace was abandoned. Tamriel was sure something terrible had happened. The sooner he reached Itheria, the better he would feel.

The Green City called Itheria was built hundreds of years before by the Elfin Lady Rheis, standing upon the jungle canopy at the heart of the rainforest covering the small island of Ikaria. Rheis wished to create a safe haven for the followers of the Old Gods forced from their homes in the Atland by the vicious Matriarchs, serving as both queens and high priestesses of the One God. Rheis used the power of her talisman, called the Autumn Crown, to draw mighty spells of protection around the island so that neither the forces of darkness, nor the followers of the One God could enter uninvited into her domain.

The fact that the defenses had fallen meant the Elfin Lady Rheis was in trouble and Tamriel was ready to come to her aid. He had long been smitten with Rheis but her affections were directed towards the Wandering Wizard, Anaximander. If she was in trouble, Anaximander was also likely in peril, leaving only Tamriel to resolve the situation. He clutched Aras close to his chest, wrapped beneath the folds of his green robes, and steadied his quick pace. The road to Itheria would take only a couple of hours to travel but it felt like an indeterminable amount of time. Tamriel decided he would use another road. He chose a grassy mound just off the Jade Road and drew a circle around himself in the dirt with the bottom of his staff. Once the circle was complete he spoke a soft spell that was barely audible over the wind rustling through the mangrove trees.

"Golau'r seruchod yn cymryd...i mi yn awrat y thinas wair."

A narrow beam of light descended from the heavens and engulfed Tamriel and Aras in its brilliance, carrying them away over the trees so fast that, within a blink of an eye, their feet had touched down upon the cold marble steps leading up into the heights of the trees where Rheis' palace stood like an emerald tiara crowning an giant mangrove tree. He cautiously mounted the stairs, careful to be observant of his surroundings. Like the village, the palace was completely devoid of life. It was as though all the people of Ikaria had evaporated into the wind, like they had never even existed. Tamriel could sense a powerful force within the palace, an entity of such might that he considered turning back to his boat and setting sail for somewhere far away, where he could be sure that Aras would be safe to one day fulfill his destiny.

As he entered the palace, Tamriel noticed that the torches on the walls were barely burning, like the air had been drawn out of the room and replaced by a vacuum of nothingness. The furniture was untouched and the paintings were gathering dust. The palace had been forgotten but, even as Tamriel shifted Aras in his sling, an eerie music began to echo through the passageways. Someone was playing a tamaris (an instrument similar to a guitar), striking strange harmonies on its thin, resonant strings. Tamriel was drawn to the music like a moth following the light of a brightly burning flame. He walked deeper into the palace with a determined pace, until he came to one of the smaller parlors in the west wing, where Anaximander was seated on dozens of pillows playing the tamaris with his eyes closed.

"Thank the Gods," exclaimed Tamriel, "I feared the worst, old friend, but knowing you're here warms my heart."

Anaximander stopped playing but he didn't open his eyes. He straightened his flowing white robes as he stood and took a deep breath.

"Anaximander is no longer here," said dozens of voices through Anaximander's mouth, *"he is at his eternal rest. We speak on his behalf and welcome you to the new palace of Itheria."*

Tamriel backed away from Anaximander as he realized that his friend was indeed gone. Someone, or several people, were now occupying Anaximander's body, using his mind and his power as their own.

"Where is Rheis?" asked Tamriel apprehensively.

"She is here, with us," replied the voices and Tamriel could just make out Rheis' sweet, soft tones amongst the others.

"And the Autumn Crown?"

"Gone."

"You have destroyed our only protection against Araxim and the Matriarchs. Without the Autumn Crown, without Rheis, we are lost."

Anaximander showed no signs of anger. As he finally opened his eyes to look on Tamriel they were hollow and white. Tamriel could see dozens of spirits swirling behind the lifeless irises and he was struck with fear as Anaximander began to speak.

"We see you have a baby held close to your chest," said the voices, *"is that one of the sons of the Firebrand?"*

Tamriel did not answer.

"Your silence tells us all we need to know. It is one of Caenara's twins. Where is the other?"

Again Tamriel remained quiet.

"We are not your enemy, Green Robe…we only wish to restore the balance and bring the ancient ways of Albion back to the hearts of men. Elfkind may be gone but their principles remain, etched in the annals of history. Would you rather see Araxim free his father from the void, or watch as the Matriarchs destroy the Atlandish people in the name of their One God?"

"I want only for Ikaria's defenses to be restored and for the Lady Rheis to again be made whole."

"Rheis is happier than she ever was in life…as for the protection of Ikaria, it will soon no longer be needed. I mean to make such measures obsolete."

"I recognize some of your voices," said Tamriel, having heard familiar tones amidst the many, "I can hear Braanos the Great and Maglos the Wise, I hear Lady Rheis and Daru the Seer. Who else resides now within your flesh?"

"All the Wyt Robes cut down by the Matriarch they call Faceless now abide here within…as does Rheis and the sleeping Anaximander. We are all here, each a single drop of melting snow, forming a mighty river."

Tamriel was horrified. He had expected there to be at least six souls merged into a single collective. He never expected there to be nine. He tightened his grip on his willow staff and wrapped his free arm around Aras as he began to back slowly away. He never took his eyes from the collective inhabiting Anaximander's body. Just as he reached the archway leading from the parlor back to the passage and the stairs beyond, the collective began to speak again.

"We cannot allow you to leave, old friend. You must tell us where the other child is...and give us the one you hold in your arms."

"I will not," said Tamriel forcefully, raising his staff in front of him as though he was defending himself from a vicious attacker. The staff erupted with a brilliant green light that formed the shape of a giant falcon. It bore down upon the collective with its talons stretched out like it meant to tear him viciously apart and devour his flesh as its afternoon meal. The collective remained calm and composed. He simply waved his hand, like he was dismissing the help, and the light-falcon exploded in a shower of cascading embers. As the collective locked his staring eyes upon Tamriel, he was lifted from the ground, held against his will by unseen chains. He moved slowly back into the room, struggling violently against his restraints.

"You actually believed yourself to be strong enough to fight us," said the collective, *"We are the mightiest wizards the world has known in many long years. Our power is nearly absolute...now give us the child."*

Tamriel stared at the small opal crowning his staff and focused his mind, gathering all his strength and funneling it into a single powerful spell.

"Galwaef ar y pir y nefoeth a'r mor...Na i gwared fi i ethiogeldor..."

The force of Tamriel's spell was such that each word he spoke resonated of the walls, growing to a deafening volume and shaking the foundation. Without warning, the roof was torn from the palace, exposing a dark, stormy sky beyond the boughs of the mangrove's canopy. With a loud boom, a powerful bolt of red lightning descended from the heavens and struck the collective with all its might. Anaximander's body seemed to buckle under the force of electricity coursing through it but, even as he fell to his knees, the collective gathered his strength and repelled the lightning. Meanwhile, as the collective was distracted, Tamriel was released from his invisible restraints. He dropped to the floor with a thud, protecting Aras with his arms. In a fraction of a second, Tamriel was on his feet, sprinting through the archway and down the passageway towards the staircase leading back to the forest floor. The collective attempted to follow but was delayed by a mighty gust of wind that knocked him to his knees again, and an onslaught of hail that caused Anaximander's body to be bruised and cut in many places. The waters of the nearby river rose and flooded the ground around Rheis' palace as a giant tidal wave picked up Tamriel gently and delivered him to the Bay of Aranos where his little boat was still moored.

Tamriel set sail without looking back. It wasn't until they were safely out to sea that the reality of what had just transpired set in and he realized he and baby Aras were fugitives without a safe place to seek sanctuary. The soldiers of the One God would have reported Tamriel's interference in their attempt to abduct the Orthelios twins, while Araxim would likely be hunting for Aras. The Atland was too populated, Lemuria too far away, and the Easterling Isles too savage. The Three Cities were under the thumb of the Matriarchs and the Wynterlande Forest was too close to Araxim and the Shadow-Weavers. Tamriel knew that he needed to act against the collective but he also understood the importance of securing Aras' safety. After hours spent in pensive silence, Tamriel looked down at Aras laying on a mound of cloths near the mainsail.

"I think I know where to take you little one," he said, "I just pray the man we seek can still be found."

Tamriel altered course, pointing his sailboat towards the tiny island of Walweitha near the southern tip of the Atland. Once, Tamriel founded a small commune of Green Robes on Walweitha, a tiny haven built in a narrow ravine formed by the massive cliffs that dominated the island's landscape. Before leaving to return to the Eternal City, Tamriel turned over leadership of the commune to a young Green Robe named Galeg Ro, an exceedingly handsome Atlandish man with fair skin and hair the color of molasses. His eyes were strikingly green and his body perfectly formed. Galeg was brought up by an overbearing father and entered the Green Order before he was old enough to shave. He was quiet but capable and demonstrated his skills in the uses of magic dozens of times. The commune had long since dried up and fallen into decay but it was rumored that Galeg still dwelt there in seclusion as a mad hermit.

The journey to Walweitha took less than two days. They were met by a favorable wind that helped to shunt their tiny vessel across the unusually calm water of the Southern Sea, until they came to the small, rocky island that had once been Tamriel's home. He ran their boat aground on a small beach covered in pebbles, smoothed by the force of the tide and the power of the ocean's waves. Tamriel scooped Aras into his arms and carried him along a small path left to be reclaimed by nature. He looked at Aras and smiled before turning around a bend to be greeted by an old set of wooden buildings falling into disrepair. Inside, Tamriel found the rooms vacant and dusty, the furniture overturned and the tapestries moth-eaten. There was no suggestion that anyone had been in the commune for months. The only things that remained were insignificant and Tamriel felt his hope rush out of him like air escaping from a balloon.

After taking some time to think about his options, Tamriel decided to search through the tattered leaflets and piles of books left behind in the commune, hoping to discover something that might lead him to Galeg. He was about to give up and return to his boat when he happened upon a tiny shard of paper with Galeg's name, followed by the description of a small inn on the other side of the island, in the village of Druin. Tamriel set out at once and, just as the full moon rose into the clear night sky, he arrived in Druin and found a ramshackle little public house called 'The Sea Falcon'. The pub was practically empty. There were three old men sitting near the hearth drinking ale and laughing at each other's incoherent jokes, while the barkeeper stood behind the counter nipping at the potato-skin spirits. A narrow set of wooden stairs spiraled up to the second floor near the back of the room and there were several tables spread throughout. Tamriel moved slowly to the counter and addressed the barkeeper.

"Excuse me, barkeep. Can I ask for your help?"

"What'ya be needin'," replied the barkeep with a thick West Lemurian accent.

"I need a pint of goat's milk in this skin," said Tamriel, handing a small leather feeding pouch to the barkeeper, "and a cask of mead."

A few moments later the barkeeper returned with the milk and mead. Tamriel began to feed Aras with one hand and drink mead with the other while the barkeeper returned to his potato-skin spirits. When Tamriel had finished his mead, he ordered another cask.

"How long have you been the barkeep here?" asked Tamriel, striking up a conversation with the particularly unattractive West Lemurian man.

"I been here fer years," replied the barkeeper, "started just a few months after the place opened."

"Then you must know my friend, Galeg Ro," continued Tamriel, "I believe he owns this place. He's a tall man in his forties, with a bald head, a large waist, and an overall jovial demeanor."

"Never heard 'a him...the Sea Falcon's owned by a man named Draed...Gyrdhan Draed. Been boss here for five years now."

"And where is this Gyrdhan Draed?"

"He'd be in his house 'bout now," grunted the barkeeper, "but he ain't fond 'a company."

Tell me where I can find him," said Tamriel with an eerie voice that was almost imperceptible above the roar of the fire. The barkeeper's eyes went vacant, as though he'd been hit on the head with a large mallet and left thoroughly concussed.

"He lives behind the bar, in the cherry wood cottage along the dead end road, but I be warnin' ya, he dunna like visitors."

"I'll take my chances," said Tamriel before rising from the bar and exiting the inn. He followed the little lane as it twisted around the inn and began moving off towards a thicket of alders in the distance. There, near the edge of the trees sat a small cherry wood cottage with smoke rising lazily from its chimney. The cottage was surrounded by a short wooden fence and gardens with exotic flowers growing in them. Tamriel said a silent prayer to the god of light, hoping he was in the right place. He passed through the gate, mounted the stairs leading to the porch, and knocked on the door.

"Somebody better be dyin'," growled a deep baritone voice from inside as Tamriel heard massive footsteps lumbering slowly towards the porch. Seconds later, the door swung open and Tamriel was greeted by the largest man he had ever seen. He easily stood over nine feet tall and had a body the size of a bear. His head was covered by thick, matted brown hair with a matching wiry beard, and his skin was the color of honey. He looked down at Tamriel with his enormous blue eyes and exhaled a sigh that sounded a lot like a growl.

"I'm sorry, sir," said Tamriel, backing away a few steps, "I was told I might find a friend here, his name is Galeg Ro."

Without warning, the massive Gyrdhan reached out his hand and plucked Tamriel up by the neck, tossing him like a ragdoll into the house and slamming the door behind him. Tamriel landed on his butt, careful to keep his arms wrapped around Aras to protect him, and inadvertently dropped his willow staff. Gyrdhan clomped towards him with his fists balled and fire in his eyes as Tamriel searched desperately for his weapon, wrapping his fingers around its narrow shaft just in the nick of time.

"*STOP,*" commanded Tamriel with a powerful basso voice and Gyrdhan froze in mid-step, held there like a statue crafted from bronze.

Tamriel rose to his feet and straightened his robes before checking to see if Aras was alright. He was looking this way and that way in hyper curiosity but he wasn't crying or hurt in any way.

"Why did you attack me, sir?" asked Tamriel without lifting his spell.

"He said you would come," replied Gyrdhan gruffly.

"Who said? Of whom are you speaking?"

"I ain't tellin' you squat," spat Gyrdhan.

"I am not your enemy. I am looking for my friend."

"You ain't no friend to Galeg. He'd 'a told me about you."

"Finally the truth. You do know Galeg Ro," said Tamriel, "tell me where he is."

"I ain't sayin' anythin'. Yer gonna have to kill me," replied Gyrdhan, "go ahead…do it, you are the great wanderin' wizard, aren't ya?"

"You think I'm Anaximander?" laughed Tamriel.

Gyrdhan looked thoroughly confused as Tamriel dropped his spell, allowing Gyrdhan to move again. The massive man scratched his beard with a quizzical look.

"If ya ain't Anaximander, who are ya?"

"My name is Tamriel Ecthelion…I am the last High Wizard of the Green Robes. Galeg Ro is my subordinate and my friend. In these times of peril, there are few to whom I can turn, especially now that Ikaria has fallen and the Elfin Lady is no more. I need a safe place to hide this child and I hoped Galeg could provide such a home."

"He might 'a helped ya if he was still here, but he's been gone for months. Told me he was goin' to Ikaria to confront the wanderin' wizard. He said the wizard has lost his mind and killed the Elfin Lady. I was to remain behind and wait for his return. If he didn't come back, he warned me the wanderin' wizard might 'a come callin' and told me I should kill him."

"He was right. But I don't think Anaximander knows about this place…we should be safe. I must ask you a favor. Take the child and care for him. He needs a gentle hand and a caring spirit. I can sense both in you now that you have calmed yourself. The baby will be safe here. I know this to be true. Why else would the old gods have brought me to you?"

Tamriel removed Aras from the sling he'd carried him in since departing the Atland. As he handed the baby to Gyrdhan, he took note that Aras looked immensely small in the massive man's gentle grip. Gyrdhan looked kindly at the child as he began tugging on one of his large fingers. He smiled and revealed a side of himself he rarely showed. Tamriel turned on his heels and began leaving the cottage.

"Where are ya goin'?" asked Gyrdhan.

"Like Galeg, I must take my turn facing the monster Anaximander has become," replied Tamriel.

"What's the baby's name?"

"Aras…Aras Orthelios," said Tamriel, "Keep him safe, friend. He's the last hope for our failing future."

Chapter Four
"The Wynterlande"

Arad got up before dawn and quietly ate his breakfast before taking to the fields to begin his daily chores. His routine was the same every day, designed specifically to avoid his mother and her violent mood-swings. She rarely left the house, spending her lonely days sitting at the dining table near the hearth, weaving tapestries and ill-fit clothing for Arad. She usually never spoke more than three words to Arad throughout the day but, occasionally, she would rise from bed in a terrible rage and bear her contempt down on her son with brute force. She never hit him but her words were often as pointed as a freshly sharpened knife tailored to wound Arad as deep and fatally as any weapon. It was well-known that his mother was a sorceress with a terrifying understanding of the darkness in the Art but Arad had never witnessed her using her powers. She didn't need to use magic to make Arad afraid of her. Her words were powerful enough.

Arad knew very little about his mother's life but what he did know made him sympathetic towards her outbursts. Jadzia Hanara was one of the four daughters of a wealthy knight long since dead. As a young woman she witnessed the death of her four sisters at the hands of a dark witch and returned home to find her father had succumbed to a fatal illness while she was gone. These losses were too much for Jadzia. She vowed she would find a way to seek her revenge and set out to blackmail the same witch that killed her sisters into granting her eternal life. She hadn't aged a day since, remaining forever twenty-one with exotic beauty and unparalleled charm. She then set out to learn all the intricacies of the Art, especially those dark spells and enchantments which require very little patience or dedication to master. She developed a violent temper and a penchant for cruelty but, deep beneath her cold and stoic exterior, she remained a sad and fearful child. She went to the nearby crypts nearly every day to visit the graves of her sisters, taking them flowers and beautiful rocks. Arad would occasionally follow his mother to the crypts but she always knew he was there. She would scream at him with a harsh tone to stop being such a curious brat and to return home, to his room, and remain there without supper. The kindness Jadzia felt towards her sisters did not translate to Arad and, each day that passed, she became crueler and more abusive.

Upon reaching the age of thirteen, Arad was given new responsibilities which came with the freedom to avoid his mother on a regular basis. The village chieftain, Fenryr Adami, required all the male villagers to participate in maintaining the crops and herds that provided them with food. Their village sat on the southeastern edge of the massive Wynterlande Forest in a climate zone with short summers and long, harsh winters, limiting the grow season and requiring more work from the villagers than other settlements to the south. Arad was assigned to working the crop, taking to the fields each day to pull weeds and spray tonics to keep the bugs away. He also tended the beehives, extracting honey and storing it in the village larders. Arad had always been an awkward boy. He was Atlandish in appearance, tall with a narrow frame and fair skin. His fiery red hair fell to his shoulders and his face was covered with faded freckles. His strikingly silver eyes were eerie and his stare often caused the other children in the village to shudder. The villagers were not of Atlandish descent, despite living in the Atland. They were a mixture of Easterlings and Lemurians who had come to live on the boundaries of the forest years before after the rise of the Temple of the One God in their distant homelands. The other children called Arad a native and freak and never allowed them to spend time in their presence, leaving him to spend his days alone.

That morning was no different than any other. It was nearing the onset of winter, when the village gathered for the harvest celebrations. Arad always loathed the festivals that followed the gathering of the grains and other vegetables growing in the fields. While the villagers danced and made merry in thanks to the Old Gods, Arad watched from afar or disappeared into his house with his mother to endure her temper and loathing. He spent the morning doing his duties, spraying the plants and pulling the weeds before the noontime bells rang, heralding the hour lunch break for the villagers working the fields. Arad ran home to find his mother in the kitchen, rehydrating a piece of dried trout to make a fish stew for dinner. Her eyes were narrowed into their usual glare and her body was taut and rigid.

"Hello, mother," he said as he grabbed a lump of bread, some cheese, and a tomato for his lunch.

"Why is it that you always insist on speaking to me when you come to have your lunch?" hissed Jadzia.

"Because you're my mother and I respect you," said Arad.

"Interesting choice of words...respect, hah. Other children tell their mother how much they love her and you, you say respect. You're a terrible little boy..."

"And you're a terrible person," snapped Arad.

"You have no idea...I think it's time I take you to visit my sisters."

"I have to get back to the fields."

"You're taking the afternoon off. I will speak to Fenryr...he'll understand."

Jadzia led Arad away from their tiny village and into the outer groves of the forest, where the old village crypts stood like crumbling stone houses to protect the dead. There were at least four dozen crypts, some large, some small, some freshly built and others older than the Theocracy of the Eternal City. Jadzia and Arad approached a particularly dilapidated and small crypt deep in the outer groves and pulled the heavy iron door open with little effort. The interior of the crypt was filled with cobwebs and smelled of dank mold. A rat scurried by as Arad entered and Jadzia lit a torch.

At the center of the crypt were four stone tables and, upon three, were laid the remains of Jadzia's sisters. They were wrapped in thick purple shrouds that concealed their slowly decaying flesh. Only their closed eyes were visible from beneath the velvet cloth. Their hands were crossed, each touching their shoulders, and their heads were laying on small stone pillows. They looked completely at peace as Arad examined them each closely.

"Rise," said Jadzia with a terrifyingly eerie voice and Arad caught the glimpse of her silver ring glowing from the corner of his eye.

Suddenly, to Arad's absolute horror, the corpses of Jadzia's sisters began to twitch, each taking a raspy breath and opening their hollow, red eyes. They wheezed as they sat up and swung their legs down to stand in front of Arad and Jadzia. Arad looked from his undead aunts to his mother and back again, backing away towards the doorway leading out of the crypt.

"Where do you think you're going?" mocked Jadzia before waving her hand and causing the iron door to slam shut with a thud, "I want you to meet your aunts."

"Why did you bring that thing here?" spat one of the undead sisters, pointing towards Arad, "We're hungry and you bring this tasty treat into our midst…he looks delectable."

"Enough, Aneira," said Jadzia, "You will not eat Arad and that is a command."

"Hsssss," replied Aneira.

"Why have you woken us?" asked one of the other sisters, "Do you have another mission for us to complete?"

"I want you to tell Arad how you have come to stand here before him, alive and yet still dead," said Jadzia.

"Your mother holds our souls prisoner and refuses to let us die," said the same sister, "Aneira, Oryne, and I wish for nothing more than to pass on to the other side but your mother is afraid to live without us. At first, we thought it was because she feared being alone but she has you now and still she wakes us from our eternal sleep to do her bidding, without a care for what we want…she has no feelings."

"You see, my son," said Jadzia with a smile, "Now you can understand how terrible I truly am. I think you should stay here with your aunts for a while and learn about the pain I have forced them to endure."

With a snap of her fingers, Jadzia vanished, leaving Arad with the three undead sisters beginning to advance on him menacingly.

"Do you love your mother?" asked Aneira.

"I respect my mother," replied Arad.

"That wasn't the question," interjected Oryne, the sister that had yet to speak, "Do you love her?"

"Do you?" countered Arad.

"I used to," replied Oryne, "when we were young, she was innocent and sweet. She dabbled with the darkness in the Art but it was only out of naivety, not a need for revenge. But after our deaths, she changed. She sought out a great evil to release us from our imprisonment in the beyond and bring our spirits back into her possession. The Master resurrected us and gave command of our futures to Jadzia. It was then that my love for her began to fade…she has become a monster. What about you, boy? What do you think of our little sister?"

"I think I hate her," yelled Arad, "I can't stand her mood swings and her contempt for me. She can be kind to other people in the village and I think she might be in love with our chieftain, but to me, she is cold and hard. I hate her with every fiber of my being."

"Good," laughed the other sister, Idris, "I think you're ready."

"Ready for what?" asked Arad.

"How old are you now, boy?" asked Aneira.

"Fourteen," replied Arad.

"Old enough," sneered Idris.

"Let's begin sisters," said Oryne.

One by one, the sisters unwrapped their shrouds. Their naked bodies were revolting to behold. Their skin had all but rotted away while their exposed musculature was gray and stringy. Pieces of their face were missing, exposing their skulls, and their hair was nothing more than strips of lifeless, gray hay. Arad backed against the wall, trying desperately to push the iron door open, but he was unable to escape. Aneira reached him first, grabbing him by the back of the neck and forcing him back to the center of the room. She was joined by her other sisters. They hoisted Arad up onto the stone table that had been empty when he and his mother entered.

"Close your eyes," commanded Oryne but Arad did not obey.

"Close your eyes or we will eat you," barked Idris and Arad felt he had no choice but to obey. He closed his eyes and was greeted by the usual darkness that exists when one stares at their eyelids. He heard the rustle of his aunts' rotting bodies as they each took up a position standing over him. Then he felt their hands. One on his thigh, one on his chest, one on his forehead. Their touch was cold and he smelled the sickeningly sweet smell of rot as they began to speak in unison.

"Taith awr mawyn ysbryd i galon…ei fodoryn ala'r ydym dal yn gyfan."

Suddenly, Arad was drawn into the realm of dreams as his soul left his body, traveling through the air at the speed of light. He could see nothing but a transcendent blur until he came to float before his mother as she walked back to the village from the crypts. Then he was drawn downward into the silver ring she always wore on her right middle finger, into a room with sparkling red walls and no door or windows. He hit the floor with a thud before standing to straighten the strange gray robes he was wearing.

"Sorry for the bumpy ride," came a voice from behind Arad. He turned around to see three beautiful young women standing in front of him naked. The oldest possessed an ageless face and strong jaw, while the next oldest had soft features and a full-figure. The youngest of the three was the least attractive, with dowdy features and a large nose, but she also looked like the warmest. All three bore kind looks and smiled as they came to stand in front of Arad.

"Aunts?" asked Arad in confusion.

"Yes, it is us," replied the oldest sister, Idris, "or, rather, it is us as we were meant to be."

"Why did you bring me here?" asked Arad.

"What must be done needs to be achieved in a place where your mother cannot see us," said the second sister, Aneira.

"I don't understand," said Arad.

"One day soon, a man will come in the night and steal your soul," said Oryne, "he means to turn you towards the darkness and plunge you into the realm of hatred, as was done to him and your mother."

"There are things that can be done to the soul," continued Aneira, "things that could render you a monster. And we cannot allow that to happen. This violence has gone far enough…"

The sisters moved to surround Arad in the same way their undead bodies had done when placing him on the stone table in the crypt. Each placed their hands upon him and began speaking another spell.

"*Archaed ei enaid rhag y tywylleth,*" said Idris.

"*Gadw'n thiogel rhag afyr,*" said Aneira.

"*Gadael i'r golau yn ei enaid thiodef,*" said Oryne.

"*Faer un dyrnod galfod yn gadwedig,*" they said together.

Arad felt his skin begin to toughen, as though he were standing there as hard as the crystalline walls of the room around them. He also started to feel as light as a feather, like he could take off and fly and his features were changed. His ears grew larger and came to a point. His eyes glowed molten silver from corner to corner, and his skin was the color of milk. He was no longer the frightened teenager ostracized by his peers. He was something stronger and more graceful. But even as those feelings began to set in, he was yanked from the room with red crystal walls and began soaring through the air back to the crypt in the outer groves of the Wynterlande Forest. He found himself taking a breath of musty air and opened his eyes to be greeted by the undead corpses of his aunts. They were wearing their shrouds again and were grouped together at the edge of the crypt. Arad had to struggle to remember what he had experienced in the heart of his mother's ring but, the more he chased the memories, the more they faded. He sat up in confusion and apprehensively jumped off the table.

"What did you do to me?" he asked his aunts.

"We have done nothing," said Idris.

"Nothing you won't thank us for in the future," said Aneira.

"You must trust us," said Oryne, "and never speak of this to your mother…"

"Speak of what?" asked Arad.

"Exactly," replied Oryne.

Arad spent the night with his aunts in that decrepit crypt in the woods. They did not speak to him again. They laid down on their stone beds and closed their eyes. Arad would've thought they had returned to the grips of death had he not seen their chests rising and falling in rhythm with their breaths. Arad never slept. He sat by the iron door with his knees curled into his chest and desperately tried to recall what his aunts had done to him. He couldn't even remember that his spirit had left his body. All he knew was he had been forced to lay down on the stone table before everything went dark. He thought they might've tried to eat him but he had no bite marks or chunks of missing flesh.

Jadzia returned as the sun rose the next morning. She threw the iron door open with the power of her ring and stared at Arad apathetically.

"Are you ready to go home?" she asked coldly.

"Yes, mother," said Arad.

"And you will never again speak to me the way you did yesterday," added Jadzia.

"Yes, mother," repeated Arad.

"Then I think you've learned your lesson," said Jadzia.

Jadzia and Arad returned home in silence. She had a breakfast of cold boiled eggs and toast waiting on the dining table. Arad ate quickly without speaking a word.

"I spoke to Fenryr and he will excuse your absence from the fields this once," said Jadzia, "but you better hurry or else you're going to be late and that, my son, would be unforgivable."

Arad did as he was told and rushed to the fields, grabbing his gardening tools and sprayer from the shed at the edge of the rows of grain growing in the shade of the nearby trees. He could no longer remember anything about what had happened in the presence of his aunts. He thought his experience in the crypts had been a nightmare and was convinced he had woken up in his bed that morning. It might have been the power of his mother's magic or that of his aunts but, whatever the case, he was stripped of his memories of that afternoon forever.

After that day, Arad began to change. His youthful timidity and awkwardness gave way to a newfound athleticism and elegance of speech. He became charming and beguiling, with girls and boys hanging on his every word. His body filled out with muscles and his face took on a gorgeous hue. The children that had called him a freak began to chase after him and the elders of the village remarked on his ability to be good at anything to which he put his mind. Jadzia continued to treat him with contempt but her menacing nature softened somewhat and she showed pride in the compliments she received from the other villagers about her strapping son. The spell meant to protect Arad, to harden the walls of his spirit had also brought him strength and the courage to stand as superior to his peers.

A few months later, Jadzia returned to her sisters' crypt and woke them. They sat just outside the crypt under the light of the full moon for a while a listened to the sounds of the frogs in the nearby pond.

"What did you do to Arad?" asked Jadzia after nearly an hour, "he's not the same boy anymore...he's stronger somehow."

"We did nothing," said Idris.

"Don't lie to me," countered Jadzia angrily.

"We only told him that he must be stronger than you and not give in to your taunts and sharp words," said Oryne.

"I don't believe you," said Jadzia.

"Whatever we did, we did for the future," said Idris, "there will come a day when we will need that boy. He has to be ready to face his doom..."

"You didn't tell him about the Master, did you?" asked Jadzia.

"Of course not. We told him nothing," said Oryne, "we are blameless in whatever might come of the boy. You on the other hand, are responsible for the child. It is you who will be found guilty if he is not ready to take up the mantle forged for him at birth."

Chapter Five
"Fight and Flight"

"Tell me a story," said Aras.

He was lying on the bearskin rug near the hearth in the warmth of a gentle evening fire. Gyrdhan was seated on an enormous stool in the kitchen plucking a freshly beheaded chicken. They had just returned home from a long day's work at *The Sea Falcon*, and Aras was glad to stretch out on the soft fur. When they were at the inn, Gyrdhan worked Aras to the bone but at home, the boy was allowed to relax. Some nights they brought dinner home from the inn. Most the time, Gyrdhan prepared their meals.

"Did you hear me?" asked Aras.

Silence.

"Gyrd," shouted Aras.

"What?" replied Gyrdhan with a deep, gruff voice.

"Tell me a story."

"Fer the sake 'a the old gods," shouted Gyrdhan, "yer gettin' too old for stories, Ari. Yer nearly sixteen."

"I didn't mean I wanted to hear about wood hags and giants. Haven't you told me a million times that you've been everywhere and seen everything worth seeing in Albion?"

"Hmph," grunted Gyrdhan.

"Well," complained Aras.

"Yer gonna have to be more specific…exactly what and where do ya wanna hear 'bout?"

"Tell me about your parents."

Aras had lived with Gyrdhan since he was a baby. He thought of him as his big, lovable father. Outside the walls of their small cottage,

Gyrdhan was a fearsome and stubborn man with a quick temper and powerful shout. However, when he thought no one was looking, or when it was just the two of them, he would let his softer side show. He laughed and smoked and even sang. But he would never talk about his parents.

"I ain't talkin' 'bout my folks," barked Gyrdhan, "pick somethin' else you wanna know…"

"Okay…tell me about the Elfin Lady of Ikaria."

"Never knew her."

"Come on, Gyrd."

"Alright, alright…her name was Rheis and she was the prettiest creature ever to walk 'neath the stars. Folks called her the Autumn Queen 'cause she was ageless and 'cause 'a the magic crown she always wore top her head. She used that crown to build the Green City on the island called Ikaria to escape the persecutions 'a the One God. Fer a long time, the Green City was a haven fer the folks that kept followin' the old ways but, after'n Rheis disappeared, the city crumbled to dust…"

"What happened to her?" asked Aras, listening intently.

"She died."

"I know she died…I want to know how."

"The Wanderin' Wizard," said Gyrdhan, lost in thought.

"Who?"

"His name was Anaximander…he was once the greatest champion of the old ways but he got greedy, wanted more power. He broke his mind and let others take over his body. Now, folks call him the Collective. He's a terrible creature'd just as soon strike ya down than give ya the time 'a day."

Aras heard the local priests talk about Anaximander often but, whenever he approached, they would quickly change the subject. Aras wondered why no one wanted him to know about some wandering wizard who lost his mind but he never got a straight answer. Judging by Gyrdhan's face, he wasn't going to get the answer that night either. Again, he decided to change the subject. He had recently learned about the Atland in school and decided that would make a more appropriate topic.

"Did you ever visit the Atland?" asked Aras.

"Many times," replied Gyrdhan before shoving the freshly plucked chicken into a pot of boiling water with some potatoes and carrots. He wiped his hands on a large dish cloth and then lumbered over to his oversized chair next to the bearskin rug. He picked up his pipe and lit it, taking it a lung full of smoke and exhaling with a sigh.

"The Atland is beautiful," he continued, "a place the like 'a which I ain't seen anywhere else in the world. There's forests with trees of red, white, gray, and green and they bear flowers that fill the air with a sweet smell. The mountains are so rich with gems and crystal that they sparkle and shine when the sun rises in the mornin'. And the Eternal City…oh, what a sight to see…it has golden walls and roads made 'a waterways. The towers and palaces are the oldest buildins standin' in the world and the people used to be the most invitin' of all the races 'a Albion."

"What do you mean, they used to be?" interjected Aras.

"Things have changed in the world, Ari. Since the rise 'a the One God's matriarchs, the Eternal City has fallen into ruin and the Atland is full 'a thieves and vagabonds. Violence rules that land now and it's all by order 'a the matriarchs. They might as well just call it as it is. They're queens now…the most powerful women in Albion."

Gyrdhan paused long enough to rise from his chair and stamp out the contents of his pipe. He returned to the kitchen and stirred the contents of the cauldron, releasing a pleasing smell into the air that caused Aras' stomach to growl. Amongst his many talents, Gyrdhan was an excellent cook. Aras watched him as he spooned some of the cauldron's contents into his mouth and then added a few spices with a grunt.

"How many matriarchs are there?" asked Aras once Gyrdhan had replaced the lid on the cauldron.

"There's five 'a them. Four juniors and one senior. She's the one with all the real power. They call her Faceless…"

"What a weird name," said Aras.

"It ain't her name, it's just what they call her," continued Gyrdhan, "no one knows her real name, or even what she looks like. She keeps herself all covered up and wears a veil over her face. Adds mystery, I s'pose. Not that she needs it. She's a terrifyin' woman commandin' legions of fearsome soldiers. Won't catch me crossin' her, no sir."

Gyrdhan stopped again to serve dinner. He spooned the contents of the cauldron into two large wooden bowls that he set gently on the table, each with a matching spoon. He also produced a loaf of day-old bread and a pitcher of milk before sitting down, nodding at Aras to join him. They always ate in silence, perhaps because Gyrdhan usually shoveled his food into his mouth so fast he had no time to talk but Aras also thought it was because Gyrdhan wished to observe some cultural formality with which Aras was wholly unfamiliar.

After dinner, Gyrdhan washed the dishes in the kitchen basin before setting out for one of his solitary evening strolls through the nearby woods. He never invited Aras on his sojourns and Aras never tried to insinuate he wished to go. Aras sprinted up the narrow stairs to the second level of the cottage and stripped off his clothes, exposing his lean and hairless body. He had lighter skin than the townspeople and his hair was a vibrant shade of red. He had light freckles all over his face and his eyes were the color of tarnished silver. He was a handsome young man by any standard but he had trouble acknowledging it. When he gazed into the looking-glass he was greeted with a plethora of self-criticisms preventing him from being happy in his own skin. He disliked his sharp, slightly large nose, and despised the sharp contours of his sallow face. He always thought his ears too large for his head and was disgusted by his freckles. His feet were too wide, his dick was too small, and he had yet to start sprouting hair when other boys his age already bore the onset of a beard. Most of all, he hated that he knew nothing about where he had come from, had no one to blame for the imperfections he saw all over his young body.

After his usual few minutes spent scrutinizing his looks, Aras entered the washroom and drew himself a bath. The bathtub consisted of an enormous marble basin with a giant barrel next to it, sitting over an open flame. There was another barrel next to the door filled with cold water. Aras turned a wooden lever attached to the first barrel and a steady stream of hot water began pouring into the tub. Meanwhile, Aras used a bucket to scoop cold water out of the other barrel and add it to the tub until he had produced the perfect temperature. He dropped himself into the tub and closed his eyes, thinking about what Gyrdhan had told him about the Wandering Wizard and about the matriarch called Faceless. He had learned about the modern political spectrum in Albion and knew the tyranny of the Matriarchs was very real and very terrifying. They used their authority over the Temple of the One God to force the Atlandish and Lemurian people into subservience and imposed upon them harsh laws that prevented the worship of the Old Gods or the practice of the Art.

Aras was familiar with the Art. He began learning it when he was four years old from the local apothecary, Aslan Farr. Aslan had been a priest of the Blue Robes before the order was disbanded by the aggressions of the Matriarchs. After the death of most his peers, Aslan returned to the village in which he had grown up and started his apothecary. Aslan was almost seventy years old when Aras started learning the Art from him but his poignancy and abilities had not been effected by his advanced age. He taught Aras how to conjure spells and draw circles of protection, how to glamour and control the will of men through subliminal autohypnosis. Aras learned how to invoke Sendings and call the elements to do his bidding. He was made aware of the High Secrets of the Art and, most importantly, he was instructed on the channeling and harnessing of the energy called *The Pure Light*.

Aras excelled at all aspects of the Art but he rarely utilized his skills. There was no call for magic in their peaceful and quiet town. He could use his powers to help him with his chores or to ingratiate himself amongst the other young townspeople but Aslan taught him to be cautious and never to use magic unless there was no other recourse. In all other areas of society, Aras proved to be somewhat of a failure. He wasn't athletic or overly strong, nor was he the smartest of his peers. He found interactions with the other townspeople to be difficult and preferred to spend his time alone or in the company of his best and only friend, Darendon Kyree. Gyrdhan never pressured Aras into doing things that made him uncomfortable and was overwhelmingly encouraging of Aras' study of the Art.

"You are always in the bathtub," came the voice of Aras' friend, Darendon, as he entered the washroom unexpectedly.

"I like to be clean," said Aras, "there's no crime in that."

"I guess not," said Darendon, pulling his tunic over his head and dropping his trousers to reveal his taut, muscular body. Darendon was a year older than Aras but his athletic physique was far more developed. His olive skin was covered with a light dusting of black hair to match the silky locks growing wildly from the top of his head. He strolled over to the bathtub and jumped in alongside Aras, scooping the water over his head to drench his hair and wash his face. Aras and Darendon had been taking baths together since they were toddlers so there was nothing strange or overtly sexual about Darendon's decision to get in with Aras. Darendon let Aras wash his back as he flicked his fingers across the surface of the water. The boys dunked their heads beneath the water at the same time and stayed under as long as they could, a little contest they played to judge which of them was stronger. When they surfaced they were greeted by three tall, fearsome looking men dressed in red robes emblazoned with the image of a golden crown overlaid with a white rose in full bloom.

"He must be one of them two," grunted one of the intruders.

The three men rushed towards the bathtub, intending to pluck Aras and Darendon out of the water and haul them off in captivity. They seriously underestimated Darendon. Where Aras had been studying the Art since he was a toddler, Darendon had been preparing to become a Knight of the Old Guard. He was nearly unparalleled amongst his peers in his fighting skills and tactical training. He leaped from the water like a frog jumping off its lily pad and came down on the first of the three man, knocking him to the floor and disarming him of his sword, a strangely shaped blade with a large ruby set in its hilt. Darendon swung the sword towards the next intruder but the intruder held up his own blade which glowed a dull, fiery orange.

"Dareg dalhanir azarag marek kahr," said the intruder and Darendon was thrown across the room like a ragdoll, crumbling unconscious onto the floor. The first intruder retrieved his sword and kicked Darendon in the gut for good measure.

"That must be him," said the intruders, pointing towards Aras.

The intruders resumed their path towards the tub. Aras backed into the farthest corner and attempted to make himself small as they reached out their hands to grab him. He instinctively put out his hands in front of him and shouted a spell he learned when he was seven.

"Rhoi'r gorau i," he said.

For a split second the intruders froze in mid-step like they had been covered with quick-drying glue. But the effect was only temporary and soon they had plucked Aras from the bathtub and hauled him downstairs towards the front door. Aras tried to conjure another spell but they gagged him with a washcloth and bound his hands with a rope one of them had been carrying. He was soaking wet, covered in soap, and completely naked as they shoved him out into the cold night air. The street lamps had been doused and the streets were pitch black but, as they passed the gate at the edge of the property, the silhouette of an enormous figure emerged from the nearby trees and began running furlong towards the intruders holding Aras captive.

"Get yer hand of 'a my lad," bellowed Gyrdhan as he bore down on the three intruders. Each of his massive fists landed a punch square in two of the intruders' jaws, knocking them to the ground and releasing Aras from their clutches. Just as Gyrdhan turned to face the other intruder, Darendon came running out the front door and through the gate, brandishing a large stick Gyrdhan used to barricade the door when he and Aras went to sleep each night. Darendon joined the fight as Aras cowered next to a tree.

"What do a bunch 'a Red Robes want with my boy?" shouted Gyrdhan as he faced off against the tallest of the intruders.

"Piss off," spat the intruder fighting with Gyrdhan.

"We know who you are," said the one fighting with Darendon, "you're Gyrdhan Farr, the runt-giant buffoon who used to serve as a lackey for the Green Robes. And that isn't your boy. He belongs with the Collective."

"So that's who sent ya," said Gyrdhan with a grimace before socking the Red Robe in the gut so hard he crumpled over onto the ground and didn't move again. With the greatest of the intruders out of the way, Gyrdhan made short work of the other two. They conjured various kinds of spells to protect them but they had no effect on Gyrdhan. He bore down on one and wrung his neck like the chicken he had served for dinner. Darendon defeated the third intruder, using the Red Robe's sword to run the intruder through.

Once Gyrdhan had buried the three Red Robes and disposed of their swords he and the boys returned to the cottage. Aras and Darendon each washed themselves again and then dressed in warm wool tunics dyed forest green and black leather breeches. Gyrdhan poured them some hot tea and they sat on the rug by the fire while Gyrdhan busied himself gathering blankets and food together in a large satchel. He filled three water-skins and produced a large bag of silver from a place beneath the floorboards.

"What are you doing?" asked Aras.

"It ain't safe here no more," replied Gyrdhan hurriedly.

"Who were those men, Gyrd?" said Aras.

"They were messengers," said Gyrdhan without stopping, "we gotta get outta here 'fore he gets here. Yer gonna have to come with us, Darendon. It ain't safe for you here no more either."

"I don't understand," said Aras, "whose coming?"

"The wanderin' wizard," grunted Gyrdhan.

"Anaximander?" said Aras, "What would someone like Anaximander want with me?"

"Never mind that," barked Gyrdhan, "ya need to get ready."

In less than an hour, Gyrdhan had finished packing and shoved two large packs on Aras and Darendon's backs. Gyrdhan put out all the lanterns and locked the door before they set out down the narrow road leading through the town. They continued on towards the thicket of woods beyond and soon emerged on a wide sandy dune that stretched out towards the nearby ocean. They walked along the dune to a small lagoon where a village of easterling immigrants had sprouted up a few decades before. Gyrdhan paid nearly half his silver to hire an easterling boatman for safe passage away from the island that had been Aras' home his whole life.

"Where are we going, Gyrd?" asked Aras once he, Gyrdhan, and Darendon were safely aboard a small easterling schooner headed out into the open sea.

"We gotta go somewhere Anaximander ain't gonna think to look fer ya," said Gyrdhan, "somewhere we can get protection…I think I know a place but it's gonna take us a while to get there."

"What place?" asked Aras.

"The Norn Mountains," replied Gyrdhan.

Chapter Six
"Nameless Truths"

Faceless and her manservant, Goran, entered the Great Hall at the heart of the Palace of Silver Light by way of the royal entrance. She was dressed in her usual heavy purple robes emblazoned with the Yellow Rose of the One God and a silky gray veil covering her face. No one ever saw Faceless without her veil and many of the Atlandish converts were circulating the rumor that she was hideously deformed. She greeted these rumors with apathetic indifference and carried herself with regality and personal piety. The other four Matriarchs, whose names were Lylid, Draena, Anorra, and Elora, had a different theory about Faceless' veil. They had come to believe that she was hiding her identity because she was wanted by someone and, if she exposed herself, she might be assassinated. The sisters, Anorra and Elora, were faithful followers of Faceless and never questioned her authority over them or the story she told them about her younger days. Lylid and Draena were a different story. They had started out like Anorra and Elora but, over the last few months, they had begun to have their doubts about their mysterious leader's intentions.

After exterminating the Wyt Robes and taking control of the Eternal City, Faceless had statues of the One God erected in every district but she insisted the statues be covered by thick purple tapestries and declared that the removal of the tapestries would be punishable by death. She stationed a guard at every statue around the clock to prevent passersby from taking a quick peak and ordered that the Tetrarchs only worship at these enigmatic sculptures. Lylid and Draena couldn't understand why the One God needed to be covered, especially after the victory of expelling the Old Religion from the Atland. Whenever they attempted to speak to Faceless about it, Faceless would react harshly and chide them for questioning her judgment. Was it not she who had secured the victory against the Wyt Robes? She would not stand for dissension, not even from the other Matriarchs who were viewed publically as her equal.

The only person ever to look beneath a purple tapestry at the face of one of the hidden statues was the former leader of the Gray Robes, whose name was Gareth. He saw the statue the night the Matriarchs took the Eternal City and then was struck down the next morning by unknown causes. If he had lived, he would have told the world that it was not the face of the One God that greeted him but the stern and unfeeling visage of the dark deity called the Nameless Goddess, the Poisoner in the Well, and the Dark Lady. A fact that Faceless would kill to keep hidden. The Nameless Goddess had long ago fallen from grace, imprisoned in the waters of a dark well somewhere in the forgotten woods of Albion, cursed to live for an eternity as a ghost of her former self, a hollow echo of a fiery spirit chilled by the frigid waters serving as her everlasting prison. If the other Matriarchs were to discover the truth about the statues beneath the tapestries, they would question Faceless' fidelity and her devotion to the One God. Luckily, no one except Gareth ever tried to see the face beneath the cloth, a face that would strike fear in their hearts and bring chaos into a world they were trying to order.

Lylid and Draena sat in chairs to Faceless' left, while Anorra and Elora sat at her right. Goran stood behind Faceless' large marble chair and two stewards were situated at the base of the stairs connecting the royal plinth to the rest of the Great Hall. They were all silent as the doors opened and a large assembly of Tetrarchs and Atlandish noblemen loyal to the One God poured into the Great Hall, filling it with chatter and murmurs.

"Thank you for joining us, my Lords and Brothers," said Lylid to the assembly of men standing before her.

"We are eager to know why you've called us here," replied one of the noblemen near the front, an especially rotund man named Varo.

"We wish to discuss three pressing matters with you, our loyal followers, as we sweep the Atland clean of the Old heresies," said Anorra, "the first of these matters is the question of a government."

"You don't mean to rule?" said a Tetrarch by the name of Eahald, "we assumed you would establish yourselves as sovereigns."

"You misunderstand, Brother Eahald," replied Anorra, "we are the heads of the Temple, leaders of the true faith. It is, and will be, our sovereign obligation to ensure the law of the land reflects the rule of the One God. But we haven't the time to establish the law, or to monitor each city, town, and village in the Atland. Therefore we propose that you gentlemen present here form a government in our name. Elect whom you wish and establish governance as you see fit. We are not interested in the details. Our only concern is that the law of the One God be the law of the realm. There can be no deviation from the true faith."

"The next issue we mean to address is one of a more prudent nature," said Draena, "there has been a great deal of dissension in the outlands of the Atland. The followers of the Old Religion are still present in those parts of our dominion, spreading their lies and their heresies amongst the poor, unthinking masses. We cannot abide the continued presence of the Old Religion in the Atland. The Eternal City has shown that conversion is not only possible, it's pleasing to the people. We must send emissaries to the Outlands to preach to the villagers and reach the Tribes beyond our direct influence. Who here will volunteer to undergo such a mission?"

"I think I speak for all the Tetrarchs here and everywhere in your dominions when I say any of us would be glad to take up this righteous call to bring more people into the fold," said a High Tetrarch named Maren, "but what if we encounter resistance or violence? We are not warriors and we have no magic."

"You needn't worry about magic," interjected Faceless from beneath her veil, "there is no magic in the living world that can bring harm to us or any of you. The One God has blessed us and we must trust that he will not abandon us now, in our hour of glory. But to put your mind at ease, a contingent of my personal guard will accompany the emissaries on their journey. Does that soothe your fears, Brother Maren?"

"Yes, my Lady, and I will be the first to volunteer," said Maren with a deep bow.

Four other Tetrarchs and two noblemen also volunteered and together they left the Great Hall to prepare for their journey to the Outlands. The remaining men began to talk amongst themselves, whispering about their order to create a government, but their attention was redirected to the Matriarchs when Faceless began to speak again.

"The final matter is one that warrants my personal attention," she said authoritatively, "we must move beyond our borders if we mean to truly bring peace to Albion. The Atland and Lemuria are the greatest kingdoms in the living world and each now stands in the glory of the One God. But there is another powerful nation we must turn our attention towards. Ikaria."

"Forgive me, my Lady," said a nobleman named Hareth, "but how is Ikaria a threat to us? No one has seen the Elfin Lady in years and its rumored the Green City has crumbled into ruins. They have no standing army, no weapons, no resources of any kind."

"The most powerful practitioners of the Art have taken refuge in Ikaria," snapped Faceless, "the Wyt Robes were but one of the wizarding clans. The others are still out there and they still pose a risk. We have to attack them now, while they're not expecting us. I propose that every adult man able to bear arms be called to duty and sent to crush the isle of Ikaria, once and for all."

The men in the Great Hall were dead silent as they looked at one another, each hoping one of the others would speak up against such madness. Never in the history of the Atland had men been summoned to war without volunteering and an act of such despotic cultural irreverence would surely lead to a revolt or uprising. As the men silently stressed about Faceless' demand, a cloaked figure entered the Great Hall by way of the royal entrance and whispered into Goran's ear. In turn, he leaned down and spoke quietly to Faceless through her veil.

"My Lords and Brothers," said Faceless, "I am afraid something pressing has arisen and we must cut this parlay short. Go now to your homes and your halls and decide what form your government shall take."

Faceless rose from her chair, followed by the other Matriarchs, and they left the Great Hall through the royal entryway, emerging in a narrow passage that led to a small parlor connected to a kitchen, a sitting room, and a set of sleeping chambers. The cloaked figure who had whispered to Goran was sitting in the parlor, looking out the window at Atlantis, across the wide waterways separating the royal estate from the rest of the city. Faceless motioned towards the other Matriarchs and they continued into the sitting room while Goran stood guard at the door between the two spaces.

"Goran tells me you bring news from the Green City," said Faceless.

The cloaked figure removed his hood to reveal an older man with graying hair and a thinning beard. Faceless recognized him at once as the Grey Robe known as Neran Kalenti. A few years before, when Faceless and the other Matriarchs took control of the Temple and the kingdom of Lemuria, they had come across Neran Kalenti. He was a wizard of some renown but he had been exiled by his order for failing to declare allegiance to the Black Prince before he was removed from power. Neran was never good at pretending and the only thing he desired was wealth and power for himself. He made an arrangement with Faceless, that first week they were acquainted, that he would move to Ikaria and join the rebel Grey Robes in their service to the Elfin Lady but that he would report their dealings to Faceless as a spy and a secret ally.

"I have good news and I have bad news," said Neran, "which would you like to hear first?"

"The good news, of course," answered Faceless.

"Our enemies are no more," smiled Neran, "the Wandering Wizard has lost his mind and, in his insanity, he murdered the Elfin Lady Rheis. Without them the wizarding clans are in disarray. They'll never think to try and return to power here while they are faced with this crisis."

Faceless didn't react.

"And the bad news?" she said apathetically.

"The Autumn Crown has disappeared," replied Neran in almost a whisper, "at first I thought Anaximander stole it after killing Rheis but he hunts for it relentlessly…no one knows where it has gone."

Unlike with the good news, Faceless reacted by clenching her hands into tight fists and, even though she wore a veil to conceal her face, it was apparent by her body language that she was displeased. She rushed out of the parlor and down the narrow passage leading back to the Great Hall without her manservant or the other Matriarchs. When she reached the open courtyard beyond the Great Hall and found it empty, she produced a small ruby talisman from beneath the folds of her robe. It consisted of a golden pendant in the shape of a teardrop with the ruby at its center. The pendant bore strange markings that looked like the runes of Elfkind and it hung from her neck by a thick golden chain. The ruby glowed faintly as Faceless held the pendant in the palm of her hand and spoke with an eerie, otherworldly voice that filled the air with a chill and cast strange shadows across the light of the torches shining down onto the courtyard.

"Asha rim akarabet alir atani," she said and suddenly she vanished into her surroundings. Though she was still standing there, she could not be seen by the eyes of any living creature as she made her way to the nearby waterway and stepped onto it, as though it were a road made of stone. With one final look at the Palace of Silver Light, she took a deep breath and then started running, not like a person runs towards a finish line, but like a powerful wind gusting across a meadow. She moved so fast that, even if she weren't cloaked

by a spell, she would seem like nothing more than a colorful blur, a mirage moving outward, beyond the crumbling walls of the Eternal City and into the waters of the ocean. She moved across the violent waves and treacherous tides of the Southern Sea like a bullet freshly shot from a smoking gun until, in only hours, she came to the shores of Ikaria. If the Elfin Lady Rheis were still living, and the Autumn Crown were upon her head, Faceless would have crumpled against the strength of an unseen barrier as she approached. As it stood, she was able to reach the beaches and enter the lush rainforest serving as the home of the Green City. She came even to the stairs leading up to Rheis' palace on the boughs of the mangroves before her shrouding spell was nullified and she could be seen by others.

"We felt you coming," came a series of voices carried on a cold, gentle wind.

"You didn't think I would remain in Atlantis when the Autumn Crown has gone missing," replied Faceless, "why don't you all come out where I can see you...I'd like to know to whom it is I'm speaking."

"Oh...but you do know us, and we know you," said the voices, "the real you hiding beneath those robes and that ridiculous veil. We are not as blind as the morons who follow you as Faceless, the Champion of the One God when you are really thus..."

Suddenly it was as though giant invisible hands reached out and tore at Faceless' robes until she stood there naked and unveiled, with only the Amulet of the One God remaining around her neck. Her wild, raven black hair fell coarsely down her back and her once beautiful alabaster white face was contorted into something monstrous by her fear and hatred. Her red eyes gleamed with a hint of anger and her lips were curled into a bloodcurdling smile. She made no attempt to cover her naked flesh. Instead she curled her long white fingers around the amulet which glowed in response.

"You've seen me," she laughed, "it's only fair that I should see you. Come out, come out wherever you are..."

Her spell was not needed. The wizard, Anaximander, stepped out from the shadows near Rheis' throne. He was dressed in a bright white cloak and his head was shaved in the style of the Wyt Robes. But he looked much different than the last time Faceless had encountered him. His eyes were hollow and lifeless, as though he were no longer living and yet still breathing and standing before her. His face was bereft of the usual emotion he wore pinned to his sleeve and he was absent his traditional oaken staff.

"There is no need for violence," said ten voices from Anaximander's mouth, "we will show ourselves willingly, after all, without you, we would not exist as we are today. We are all here, all your many enemies. If you focus you will hear us as we used to be. Then you will know."

Faceless bent her ear to the words escaping from Anaximander and began to understand. She could hear the voices that made the prophecy about the twin souls rising to destroy her. The voices of the men she burnt on the pyre as heretics. All the Wyt Robes were present inside Anaximander, all her greatest enemies indeed. But there were more, three more, two men and one woman. She couldn't identify the men's voices. It was the woman's voice that intrigued her. It was the voice of the Elfin Lady Rheis and it was to her that Faceless spoke.

"Where is the Autumn Crown, Rheis?" said Faceless.

"We do not know," answered all ten voices, "it was given over to a cloaked figure whose identity was never revealed. Rheis asked her friend, The Yellow Lady, to send her a messenger to spirit the crown away in a manner that would keep its location secret. The crown is no closer to you than it is to us…"

"I think you're lying," sneered Faceless.

"We can assure you we are not," answered the Collective, "if we knew the whereabouts of the crown, it would be sitting atop our head and we would use it to destroy you…for any servant of the Nameless Goddess is our enemy, especially the one who set us upon the pyre."

"You think I'm her servant," laughed Faceless, "I am no servant...I am the Nameless Goddess."

Anaximander's eyes widened as he put his arms out and threw a giant fireball in the Nameless Goddess' direction. The Nameless Goddess smiled as she reached out and caught the fireball like it was a baseball, causing it to turn to a massive sphere of ice that she hurtled back at the body that once belonged to Anaximander. The Collective shouted some indecipherable words and the ice ball shattered into a million pieces. He moved to throw another spell at the Nameless Goddess but she had vanished into thin air. The Collective drew a powerful sphere of protection around himself but, before he could close the circle, the Nameless Goddess appeared in front of him. She reached out her hand and touched her finger to his forehead, causing him to rise up into the air like a marionette and then succumb to hundreds of seizures.

"You may be the greatest minds that have walked in Albion for a thousand years," smiled the Nameless Goddess, "but I am the goddess of the darkness with the power of the One God under my control. You never stood a chance...I will find the Autumn Crown and I will use it to destroy these twin souls. And you...you will *disappear.*"

With a great puff of gray smoke, the Collective disappeared, leaving the Nameless Goddess standing alone in Rheis' palace. The Nameless Goddess wondered for a moment where the people of Ikaria had gone. The villages were abandoned and the Green City vacant. There wizarding clans were nowhere to be found, vanished just like the Collective and the Autumn Crown. With a sinister grin, the Nameless Goddess replaced her purple robe and pulled her veil over her head, becoming Faceless once again.

Chapter Seven
"A Light in the Darkness"

On the morning of Arad's sixteenth birthday, Jadzia woke him before sunrise and instructed him to dress in his warmest furs. It was winter in the Wynterlande Forest and the entire village was buried in four feet of freshly fallen snow. Arad did as he was told without complaint and soon the pair were out in the elements, on the Northeastern Road leading into the heart of the forest and beyond. The sun rose into the sky as they passed the border of the woods, though its light was muffled by both a thick layer of gray clouds and the canopy formed by the boughs of the ancient trees comprising the Wynterlande Forest.

In the last two years, Arad had changed a great deal, both physically and emotionally. He had become hard and unfeeling, a byproduct of his mother's constant berating and abuse. He was quick to lose his temper and treated others like they were nothing more than pawns on a chess board. His heart had gone cold but his soul still burned with fiery passion. There were moments when his unkind nature would melt away to reveal a frightened, caring child. Jadzia did all she could to ensure those moments were few and far between, driving Arad to display only his darker, more menacing qualities. She applauded his abuse of others and nurtured his superiority complex until he felt that no one was his equal. She also encouraged Arad to begin studying the darkness in the Art. He proved himself to be a capable practitioner of magic and his power began to rival that of his mother but he lacked focus and resolve. Jadzia pushed him hard and praised him little and she refused to allow him to visit her sisters after their initial meeting. Arad still dreamt of escaping from his mother's influence but he didn't know if that would be possible, without serious consequences.

"Where are we going?" asked a drowsy Arad as they walked briskly along the Northeastern Road.

"You'll see," replied Jadzia.

They continued on for nearly five hours, stopping only once by a stream to fill their waterskins and eat a small meal of berries and dried venison Jadzia had packed in her knapsack. As cold and callous as Jadzia was verbally, she always made sure that Arad's basic needs were met. She sewed new clothes for him every year from linen spun by her own hand. She had considerable wealth she inherited from her father and she used it to fill their home with fresh foods and firewood to keep Arad fed and warm. It was Jadzia's duty to raise Arad and, while she was harsh and unfeeling, she was diligent in her maternal obligations. That particular day, Arad was dressed in furs cured and sewed by Jadzia just days before his birthday.

As the sun reached its midday zenith, Arad and Jadzia emerged from their long road through the forest onto a wide grassland stretching out towards the Norn Mountains far to the north. There, next to a small creek, stood the Red Tower gleaming like a ruby sitting in mud. Arad had never seen the Red Tower but he had heard the stories telling of its long history as a place of hope and perseverance. The tower was the residence of two She-Elves, both called the Red Witch by the Tribes and Gnomish-Men living in and around the Wynterlande Forest. The first Red Witch vanished the day nearly all the Elfkind disappeared forever. The handful of survivors dispersed into the wide world and most were never seen again. The second Red Witch was one of those survivors, taking up residence in the tower at the edge of the Wynterlande Forest as heir and successor to the first. She was murdered by the evil Black Prince and, as far as the rest of the world knew, the tower had been vacant ever since.

Jadzia looked nervous as she crossed through the gates at the edge of the gardens surrounding the Red Tower, like she had done something wrong and was waiting to be punished for her crime. She walked a few paces ahead of Arad and never looked back, though she knew he was still there. She could hear him breathing. When they arrived at the massive oak doors marking the entrance to the tower, Jadzia pushed them open and disappeared into the darkness on the other side. Arad hesitated for a moment as the fear of the unknown overwhelmed him. He considered turning around and running back into the forest but Jadzia lit a torch with a small fireball, revealing the grandeur of the entryway and peaking Arad's curiosity.

The wide passages and hallways leading towards the heart of the tower were absent any furniture or trappings that would suggest it played home to an occupant. There were cobwebs forming in the corners and the building was overly drafty, like a cold, stale wind was wafting through the corridors. Arad wondered about the history of the building. It seemed as though no one had been there for years. Then he saw a dull light glowing from an open door at the end of the passageway and heard someone pacing back and forth with heavy feet. When they entered the room, Jadzia rushed over to the tall elderly man near the wall and bowed to him dramatically before turning to face Arad.

"Arad, I would like you to meet my friend and teacher, Araxim," said Jadzia with a slight tremor in her voice.

"It is very nice to meet you, Arad," said Araxim, "I've been looking forward to this moment for a long time."

"You have?" said Arad in irritated confusion.

"Oh, yes," replied Araxim with a smile, "that will be all, Jadzia."

Jadzia turned around and rushed out of the room, closing the door behind her and leaving Arad alone with Araxim. Araxim was at least six and a half feet tall with a bony, thin body covered by the layers of his gray robes. He surveyed Arad with an expression of superiority, causing Arad's blood to boil as he was overwhelmed with anger.

"Very good," smiled Araxim, "your anger will give you strength…Jadzia tells me you know how to use magic?"

"Yeah...what's it to you?" barked Arad.

"Do you know anything about the wizarding clans?" asked Araxim.

"Who doesn't...there were six of them before the Wyts were exterminated. There are the Greens, the Greys, the Browns, the Blues, and the Reds, but they've all followed suit and disappeared."

"Not all."

"So...you're a wizard?" smiled Arad menacingly.

"I was born into the caste of the Grey Robes," said Araxim, "I joined the Order at the age of fifteen and devoted my life to the service of our Master, he who gives us our power and binds us to our righteous cause. It was my destiny, just as it is yours."

"I'm no wizard," sneered Arad.

"But you are. You are a legacy of the Orthelios bloodline. Your father's grandfather was a member of the Grey Order, just like his father, and all his forefathers before him."

"You knew my father?"

"Sadly, I never had the pleasure of making his acquaintance. He didn't pursue a life in the Order. He became a Knight of the Old Guard instead and, from what I hear, he was a force to be contended with. I did know your great-grandfather, Idran, very well. He was my teacher. He taught me everything I know. Now I will teach you."

"I already know how to use magic," huffed Arad.

"Yes, your mother tells me your skills are quite impressive," said Araxim, "but you have barely scratched the surface. The real power of magic rests with the wizarding clans, kept secret for centuries by our Orders. With my help I can impart that hidden wisdom to you and give you a strength you've only ever imagined."

"Why?" asked Arad suspiciously, "What's in it for you?"

"I made a promise to my Master that I would bring you into the Order. It's your destiny to be our champion, Arad. You were born with great power. You only need to learn how to access it, to make it work for you as a weapon to instill fear into the hearts of others."

Arad was suddenly overwhelmed by a sense of fear and panic. He was miles away from the only home he had ever known in the presence of a powerful and cunning wizard who could no doubt destroy him with the blink of his eyes. Arad trembled slightly, causing Araxim to walk over and extend his arms to stabilize him. Arad recoiled as Araxim touched him.

"I mean you no harm, boy," said Araxim gently, "I would never dare to hurt our savior."

"Savior?" said Arad, "How am I your savior? I'm nobody."

"You're wrong. You're very special. You have a power within you that cannot be matched, inherited from your Orthelios forefathers and from the bloodline of your mother."

"I hate my mother," Arad blurted out without thinking.

"You've never met your mother."

"But…"

"Jadzia is not your mother. I placed you in her care when you were a baby, after she rescued you from death."

"I don't understand. If Jadzia isn't my real mother, who is?"

"I'll show you," said Araxim before leading Arad to the back of the room and through a narrow archway. On the other side was a tall spiral staircase leading ever upward into the lofty heights of the Red Tower. Araxim mounted the stairs and Arad followed.

After several minutes of exhausting climbing, they came to a large landing with no door or windows, standing like a balcony overlooking the staircase spiraling back down the way they had just come. Araxim stood there on the landing for a moment searching through the many interior pockets of his shabby gray robes until, at last he produced a small rectangular box and a long wand hewn from blackthorn and tipped with a crystalline point. Araxim tapped the wall opposite the stairs with his wand and muttered a spell under his breath. The wall suddenly gave way as the red bricks began to rearrange themselves, forming an archway where seconds before one did not exist. The chamber opposite them was almost completely dark, except for a dull silver glow emanating from the opposite side of the room. Araxim and Arad entered and Arad was immediately drawn to the light. It looked like a strangely shaped lantern. It was oblong and oval, like someone had sat on and squished a ball of clay.

"What is that?" asked Arad as his curiosity got the best of him.

"Your mother," replied Araxim.

Sure enough, as they moved closer, Arad began to see a creature lying at the heart of the soft silver light. It had the same general characteristics as a woman: breasts, arms, legs, a torso, a head, that sort of thing. However, its skin was as white as freshly fallen snow and it lacked a nose or any distinguishable characteristics. Strange, branch-like hair grew in droves from atop its head and its ears were long and pointy. As Arad gazed into its large, molten silver eyes staring blankly at the ceiling, he knew what type of creature sat before him. His mother was Elfkind.

Araxim moved to stand over her and opened one side of the small box in his hands, revealing a glass window through which the same soft silver light was glowing.

"She's dead," said Arad angrily.

"No," replied Araxim, "she is in a state of non-death. I couldn't let her die. She's the last of her kind. Imagine what she could tell us, the vast wisdom she could share. Sadly, she was never very cooperative. I was forced to resort to extreme measures to contain her. I split her soul from her body and imprisoned it within this box. As long as I possess this, I control her every thought and her every movement."

"Just like Jadzia and her sisters."

"Not quite. The Shadow-Weavers are dead. Jadzia uses their souls to bring reanimation to their flesh, but she cannot restore them to life. Your mother can be returned to the world of the living because she is not dead. Let me show you…"

"Esgyn Caenara," said Araxim.

The light within the box pulsed brightly for a few seconds before the light around Arad's mother echoed with the same pattern before all the torches lining the walls of the chamber burst to life and Caenara herself was wrapped in fire. The violent red flames licked at her skin but they did not harm her as she rose to hover in the air above the table upon which she'd been lying. Her silver eyes glowed with a fiery intensity as the fire around her formed the silhouette of a mighty raptor.

"Ni fyddaf yn cael ei gynnal gartharor yma," she spat and as she did bolts of fire flew outward from the raptor towards Araxim. Araxim wrapped his hand around the box and drowned out the silver light emanating from it with the darkness of his robes. The fiery raptor around Caenara vanished as she fell back to the table. She was still conscious but she seemed violently drained of her energy. She didn't even have the strength to lift her head.

"Why have you awoken me?" she said weakly.

"I thought you might like to meet your son," said Araxim, pointing towards where Arad was standing in awe. Caenara looked at Arad and a weak smile appeared on her face. She examined his every feature from his long red hair to his tall, lean body. She seemed impressed, though her present condition kept her from any true emotional reactions.

"My son…my Arad," she said in almost a whisper, "You look so much like your father. But you have my eyes. I prayed I would live to see this day. The gods have brought you to me for a reason. They knew I needed to see that you were safe. Now I may die in peace."

"You're not going anywhere," hissed Araxim.

"Oh, yes she is," replied Arad as he conjured a powerful bolt of lightning and sent it cascading towards Araxim. Araxim grinned sarcastically as he pointed his wand at the lightning, absorbing it into its tip so that he stood there unharmed and amused. He replied by slamming the window in the side of the box shut, causing Caenara to fall lifelessly to the table, returned to her comatose state of non-death. Arad called the shadows cast by the dozens of torches, compelling them to attack Araxim but again he raised his wand and the shadows turned on Arad, wrapping themselves around him like shackles binding a violent prisoner.

"I told you," said Araxim, "you are powerful but your strength is no match for that of a wizard. The only way you'll be able to kill me and free your mother is to learn the ways of the Grey Order, to become my apprentice."

"Why would I ever agree to that?"

"If you become my student and allow me to indoctrinate you into the Grey Order, I will free your mother. If you do not, I will kill her. The choice is entirely up to you…"

"Fine," said Arad with a tone of disgust, "But I will hold you to your promise…when do we start?"

"Now," replied Araxim before snapping his fingers and causing both him and Arad to be swallowed by shadows. In the blink of an eye the shadows dissolved and Arad found himself standing in another chamber within the Red Tower. This one was at the top of the tower with windows stretching across one of the walls. Arad could see across the top of the Wynterlande Forest. It looked like a sea of green and white stretching outward towards the distant horizon. The room itself was filled with various cabinets and tables, chairs and mirrors but what drew Arad's attention was a long ornate wand sitting at the center of the chamber. It was crafted from intricately polished blackthorn with a strand of gold and a strand of silver wrapping around it in a spiraling pattern, from its wider base to its narrow tip. Upon the metal was written various runes in the ancient language of Elfkind and it was tipped with a purple moonstone point.

"It's beautiful isn't it?" said Araxim.

"Yes, very," replied Arad.

"It belonged to your great-grandfather. Now it is yours."

Araxim gestured for Arad to take the wand but, before he could wrap his fingers around it, a hauntingly terrible spell spilled forth from Araxim's mouth like water erupting from a geyser.

"Yn dod allan oddi eyerth coref a yn y roedth thon hawyn."

Arad was overcome by an unbearable pain in his stomach, doubling over in agony before he felt something being ripped from his body, torn from the depths of his being like the pit being cut from the heart of an olive. As Arad began to scream an orb of light materialized in front of him, soaring across the air towards the wand. However, before it could reach its destination, Araxim spoke another spell.

"Rhoi'r gorau i."

The orb stopped in midair before Araxim walked over and plucked it from the air with a look of confusion on his face. When one openly practices the darkness in the Art, it has an effect on the light of the soul, transmuting its natural brilliance with shadows so that it takes on a dirty grayish hue. Yet Arad's soul continued to glow with a brilliant mixture of golden and silver light, as though all his anger, hatred, and selfish intentions had never penetrated his spirit, never tarnished its natural beauty. Araxim studied it closely while Arad stood there in a daze. Araxim walked over to the cabinet nearest to the windows and produced a box similar to the one holding Caenara's soul. He opened it by pressing a hidden trigger and jammed Arad's spirit inside before squeezing it tightly. Arad fell unconscious to the floor, his eyes staring lifelessly at the ceiling.

Araxim left Arad there and rushed out of the room, down several corridors and even more stairs before he arrived back in the main hall of the tower. Jadzia was sitting on the steps near the entrance with her head in her hands. She stood when she saw Araxim, who struck her hard across the face as soon as she was in reach, knocking her to the floor with the brute force of his fearsome blow. It took her a moment to recover and when she did, she stayed on the floor.

"You idiot," spat Araxim, "you swore to me the boy would be ready. How many times did you tell me he had begun practicing the darkness in earnest? How many times did you reassure me everything was going according to plan? You lied…"

Araxim pointed his wand at Jadzia and she was lifted from the floor, screaming in absolute agony as her skin began to be burned by invisible flames that left no mark but convinced her mind that she was on fire. Her eyes began to bulge from her head as she became convinced her head was in a vice and, worst of all, it felt like someone was jamming a red hot poker into her vagina. She screamed again and again until Araxim was convinced she had endured enough. He dropped her in a quivering pile on the floor and stowed his wand in one of the interior pockets of his robe.

"I promise I did everything you ordered me to do," said Jadzia in a whisper, "I swear…"

"Something did not go according to plan," hissed Araxim, "and it changes everything."

Chapter Eight
"The Gentle Giant"

The journey that took Aras away from the only home he'd known since infancy took nearly three months to complete. He spent his sixteenth birthday on a tiny freighter crossing the Straights of Katar from the Free City of Alkonath to the Principality of Darthonia. Gyrdhan chose an erratic and unpredictable path in case they were followed. It felt as though they had crossed the breadth of the known world as they journeyed first from their home to the distant isle of Lemuria, then to the Easterling Islands before setting out for Alkonath where they met one of Gyrdhan's old friends who gave them food and provisions. When they once again set out after only a single night's stay, Aras and Darendon grew restless. Once they reached Darthonia, they camped on a white sand beach under the light of the bright winter stars. Darendon went to sleep early, while Gyrdhan and Aras hunkered down next to a roaring fire.

"How much longer are we going to do this?" asked Aras.

"Do what?" replied Gyrdhan.

"Live like nomads," said Aras, "I thought you said we were heading for the Norn Mountains."

"We are. We're just takin' the long way 'round. I thought the wanderin' wizard might 'a sent his minions to follow us. But I don't think they have kept up. We'll set out fer the mountains in the mornin'."

Aras was relieved to hear their long journey would be drawing to a close but he was also overwhelmed by fear as he thought about the distant mountains that would become his haven and safe harbor. He had heard stories about the inhabitants of the Norn Mountains that would strike terror into the heart of any man. Darendon's father used to tell them bedtime stories that would bring them nightmares and cause them to wet their beds. He told them about the vicious giants who dwelt in the high passes of those frosty mountains. They were said to stand over ten feet tall and had the strength of ten men but they were dim and slow. They attacked and ate anything that moved, including their own children, and were content to live in squalor like violent cavemen. Gyrdhan could sense what Aras was thinking by the expression he wore heavily on his face.

"The stories that Darendon's father told ya were only partially true, Ari," said Gyrdhan, "The Norn Giants are barbarians true enough. They war with each other all the time but they aren't cannibals. They're just like men, only a bit larger. Some 'a them aren't so bad..."

"How would you know?" asked Darendon who emerged from the tent with a look of curiosity on his face.

"They're my kinfolk," said Gyrdhan suddenly, "don't tell me ya never suspected I was a giant..."

"We just assumed you were a really big guy," said Darendon.

"I kind of knew you were a giant," admitted Aras, "I read a letter you keep hidden in your undergarment drawer. It was from your mother asking you to please come home and rejoin your people. She talked about a giant named Treax and someone called Locutia."

"Treax is my father," said Gyrdhan, "and Locutia is a woman I used to know when I was your age."

"She was your girlfriend?" asked Darendon.

"We were close but she chose faith over her feelings for me," said Gyrdhan sullenly, "she joined the Order 'a the Veil once we were eighteen. Priestesses 'a the Veil are not allowed to marry or even spend time in the company 'a men...I never saw her again."

"But your mother's letter," began Aras.

"If ya had finished readin' it, you would 'a seen my mother was writin' to let me know Locutia had died and askin' me to come home fer the funeral ceremonies. I wanted to go but I couldn't bring myself to make the trip. I was still hurt."

Gyrdhan chose that moment to retire for the night, standing and lumbering into the tent with the weight of the world bearing down on his shoulders. Aras and Darendon eventually fell asleep by the fire, each dreaming of the other as the moon crossed the sky and the sun began to rise. Just after dawn, Gyrdhan rose and woke the boys. They ate apples and some nuts Gyrdhan had bought in Darthonia before boarding their little skiff and setting out across the waters of the Gulf of Ulna towards the northwestern tip of the Atland. The entire trip took only three days and soon they were within sight of a wide peninsula covered by a thick evergreen forest. The temperature had dropped by several degrees and the landscape was covered by thick layers of snow and ice. A frigid wind howled across the choppy water of the gulf and Gyrdhan was careful to avoid the numerous icebergs bobbing on the waves of the sea like corks.

"That's the Wynterlande Forest," said Gyrdhan as they hugged the shore to avoid the tumults of the large waves, "it used to be a place where the old ways were strong but now it's been abandoned. Terrible shame, it's a real pretty place. And those, those there are the Norn Mountains."

Beyond the Gulf of Ulna, where the peninsula of the Wynterlande Forest met the rest of the Atland, stood dozens of tall, snow-capped mountains, stretching outward towards the inland parts of the small continent. The mountains were very majestic as they stood there, their lower slopes covered by evergreen trees, their higher passes packed with snow and ice. Yet they also looked intimidating and Aras wondered if he and Darendon possessed the stamina to endure life in such a cold, inhospitable environment. Gyrdhan continued talking as he rowed the skiff along the coastline of the forested peninsula.

"The only people that live in the mountains are the giants…but there are men who live in the hills to the south and in the Frozenland to the north.

They aren't like the men you boys grew up 'round. They're barbarians and they don't mind killin' their own if it means they're gonna gain power over their people. They ain't meant to be crossed."

"What about the people who used to live in the forest? Were they barbarians too?" asked Darendon.

"Nah," replied Gyrdhan, "they were Atlandish people. Mostly 'a the tribes of Fornos. Then there was the Dunmors...they were gnomish-men, real little fellas with hardy bodies and gentle spirits. I dunno but I think they're all gone now..."

"Were there ever any elves?" asked Aras.

"Not really...only one, an Elf-Witch that lived in a tower on the edge of the forest," said Gyrdhan, "but she's been dead a long time, just like the rest of 'em."

"You don't think Anaximander will look for us here?" asked Darendon with a tone of genuine concern.

"I dunno but I never really told nobody 'bout my parents, so he shouldn't know anythin' 'bout my ties to this place."

For the next few hours they went about their business without really talking. Gyrdhan continued to row the skiff while Darendon cooked some freshly caught bass for their breakfast. Aras practiced magically calling the wind to help push them faster across the choppy water and soon they were approaching a small harbor with a rickety old dock, just northeast of the Wynterlande peninsula. Gyrdhan tied off their boat and gathered their provisions into his massive pack before they disembarked, setting out on a narrow dirt trail winding its way across a hilly grassland towards the mountains in the distance. It was immensely cold and, even with his multilayered furs, Aras was shivering. Darendon fared better but even his usual rough, warrior demeanor was beginning to crack.

They continued on foot for two days, spending the first night by a little creek amidst a small grove of furs and the second night against the wall of a narrow ravine. Gyrdhan hunted the first night and returned to camp with a small boar that he skinned and set out to cure on a hand-built tray resting on stilts above the fire. The meat would feed them for days and, along with the nuts, berries, and dried fruits they brought with them, they were in no danger of starvation. They were, however, susceptible to the cold and found themselves moving slower than they otherwise would have.

On the third morning, as the path began to steadily slope upwards towards the high passes of the cold mountains, Gyrdhan took a detour from the trail, leading the boys into a thicket of evergreens where he uncovered a hidden cave by shifting a large boulder a normal-size man would find impossible to move. He disappeared inside for a few moments, returning with weapons in tow, two normal sized longswords for the boys and an enormous double-bladed axe for himself. As he handed a blade to Aras, Aras handed it back with a dramatic gesture of passivity.

"Yer gonna need it," said Gyrdhan, trying to return the sword but Aras again refused it.

"I think I can take care of myself," said Aras.

"Except magic don't work on giants," replied Gyrdhan, shoving the sword into Aras' hands more forcefully. This time Aras accepted it, pulling the scabbard belt over his torso so the blade hung down his back.

"Don't worry, Ari, I won't let anyone hurt you," said Darendon with a wink in Aras' direction. Aras felt a spark of warmth rise from the pit of his stomach and his knees buckled slightly. His pupils dilated and the capillaries in his face burst, making him flush and hot. Even there amidst the coldest cold Aras had ever endured, he felt like he would break out in sweat from overheating. Darendon smiled wryly as he walked beside Aras, both on Gyrdhan's heels.

After returning to the trail and venturing steadily upward for more than two hours, the snow became so deep Gyrdhan began using the handle of his axe to plough a trail for the boys. Aras couldn't tell if they were still on the path or not as they walked on and on, up and up. Just after noon, they came to the base of a sheer cliff with massive stairs cut into it, leading to the lofty heights above. Gyrdhan could mount the steps like normal but the boys were forced to resort to crawling up them one at a time. They stopped on a ledge to eat lunch, by which point Aras and Darendon were utterly exhausted. That didn't stop Gyrdhan from resuming their course after only a few short minutes of rest. When they finally reached the top they were met by a thick forest of pine trees growing along a high slope of one of the tallest of the Norn Mountains.

"We're 'bout to enter the Cradle," said Gyrdhan softly, "this is where most 'a the giants on the mountain live. We gotta be extra quiet through these parts…try not to make a sound."

They moved through the thicket like church mice foraging for bread crumbs, taking great care not to break any branches or rustle any leaves as they walked along a little animal trail twisting about the thicket. A few times, Gyrdhan stopped dead in his tracks and stuck his ear out, as though he could hear something dangerous in the distance. Aras tried to ask him what it was but Gyrdhan motioned for him to remain silent. On each occasion, neither of the boys heard anything and, after a few seconds, Gyrdhan resumed his course through the pines.

The sun was beginning to settle down behind the jagged mountain peaks as the three travelers emerged from the thicket onto a small plateau with a frozen lake stretching over half of it and what looked to be an enormous pile of big granite stones. Gyrdhan moved slowly towards the pile of rocks but halted after the tall hedges on the opposite side of the lake began to rustle. A giant of no less than twelve feet stepped out into sight, his giant hands grasping a freshly killed caribou. His face was grotesque to look at, with dozens of long scars across his cheeks and one eyeball missing. His teeth were gnarled and black and his massive body was covered by layered animal furs. It took the giant a moment to notice Aras and the others. When he did, he charged them like an angry bull staring at a red banner. He jumped into the air and bore down on Gyrdhan who hit the ground with an earth-shaking thud. Aras panicked and Darendon drew his sword as Gyrdhan wrestled with the larger, stronger giant. However, before the boys could attack, the big giant stood and extended his hand to Gyrdhan.

"Long time no see, runt," smiled the giant.

Seeing the looks of sheer terror on the boys' faces, Gyrdhan patted the giant on the back.

"Ari…this is my brother, Pregg…Pregg, this is my son, Ari, and his friend, Dar…"

Pregg nodded roughly in the direction of the boys as though they were not really there before hugging his brother and walking him off towards the giant pile of rocks. Aras and Darendon followed purely out of a desire not to let Gyrdhan out of their sight. They were still in unfamiliar territory and the thought of another giant appearing terrified them.

"Where's ma?" asked Gyrdhan as he and Pregg walked a few paces in front of the boys.

"She met this wanderin' hermit day 'fore yesterday," replied Pregg, "she headed off with him into the woods and she ain't been back since. Probably helpin' him get some meat. You know how ma is and it's not often we get visitors in these parts."

"And da?" said Gyrdhan quietly.

"Where do ya think he is?" replied Pregg.

"So he's still drinkin'. Does he still wail on ma?"

Pregg avoided the question.

"Come on in," said Pregg, "I'm sure ma left some sweetbreads and I can rustle up a tankard 'a shine…and tea fer the little ones."

Pregg led Gyrdhan and the boys around the huge pile of rocks, revealing a tall doorway leading underneath it. Pregg opened the door to expose a large interior and Aras realized it wasn't a heap of rubble, it was

Pregg and his parents' home, maybe even the place where Gyrdhan had grown up. Pregg took them straight across a spacious common room complete with a hearth to a small alcove where a wood-burning stove, several counters, and a deep water basin were situated. There was also a table with four chairs. Gyrdhan sat in one and the boys in two of the others while Pregg put a kettle on the stove and produced a tin full of sweetbreads from the nearby larder. He put out napkins, two tall glasses, and two teacups, the sweetbreads, some dried figs, and a cask of whiskey before returning to the stove to retrieve the kettle. He poured the hot water into the boys' cups and added a teabag before sitting next to Gyrdhan and passing around the platter holding the sweetbreads.

"It's nice to finally meet a member of Gyrdhan's family," said Aras after shoving half a dozen sweet breads in his mouth and draining his teacup of its warm, soothing contents.

Again, Aras was ignored.

"You say ma is out with a wanderin' hermit," said Gyrdhan, "you didn't catch his name, did ya?"

"Nah," said Pregg with his mouth full of sweetbreads, "didn't ask...he's a squirrely little fella. Probably 'bout twenty years old or so. Got wiry brown hair and a little beard to match. He was wearin' a bunch 'a dirty white rags and he was barefoot. Oh yeah...he was leanin' pretty heavily on a tall oak staff...might 'a been injured."

Aras knew what Gyrdhan was thinking. He could see a look of relief wash over his foster-father's face as he leaned back into his chair and drank his whiskey. He thought the hermit may have been a Red Robe in the service of the Collective inside the wizard, Anaximander. It would've been a shock and shame to have made such a long journey only to be caught in the end and delivered to their enemy. But Red Robes carried swords, not staffs, and they would never be caught out in the open wearing anything other than their ornate crimson garments. At best, the hermit in the company of Gyrdhan's mother was a former member of the Green Robes, but if that were the case, he would be dressed in green. At worst, he was nothing more than an opportunistic beggar waiting for the opportunity to take advantage of Gyrdhan's family.

Once they had consumed all the food on the table, plus some cakes stashed in a high cupboard, Gyrdhan rose and led the boys through a couple of doorways into a large washroom with a deep bathing tub standing in its center. Gyrdhan turned a nozzle near the foot of the bath and a steady stream of warm water began pouring in. He produced a bar of soap from a cabinet near the water basin and tossed it to Aras.

"You boys get cleaned up…I'll lay out some fresh clothes fer ya. Then you should get some sleep."

The boys stripped off their layers of furs, their tunics and their breeches before slipping into the water together. The warmth felt good against their chilled skin. Aras closed his eyes and relaxed while breathing the vapors as Darendon washed his legs and his torso. Once Darendon was ready he poked Aras in the shoulder and handed him the soap, signaling Aras to begin scrubbing away at Darendon's back. This they reversed the process but, after he had finished, Darendon allowed his hands to linger on Aras' shoulders in a gentle caress.

"I'm glad I'm here with you," said Darendon.

"Me too," replied Aras, "we're on an adventure."

Darendon moved his face closer to Aras neck, so close that Aras could feel Darendon's breath on his skin.

"Just you and me," said Darendon, "me and you."

"And Gyrdhan," shouted Aras as Gyrdhan reappeared in the room with two large towels and two of Aras' nightshirts he had packed amidst their supplies. Darendon quickly withdrew from his embrace with Aras and jumped out of the bath, walking nonchalantly over to Gyrdhan and plucking one of the towels out of his hands. Gyrdhan threw the other to Aras and a few minutes later they were dressed. Gyrdhan took them to a small bedchamber near the back of the house with a giant feather bed. There was a gentle fire burning in a tiny hearth at the back of the room and Gyrdhan had placed two extra blankets across the foot of the bed.

"You two take the bed," said Gyrdhan, "I'll sleep in the livin' room."

With that, Gyrdhan retreated from the room, shutting the door behind him. Aras laid down on the side of the bed nearest the fire and covered up with one of the thick linen blankets.

"I can't sleep in this," announced Darendon before stripping off the nightshirt and sliding into bed naked. He pulled the same blanket over himself and tucked himself up next to Aras. He put his hand on Aras' knee and then very slowly began to move it upward.

"What are you doing?" asked Aras urgently.

Darendon responded by pressing his lips against Aras' and forcing them open with his tongue. Aras didn't resist as Darendon climbed on top of him, gyrating his hips and rubbing their tumescent organs together. Aras was enraptured by the experience. He had always secretly longed to touch Darendon but he never thought Darendon felt the same. Clearly he was wrong. Darendon pulled Aras' nightshirt over his head and began kissing each part of his body. When he came to Aras' member, he sucked it into his mouth with a loud slurp, driving Aras to the edge of orgasm as he lost his seed down Darendon's warm throat. Darendon licked his lips and smiled before plopping himself down on the bed next to Aras and closing his eyes. Aras wrapped his arms around Darendon, and with his head resting on his lover's chest, fell into a deep sleep.

Some hours later, the boys were awoken with a start to the sound of Gyrdhan yelling.

"I dunno who ya think ya are but ya ain't goin' anywhere near my son," he screamed.

"Gyrdhan, be sensible," said a woman's voice.

"Stay out 'a this, ma," replied Gyrdhan.

"You misunderstand me, sir," said a man's voice, "I am not asking your permission."

"I am gonna," started Gyrdhan but he was stopped midsentence by some unseen force. Then there was a small explosion and a loud crash, followed by another explosion and another crash. Darendon drew his sword and stood on the bed in front of Aras as the door swung open and the young hermit Pregg had told them about, wrapped in dirty white rags, rushed into the room with an oaken staff gripped in his right hand. With one wave of his staff, Darendon was lifted off the bed and thrown against the wall before crumpling unconscious to the floor. The hermit stared at Aras with his wide blue eyes, a distant look of recognition on his face.

"Thank the Old Gods, it's really you," said the hermit, "You have no idea what I've gone through to get here."

"And who the hell are you?" spat Aras defensively.

The hermit smiled warmly at Aras, as if to tell him he had nothing to be frightened of said:

"They call me Anaximander."

Chapter Nine
"Broken Spirits"

The darkness of his cell was so impenetrable that Arad lost track of the passing of time. He didn't know if he had been there for a month or a year. He tried to measure the days by his evening meal, making a mark that he could not see on the wall near the iron door. Then he stopped. He lost the will to care as he sat there, day in, day out, with no human contact, no light, and barely the strength to lift himself up off the pile of straw serving as his bed to pace in the darkness. The last thing he could remember of the outside world was Araxim tearing his spirit from his body to place it in his great-grandfather's wand. Then everything went dark and had remained that way ever since. The only time he was exposed to light came when the small door within the iron door would slide open each night to deliver him his food and water. It was clear Araxim was trying to force Arad to lose his mind. It wasn't working. The experience only served to fuel his anger and his hatred of all things outside his control.

Finally, after his endless entombment seemed it would never cease, the iron door was thrown open and a hideously deformed man with a hunchback and a sharp odor came lumbering into the cell. Arad attempted to conjure a spell but before he could act the hunchback knocked him over the head with the hammer he was carrying in his right hand. When Arad came around, he was strapped naked to a strange contraption clearly meant to torture him. His hands and feet were wrapped in heavy rope strung through a system of pulleys to position his so that his arms were pulled taut above his head and his legs were spread-eagle to the point that it was straining the sensitive muscles in Arad's groin. Araxim was standing in front of Arad while the hunchback was manning a lever that controlled the ropes holding Arad in his embarrassing mid-air pose. They were in a room with black walls and a rough stone floor. There were no windows and the only door was the same iron design as the one barring Arad into his cell.

"I don't know what you hope to achieve by this," said Arad with a raspy voice, "but it won't work."

"I applaud your stubbornness, Arad, I really do," smirked Araxim, "but you overestimate your power and your resolve. In my day, I used to take prisoner the greatest heroes and wizards in Albion and subject them to this method of persuasion. Each and every one of them broke. You'll be no different...trust me."

The hunchback pulled hard on the lever and the ropes around Arad's arms shot upwards so quickly it caused both of his shoulders to pop out of joint. He screamed involuntarily before hardening his face and glaring stoically at Araxim. The hunchback repeated the process again and again. Each time, Arad stared at Araxim with cold indifference. Araxim only smiled as the hunchback retrieved a strange pyramidal pedestal made of polished wood, with the tip at the highest vertical point, flaring outward to form the base about a foot below. The hunchback placed the pedestal directly beneath Arad and then returned to his lever. Arad was already writhing in silent agony from the indescribable pain emanating from his dislocated shoulders as the hunchback used the lever to lower him so that the tip of the pyramidal pedestal was nestled between Arad's buttocks. The hunchback produced two more ropes which he tied around Arad's painful shoulders and then attached to a series of heavy weights. The weights made Arad whimper, much to Araxim's satisfaction.

"Does it hurt, Arad?" asked Araxim, "Are you sure you don't want to give up?"

"Never," sneered Arad.

"Do it," yelled Araxim and the hunchback turned his lever again. This time the pulleys activated in a way that, instead of being stretched, the ropes holding Arad's hands slacked off, causing the weighted ropes to pull Arad downward with an exaggerated force of gravity. The tip of the pyramidal pedestal tore through Arad's sphincter, stretching his anus beyond its natural elasticity as it swallowed the pyramid beneath him. He couldn't help but scream in complete agony, his eyes tearing and his face flush with rage. All he could think was how much he hated Araxim, how he wanted to see him dead no matter the cost and that focus helped him to subdue the pain sweeping through every muscle of his body.

"Take him down and throw him in the tub," said Araxim after about ten minutes, "then give him a few licks from the dragon tail."

The hunchback pulled his lever and raised Arad off the pyramid. His rectum was bleeding profusely and his shoulders were crying out in agony as the hunchback undid the ropes around his hands and legs before detaching the weights dragging Arad down onto the hideous torture device below. The hunchback popped each of Arad's shoulders back into their joints, which hurt almost as much as the process of dislocating them and carried him through the iron door, across a passage, through another iron door, and into a room similar to the one they had just been occupying. This one, however, was home to two large tub-like basins, one filled with water near the point of boiling, the other with frigid shards of ice. The hunchback tossed Arad into the hot tub first. The water burned at his skin like flames licking a witch on the pyre. He fought to keep his head safe from burning but the hunchback forced him under three times. Then he plucked him out of the tub and dropped him into the ice. The frosty cold caused Arad's burns to sting like he was experiencing an acid peal. The hunchback repeated the process nine more times, leaving Arad a blubbering mess lying helplessly on the freezing stone floor.

Instead of ending the torture or providing Arad with comfort, the hunchback produced a barbed whip from a nearby cabinet and commenced to use it with brutal efficiency on Arad's back while he laid there in a state of absolute terror. The whip tore chunks from Arad's back as it bit him a dozen times. The last stroke dealt by the hunchback caused one of the barbs to hook into Arad's face just below his right eye and tore a huge gash down his cheek as it was retracted.

"That's enough," said Araxim, "bind his wounds with Alfsalve and take him back to his cell...we'll do it all over again tomorrow."

The hunchback did as he was told, wrapping Arad's wounds with moist bandages that smelled like wild mushrooms and poppies before tossing him back into the darkness of his cell. The next morning, the process was repeated and again the next day. For months on end, Arad was subjected to the same torture. He was also beaten and starved. His testicles were squeezed until he puked and he was forced to drink rancid urine. Each time he was returned to his cell, he felt himself growing weaker, his energy was sapped and his will was beginning to break. He was consumed with maniacal thoughts as he dreamed of reversing roles with the hunchback. He wanted nothing more than to inflict the same pain he had endured on others. The darkness swelled in his heart, bringing Araxim to visit him as he neared his eighteenth birthday. He carried with him the little black box containing Arad's soul.

"I want to show you something," said Araxim with a sheepish grin. He opened the miniature door on the side of the box to expose the window peeking inside. Within the box, Arad's spirit no longer burned with a bright silver and golden light. It was dark and dingy, like water infected with a toxic algae. It was as weak as Arad felt, lying there on his pile of straw.

"So what?" barked Arad.

"So, we're finally ready to begin," said Araxim before producing Arad's great-grandfather's wand from his pocket. He released Arad's spirit and drove it into the wand where it disappeared with a flash. Arad immediately felt stronger as he rose from the floor. Araxim handed him the wand and nodded for him to follow him.

Araxim led Arad up a series of spiral staircases. After a few minutes, they emerged on the main floor of the Red Tower but they didn't stop there. They kept climbing until they reached a narrow passageway with a half-dozen wooden doors lining each wall. Araxim opened the third door on the left, exposing a large bedchamber with a tall hearth, several soft linen rugs, and a giant feather bed. The light of the clear winter morning was shining in through the six large windows opposite the door. The room was warm from a hardy fire which must have been built just minutes before. But what drew Arad's attention was the two individuals chained to the foot of the bed. One was a tall, attractive female with olive colored skin, hair the color of chestnuts and eyes as black as a moonless night. The other was a young man of average height with white skin bronzed by the sun, blonde hair, and blue eyes. He had a slender, athletic body, while she had the perfect womanly figure.

"These are your slaves," said Araxim, "the girl is called Valera…the boy is Xavin. I acquired them recently from an Easterling Trader. I thought you might like them."

"I do," grinned Arad.

"Good," replied Araxim, "I'll leave you here with them for now. Get some rest. I'll send Graug with some dinner later."

Araxim withdrew from the room, leaving Arad alone with Valera and Xavin. Arad walked over to where they were chained, looking them up and down the whole way. His face was frozen in stoic apathy as he fingered the locks binding his slaves to the bed.

"How do I release these?" said Arad, pointing at the chains.

"The master has the key," whispered Valera without looking up.

"Then I'll have to find another way," said Arad, drawing his wand and pointing it at the lock holding the chain to an iron collar around Xavin's neck. Arad thought about melting the lock and, without uttering a single incantation, the wand glowed and the lock was eviscerated. Xavin stood and stretched his arms. He had clearly been kneeling there for hours.

"What about me?" muttered Valera.

"Don't worry," smiled Arad, "you'll get your turn."

Xavin and Valera's screams could be heard on the other side of the tower as they were subjected to the same kind of horrors Arad had come to know in his months of torture. When he was finished beating, raping, and whipping his slaves, he replaced their chains and crawled into his feather bed, falling into a deep, dreamless sleep, wearing a devilish grin the entire time.

The next few weeks were spent with Arad under the constant eye and tutelage of Araxim. Araxim taught him the secrets of the Grey Robes and how to properly maximize the potential of his wand. Arad learned how to walk in the shadows and call the monstrous creatures that dwell in the darkness to do his bidding. He was made privy to the conjurations of the fiercest and most dangerous spells ever created by man and steadily grew to become more powerful than he imagined he could ever become. He continued to treat Valera and Xavin like his personal puppets and toys, forcing them to endure unimaginable pain and perversions as well as feed Arad, clothe him, bathe him, and keep his bedchamber clean.

The tables were truly turned when Arad was allowed to practice his spells against Graug, the hunchback who had tortured him for nearly a year and a half. He used various burning spells, pestilence curses, hexes, and fell conjurations to render Graug a pile of crying skin. And then he would do it all over again. He had no sympathy for anyone or anything, his heart as hard as granite, his soul dark and menacing. He ceased to fear even Araxim. The only person who could still impose their will upon Arad was his foster-mother, Jadzia, who came often to see him in the Red Tower.

"Araxim tells me you're studies are coming along," said Jadzia on one of those visits.

"I am more powerful than you could possibly imagine," replied Arad.

"I know you are, I raised you," smiled Jadzia.

"How could I forget, mother," said Arad.

"It won't be long now and you'll be able to come home."

"What makes you think I want to go back there," snipped Arad.

"Where else would you go?" asked Jadzia.

Arad had thought a lot about what he would do when his training was over and he had become a Grey Robe. Many of the Grey Robes were living in seclusion within Tansapar, the Ruined City, and he entertained the idea of joining them, of rallying them into his service to build his own personal army. First he would have to deal with Araxim and Jadzia.

"Did you know about my real mother?" asked Arad angrily.

"Did I know what about your mother?" echoed Jadzia.

"Did you know she was here? Did you know Araxim was holding her captive because she's Elfkind?"

"I knew," replied Jadzia simply.

"I see. Good for you...you're more evil than I thought. Tell me something, Jadzia. Why don't I look like her? If she's an elf, am I an elf?"

"You're halfelfin," replied Jadzia, "the only one of your kind. You don't look like Caenara because your father was a man but you have her power inside your soul, hungering to escape."

Arad knew what Jadzia meant about Caenara's power. He felt something very deep inside him that he could not access, a force so great that it would bring the world to its knees in fear. One day he would learn the secret of that power and then Albion would truly come to know the meaning of suffering. He looked at Jadzia with open contempt but he didn't turn on her, he didn't attempt to inflict his usual torture on her or challenge her to a magical battle to the death. In some twisted way, he still saw her as his mother and respected her for the role she had played in his youth, however terrible she had been. There were greater enemies for Arad to focus on, one of which walked into the room as he was pondering that very thought.

"The master needs you two in the great hall," said Graug as he limped his way towards Jadzia and Arad.

Mother and son followed Graug to the main hall at the heart of the tower, where Araxim had gathered with three Grey Robes Arad had never seen before. They were relatively old yet seemingly immune to the decays of time as they retreated from the room.

"Who are they?" asked Jadzia.

"They are none of your concern," snapped Araxim harshly, "All you need to know is that the time has come for us to make our presence known...go and raise your sisters. We're going to need their help. Arad will join you at the tombs near your village in the morning."

Jadzia looked at her son for a moment before sweeping out of the room and out the front door of the tower. Arad watched her through the window as she disappeared into the shadows, taking the short route back to their home. Araxim put his hand on Arad's shoulder and led him away from the main hall. They crossed a wide passageway and entered a small parlor which served as Araxim's bedroom.

"You are about to prove if you are truly worthy to join the Grey Order," said Araxim, "this mission will determine if you will stand with us or die by our hands."

"I understand," said Arad.

"Understand this," sneered Araxim, "if you fail, you die. It's as simple as that...the mysterious stranger who took the Autumn Crown from the Lady Rheis before she died took it deep into the Atland. The other Grey Robes felt his presence as soon as he returned. You and your mother must go and retrieve the crown before our enemies have the chance to procure it. The Matriarchs would likely destroy it and the do-gooder wizards would also feel it was their duty to eliminate the threat the crown could pose on the world. We have to find it first."

"What does this crown look like?" asked Arad.

"It looks like nothing else you've ever seen before. Mortal eyes that look on its brilliance are mesmerized forever by its beauty and power."

"Where should I start my search?"

"At the heart of the Atland," said Araxim, "where it meets the Marshland Forest. That's where the augurs say the crown is residing. Find it and bring it here…"

"As you wish it, so shall it be, master," said Arad with a bow.

"Go now and meet your mother," said Araxim, "take Valera and Xavin with you if you wish. They won't be missed here."

Arad bowed again before turning to leave the room but, just before he reached the stairs that would lead him to his bedchamber, Araxim spoke a solemn warning Arad would never forget.

"Be careful, Arad," said Araxim, "I sense a change in the natural order. Something is coming that we cannot foresee."

Chapter Ten
"A Wizard's Tale"

"It's simply not possible," said Anaximander to a clearly irritated Aras, "there is no way to bring someone back from the dead. You can raise their hollow, rotting flesh to build an undead army by capturing and keeping prisoner their souls, but you cannot rejoin the two parts and make the person live again."

"But you're alive," replied Aras, "weren't you dead?"

"No, I wasn't. When the Wyts took over my body, I was forced into the deepest recesses of myself, held prisoner by the force of their combined power, as I have told you countless times before…"

It was true. In the two years since Aras, Gyrdhan, and Darendon had come to live in the Norn Mountains, Anaximander had recounted to them in full his harrowing tale, beginning with his own stupidity. Out of a desperate desire to save the wisdom of his fallen friends, the seven wizards of the Wyt Robes, Anaximander tampered with dangerous and dark magic in a vain attempt to repair the broken talisman called the Ring of a Hundred Souls. He intended to draw the spirits of the seven Wyts into the heart of the ring only long enough for them to impart their secret wisdom to him. Unfortunately, something went terribly wrong and the ring failed to absorb the Wyts' souls. With nowhere to go and no chance of escape, the seven souls did the only thing they could. They took possession of Anaximander's body, all at the same time.

Anaximander's spirit was bound to his oaken staff in the manner of the Green Robes and, from the moment they took possession of his body, the staff repelled the Collective. They conjured all their might to break the staff and set Anaximander's spirit free from the bonds of life. They believed that Anaximander's soul would journey to Avalon and then pass on to the Otherworld as all mortals do after their earthly deaths. For all Anaximander knew, he did exactly that but he did not remain there. Nine days after the destruction of Anaximander's staff, his spirit was returned to the living world, soaring through the heights of the heavens like an eagle majestically surveying the earth far below. Then, like metal drawn to a magnet, he was pulled downward to the home of a Uiwen warrior named Dergon.

Dergon Derna was an Atlandish Uiwen from the same village as Aras' father, Elam. Dergon idolized Elam as a martyr and hero, wanting nothing more than to follow in his footsteps. He learned the art of swordcraft before reaching puberty and excelled in all his martial training. When he reached the age of manhood, he joined the Knights of the Old Guard and went off to fight against the Matriarchs and the religious fanaticism engulfing the Atland. Before leaving, he declared that he would return with the head of the Matriarch, Faceless, unveiled on a silver platter for the world to see. He nearly got his wish when, as his battalion fought their way into the Eternal City, Faceless descended on them and revealed herself to be a dark sorceress. She conjured spell after spell, taking down the Knights like pins hit by a wooden ball. Dergon dove towards her with his sword extended and came within inches of her neck before he too was hit by a curse, causing his spirit to flee quickly into Avalon and leaving his body in a state of non-death. He was returned to his parents, who laid him in his bed and tended to him daily but, each morning brought more hopelessness as his parents doubted Dergon would every wake up. When he finally opened his eyes, he was not himself. He was Anaximander.

Anaximander, now housed in Dergon's youthful body, left at once, ignoring the cries of Dergon's parents for him to stay. There were many things he could not explain: why his soul had not moved on to the Otherworld, who had guided him to Dergon's comatose, waiting body, and where was he meant to start. He knew he needed to create a new talisman to restore his power to its former strength and so he set out to the nearby woods to form a new staff from an ancient oak tree. To his surprise, on the ground beneath the tree, sat his old staff, fully mended and containing inside a powerful spirit that was not his own. A force far greater than Anaximander provided a new body and a powerful weapon for his coming mission: to find the ones who would save the world.

Initially, the newly reborn Anaximander went in search of his former body, of the force called the Collective. He journeyed to the isle of Ikaria in the form of a mighty eagle but he found it completely changed. The villages were deserted and the wizards were gone. Anaximander encountered no one as he made his way silently to the heart of the Green City, cloaked with a hiding spell for added security. He climbed into Rheis' palace, expecting to find the Collective seated upon her throne but it was empty.

Anaximander couldn't figure out where the Collective went. He searched and searched but came across no clues that might lead him to his former self. If he could just locate another wizard, they could lead him in the right direction but there were no wizards in Ikaria. He finally decided to give up after a fortnight of searching. He struck the bottom of his staff against the ground and disappeared in a brilliant shower of golden light, teleporting himself through the Golden Avenues away from Ikaria and back to the Atland. He was determined to track down the child given into Tamriel's care years before, the child that would become their savior. The son of Sir Elam Orthelios and the elfin lady called the Firebrand. As he vanished, he prayed the child had grown up in peace.

Aras and the others were initially suspicious of the young man claiming to be Anaximander. It wasn't until they saw him using his formidable magic that they realized he was telling the truth. Then they began to trust him. He took Aras under his wing and began training him to use the secret magic of the Green Robes, but he discouraged him from extracting his soul and placing it in a staff in the manner of the other wizards of the Green Robes, despite Aras' evident desire to do exactly that. He knew that spirit-magic increased a wizard's power exponentially.

"Why can't I make a staff?" Aras asked Anaximander after one of their routine morning lessons.

"That future is not suited to your strengths," replied Anaximander.

"But what happens if I come up against another wizard and they have a talisman? Won't I be at a disadvantage?"

"Just because I won't permit you to use spirit-magic to create your own staff doesn't mean you won't have a talisman."

"I'm confused."

"All will become clear in time," replied Anaximander, "but now it's time for lunch."

Anaximander and Aras left the field that served as their daily training ground and mounted the steep mountain slope between them and the Cradle. When they arrived at the pile of rocks that served as their cramped home, they were greeted by Gyrdhan's mother, Svegga, and his father, Treax. They were sitting around an enormous bonfire holding meat over the hot flames with long pokers. They were both abhorrently ugly and obese. It was no wonder Gyrdhan's family referred to their youngest member as shrimp. Svegga and Treax ignored Aras and Anaximander as they made their way into the house. Gyrdhan was in the kitchen with Darendon, preparing sweetbreads and puff pastries. There were three large sandwiches on the table with a pitcher of goat's milk and some freshly harvested strawberries. Anaximander and Aras inhaled their food and downed two glasses of milk apiece before settling back into their chairs.

"How was today's lesson?" asked Gyrdhan cheerfully.

"Great," replied Aras, "I've been learning how to channel the *Pure Light* and I think I'm getting the hang of it."

"That you are," smiled Anaximander, "but I think the time for lessons is drawing to a close."

"What do ya mean by that?" asked Gyrdhan.

"I have received news from my woodland spies that the Grey Robe, Araxim, has dispatched his minions to seek out the location of the Autumn Crown," said Anaximander, "It disappeared just before Rheis was killed…ending up in the hands of a cloaked stranger whose identity remains unknown. We must find the Autumn Crown before the Grey Robes…I fear they will try to use its power to resurrect their Master. Aras and I will be leaving in the morning."

"Hold it right there," snarled Gyrdhan, "Ari ain't goin' nowhere without me."

"And if you think I'm letting him out of my sight you're crazy," added Darendon hotly.

"I thought as much," smiled Anaximander, "we must be ready to depart before first light. Go and get some rest. You'll need it."

Aras rose from the table and made his way to the small alcove that had been serving as his bedroom for the past two years with Darendon on his heels. They stripped off their clothes and snuggled into the bed, wrapping themselves around one another so that they might have been a single creature laying there quietly beneath the quilts. It wasn't until they began to kiss each other deeply that it was evident they were awake. They massaged one another, penetrated one another, and made each other explode with passionate awakening. As they settled down and went to sleep, Darendon kissed Aras softly on the chest and playfully ran his fingers through the hair around Aras' private regions.

"I love you, Ari," he said in a whisper.

"I love you too."

When Aras woke up it was nearly midnight and a loud grumbling in his stomach forced him to rise and walk to the kitchen for a late night snack.

Gyrdhan was already there, pigging out on puff pastries and a blackberry pie his mother had baked. He looked up at Aras with a start, as though he expected to be disciplined for his irreverent hunger. Aras couldn't help but laugh a loud guttural chuckle.

"Were you expecting your mom?" asked Aras.

"I weren't expectin' you," said Gyrdhan with a grunt, "what are ya doin' up? You should be restin'."

"I got hungry…mind sharing some of that pie?" teased Aras.

Gyrdhan looked down at the half-eaten pie like a greedy old miser protecting the last of his precious gold.

"Never mind," laughed Aras, "I'll have some of your mother's mountain mix."

Aras went to the cupboard and produced a large clay jar filled with a mixture of oat flakes, dried berries, sweetened almonds, honey-roasted walnuts, and some salted pine nuts. It was Aras' favorite snack and he dove into it like a swimmer jumping into a warm river. When he finished stuffing himself, he had a glass of goat's milk followed by some water. He sat back down at the table while Gyrdhan cleaned up his mess and had a few thimbles full of whiskey.

"Has the wizard told ya where we're off to?" asked Gyrdhan while washing his dishes in the water basin.

"He hasn't said a word," replied Aras.

"Ya think it'll be dangerous?" said Gyrdhan.

"It might be," said Aras, "these are wizards we're talking about."

"I ain't never liked bein' 'round a bunch 'a wizards," grunted Gyrdhan with a sour expression, "They're quick to anger and use their magic like it was somethin' they can lord over us plain folk. But the alternative is worse I 'spose."

"What is the alternative?" asked Aras, "As I see it we have enemies to fight on two fronts…"

"You're right," said Anaximander as he entered the kitchen, "If we hope to succeed we will have to contend with the forces of darkness and those of the One God. Araxim leads the followers of the Black Prince, while the Matriarch, Faceless, leads those faithful to the One God. You can bet both will have a plan and both will be after the Autumn Crown."

"Why would the Matriarchs want the crown?" asked Aras.

"To destroy it," replied Anaximander, "they've been seeking out all forms of magic for years in a quest to eradicate our presence from the world. But the crown is too precious."

"Way I see it, the only way we know we're gonna be safe is if we have the crown and the others don't," said Gyrdhan.

Aras returned to bed and dreamt about the Autumn Crown. He'd never seen it but he imagined it was wondrous to behold, likely the most beautiful piece of jewelry ever to exist. He imagined placing the crown on his head and letting its awesome power fill him, to make him stronger than any other wizard. He could call the *pure light* at a whim and banish his enemies with the blink of his eye. He looked like a king amongst peasants and reveled in his prestige and newfound power.

Aras was awoken by Gyrdhan just before sunrise. He dressed in warm furs and traveling boots as Darendon did the same and, together with Gyrdhan and Anaximander, they left the Cradle and descended downward out of the Norn Mountains towards the wide grassy plains to the south. It was the dead of winter and they were forced to wade through feet of snow before finally coming out of the hilly passes at the edge of the mountains, to the edge of a wide, rushing river. The snow was practically nonexistent, though an unbearably frigid wind was sweeping down from the north and chilling them to the bone. Gyrdhan prepared them a quick lunch and they drank from the river before continuing on their way.

They traveled for eleven days, sleeping for a few hours each night and at midday. They ate twice daily and they bathed when they came across rivers, streams, or lakes. Each day, Anaximander led them deeper into the Atlandish countryside, closer to the southern shores where the Eternal City once stood like a golden beacon before it fell into decay. Gyrdhan never let his guard down, always looking in every direction with a clearly nervous demeanor. Anaximander was far calmer, strutting along like a proud peacock, growing more comfortable in his new body with each passing step.

"Where are we goin'?" asked Gyrdhan as they stopped to hunker down for the night. They were near a cluster of rolling downs with a small creek meandering through them. The stars were clear in the crisp, starry sky and the moon was nearing full.

"To the heart of the Atland," said Anaximander cryptically.

He often answered questions with vague responses, making his traveling companions question if he really knew where they were going or if he was making it up as they went along. They knew they were seeking out the mysterious cloaked individual who took the Autumn Crown from Rheis before her imprisonment and eventual death, but Aras was not sure they knew where to find him. He hoped Anaximander was privy to information he had elected not to share with them.

They continued on their same southbound course the following morning after eating a light breakfast. Anaximander quickened his pace as they came to an old road constructed from dirt and small rocks running from northwest to southeast. As long as they were on the road, Anaximander urged them to walk fast, not stop, and make as little noise as possible. If the need arose, he and Aras could protect the four of them with a cloaking spell but that would take a lot out of them and ultimately result in a loss of their rapid pacing.

That afternoon, they reached a fork in the road where Anaximander decided to sit down on a rock and drink from one of their waterskins. The others followed suit. Gyrdhan smoked his pipe and the boys laid in the grass, Darendon with his head on Aras' stomach. The cold winter air had slowly changed to a temperate and balmy warmth. They stopped wearing their furs and switched to tunics and breeches. Anaximander kept his blue rags pulled taut over his body and Gyrdhan seemed wholly unaffected by the increase in temperature but they all expressed relief over no longer being cold.

"Are we lost?" Darendon asked Anaximander after nearly an hour had passed.

"No, we're waiting," mumbled Anaximander.

"For what?" asked Aras.

"A friend," said Anaximander.

He had no sooner uttered those words than a small fox emerged from the nearby bushes, running quickly with its tail held out behind it. It was not like the gray foxes of the Norn Mountains. It was red and smaller in stature. Its eyes were fixed on Anaximander and it stopped next to a rock near where the boys were laying. The fox began to squeak and yelp, like it was begging for food while Anaximander stared at it with unwavering intent. When the fox finished, it turned around and rushed back to the bushes. Anaximander picked up his staff and took to the left-hand fork in the road. Aras ran to catch up with Anaximander while Gyrdhan and Darendon intentionally walked a short distance behind them. Anaximander was muttering something to himself that Aras couldn't understand. He was transfixed on his own thoughts and paid little heed to the fact they were walking towards a densely populated town.

"What was that about?" asked Aras, as they turned a bend to avoid the little township.

"What?" grunted Anaximander.

"The thing with the fox back there," replied Aras, "you said we were waiting for a friend…was that him?"

"Her," said Anaximander, "her name is Ana…she's been my close friend for many years. After I decided it was time for us to take up this road, I asked her to search out clues to the identity of the individual in possession of the Autumn Crown. I told her to meet us at that fork to report her findings. I'm glad she didn't keep me waiting."

"What did she find?"

"More than I expected. She discovered the name of the man. He's called Dorin and he lives in a cottage not far from here, in the Marshland Forest. She thinks we can persuade him to give us the crown if he realizes we are on his side. Once he learns who you are…"

"And who am I?"

"You're the next master of the Autumn Crown."

Chapter Eleven
"Reflections"

The Marshland Forest was eerie and dark, nothing like the full evergreen woods of the Wynterlande. It took Arad a while to adjust to the humid, dank air, shedding his grey robes and traversing along the wet forest floor in only his loincloth. The sweat was pouring from his brow and he had a distinctly masculine odor emanating from his groin and armpits. They had crossed the Great Line between the Northern and Southern Seasons. While it was winter to the north, it was summer in the Marshland Forest. The sun couldn't penetrate the canopy above them and it was difficult to tell where to step safely. Most of the forest floor was comprised of deep, reedy bogs that could drag a body down into their depths and drown them in a matter of minutes. Jadzia was carrying a long stick that she used to poke the ground in front of her before each step, while Arad, his slaves, Valera and Xavin, and the Shadow-Weavers followed on her heels.

A few days before, the Shadow-Weavers sent their shadows out into the Atland to search out information that might point them in the right direction. As luck would have it, the shadows overheard a conversation between a young hermit, a giant, and a couple of teenagers in which they stated very clearly they were seeking out the Autumn Crown. The shadows followed them and learned they were headed to the heart of the Marshland Forest before returning to the Shadow-Weavers to report their findings. They altered their course at once and soon arrived in the boggy part of the woods. From a small fire and a large divot on the ground where a giant had slept they determined the ones the shadows were spying on had already arrived. They had no idea how far ahead of them this other search party was but Arad and his group were determined to catch up and deal them a fatal blow before they had the opportunity to take the Autumn Crown into their possession. Jadzia moved as swiftly as the dangerous terrain would allow and soon they could smell the odor of a giant on the air. The Shadow-Weavers sent out their shadows again to track down the other searchers but they never reported back, leading Jadzia and her sisters to believe the others must have a wizard or witch traveling in their company.

"It smells like a cross between a pig and a vagrant," said Idris, oldest of the Shadow-Weavers, as she stuck her shrouded nose into the air.

"I can't smell anything but algae, mold, and peat moss," said Arad.

"That's because you're not a witch," said Oryne, youngest of the Shadow-Weavers, "witches and wizards have different abilities. Wizards spend their lives learning to master either the *pure light* or the *absolute darkness*. Witches are more in touch with the sensory world, the essence of nature. I'm surprised Jadzia never told you this."

"There's a lot Jadzia never told me," sneered Arad.

"I see things are still tense between you and your mother," said Aneira, the middle Shadow-Weaver.

"She's not my mother," stated Arad simply.

"I am your mother," yelled Jadzia, causing the earth to shake violently around her and bringing the water of a nearby bog to a boil.

"Contain yourself sister!" barked Idris, "if you alert the others to our presence here they will have us at an advantage. We must be stealthy and silent until we are ready to pounce."

"If you can smell the giant then we must be getting close," said Valera in a hushed voice.

"Have you ever encountered a giant before, my dear?" asked Idris, "you don't have to be close to sense their stench. But I would say we're within a day's walk to them, judging by the campsites and resting places we've come across around here."

"The sooner we reach them the sooner we kill them," said Arad.

The truth was they were closer than they thought. The other group, consisting of Anaximander, Gyrdhan, Aras, and Darendon, was only a few hours ahead of Arad and his group. If the Marshland Forest weren't so dangerous to traverse, Arad's group would've easily overtaken Anaximander and his friends as they approached a small, poorly maintained village of Easterling immigrants at the heart of the woods.

Aras was sure they were being followed. For three days he had been feeling a strange force coming nearer and nearer. It was a familiar energy and yet also foreign. He found himself daydreaming constantly about the mysterious presence behind them in the woods. Darendon was worried that Arad might be slipping into a state of magically induced psychosis and took to walking right beside him every minute. The feeling didn't subside when they reached the Easterling village near the heart of the Marshland Forest. If anything, it only grew stronger.

Anaximander stopped to speak to the village apothecary, a particularly withered old crone named Enaret, while Gyrdhan and the boys purchased provisions from the only merchant in the forest, a shrewd Atlandish man named Bors. Bors was willing to part with any item for the right price and Gyrdhan managed to refill his large traveling pack with bread, emu jerky, a cask of wine, dried tropical fruits, and a large tin filled with cinnamon candies. Meanwhile, Aras convinced Bors to sell him a map of the forest, something that would help greatly when navigating the treacherous bogs. They were just exiting the merchant's house when they were rejoined by Anaximander with the old hag, Enaret, trailing lazily behind him.

"Excellent news," said Anaximander, "I believe I have discovered who has the Autumn Crown."

"Ja viedaju, dzie jaho sukac," wheezed Enaret as she finally caught up to Anaximander, "yon zausiody uciakau, sto chlopcyk. Jaho maci pavinna byla prylipla da jaho bos."

The confusion on the faces of Gyrdhan, Aras, and Darendon was justified as Enaret continued to rattle on with her thick Easterling accent. Anaximander placed his hand gently on her shoulder.

"Vy pavinny dazvolic mnie rastlumacyc im," Anaximander said loudly to Enaret.

"Viadoma," replied Enaret quickly.

"What's going on, Anax?" asked Aras.

"Enaret doesn't speak the Atlandish language," said Anaximander, "luckily I am fluent in the Easterling dialect she speaks. She's been telling me all about her grandson, Nahrik, who spends most his time in the hills just beyond the forest, where it's rumored the spirit of a long-dead elfin sorceress wanders aimlessly in eternal lament. Nahrik told Enaret that he befriended the ghost and she was teaching him her secrets...I think it's worth investigating."

"Ja budu z vami," said Enaret.

"What'd she say?" grumbled Gyrdhan.

"She is going to accompany us. She seems to know how to track down the ghost the locals call the Yellow Lady," said Anaximander.

"She'll just slow us down," said Gyrdhan.

"Ja mahu isci u nahu?" spat Enaret, "ja pakazu vam, nia vam vialikaje pavolna nichto. Ja maju isci u nahu z ijod hihanta, teho, sto vy mozacie byc upeunieny, vy paraj kucu asla karmy."

"How's that?" asked Gyrdhan.

"I don't think you want to know," laughed Anaximander, "but sufficed to say, you're not in danger of becoming Enaret's favorite person."

"I thought ya said she couldn't speak our language," barked Gyrdhan.

"She can't," said Anaximander, "but she can understand it."

"Heta pravilna," frowned Enaret, "ja cuju vielmi dobra."

"I think he understands that," said Anaximander to Enaret before turning to address Gyrdhan, "she is not as frail as she seems."

They left the village as soon as Enaret was prepared, walking along a trail leading towards the wetland hills just north of the Marshland Forest. Enaret kept a steady pace and, within a few hours, they reached a point where the treacherous bogs began to disappear, giving way to solid ground covered by ferns and blackberry brambles. There were a series of ponds scattered about the groves of mangrove trees in the northernmost quadrant of the forest. They sat by one of the larger bodies of water and took a quick meal. Anaximander and Aras distanced themselves from the others as they munched on venison jerky and goat cheese.

"Do you know anything about this *Yellow Lady* the villagers are talking about?" Aras asked Anaximander.

"If I do than I don't know that I do," said Anaximander, "I've never heard mention of a sorceress called the Yellow Lady in the Atland and I've been alive a long, long time. But, just because she's called the Yellow Lady doesn't mean she always went by that name."

"You never came across any elfin sorceresses in your travels?" said Aras after taking a bite of cheese.

"Only three," answered Anaximander, "but I was absent from this world for many years. By the time I returned from my journeys in the Otherworld, Theron Kalenti had cast his terrible spell and all the Elfkind were gone…almost all."

"The Lady Rheis was one of the survivors," said Aras proudly.

"Yes, and her sister, Caenara, and their mother's cousin," said Anaximander, "her name was Leanida."

"Did you know them well?"

"Rheis and I were very close, as you probably know. I looked on her as a man in love but when she gazed in my direction it was as a mother looking upon her beloved child. I always pretended it didn't bother me but it did…after all, I'm older than she was. Leanida was more of a bitter pill to swallow. I saw her as much as time would allow and encouraged her in her mission to protect the Amulet of the One God from falling into the hands of the enemy, but it made her as hard and unfeeling as the red stones of the tower in which she always locked herself."

"The Red Witch," Aras blurted out, "I've heard stories about her."

"There were actually two Red Witches," smiled Anaximander, "the first was Rheis' aunt and Leanida's mother. Her name was Xanyra. She vanished with the rest of her kin. It was then that Leanida took up her mantle and her mission, living the rest of her days sequestered in the Red Tower at the edge of the Wynterlande Forest."

"And what about Caenara?" asked Aras, "What happened to her?"

Anaximander was slow to answer, as though he was lost in some menacing memory that he didn't want to share.

"I don't know what happened to her. I only saw her once and it was not the most pleasant of encounters."

"Why not?"

Anaximander was about to answer when Enaret walked over and poked her finger in Anaximander's chest.

"My pavinny praciahva ruacca," she said.

"Adrazu," replied Anaximander before addressing Aras, "we should get going. We're going to lose the light soon enough as it is."

The screams coming from the locked houses were muffled by the sounds of the fire rapidly consuming the village. Arad was at the edge of the chaos with his wand pointed in the air, where the merchant, Bors, was hovering feet above Arad's head. Jadzia was washing with a dubious smile, while the Shadow-Weavers flitted from building to building, ensuring none of the villagers escaped from their homes.

"I don't know what you're after but this isn't the way to get it," spat Bors defiantly.

"Oh, but it is," smirked Arad.

Bors wailed uncontrollably as Arad flicked his wand and twisted him into a pretzel, his bones snapping under the immense pressure placed on them, his tendons stretched beyond the measure of anything a man should have to endure.

"Alright, alright," screamed Bors and Arad released his spell.

"Yes?" asked Aras sheepishly.

"They went north," sobbed Bors, "there were four of them and one was definitely a giant. And one looked a lot like you. They took off with our village healer, Enaret. That's all I know, I swear…"

"I believe you," said Arad before swiping his wand through the air violently, causing Bors' neck to snap, his lifeless body falling spread-eagled on the ground.

"If we hurry we can catch up to them in a few hours," smiled Jadzia.

"I want to watch," said Aras, referring to the villagers burning to death in their houses.

"There's no time," replied Jadzia, "The Shadow-Weavers will ensure things are wrapped up here and then join us on the road. Unless you want to let the others get to the Autumn Crown first."

Arad begrudgingly did as Jadzia commanded and together they ran off away from what remains of the Easterling village and into the northern portion of the Marshland Forest. In no time at all, they emerged from the swamps onto more stable ground. They found an apple core near one of the ponds dotting the landscape, confirming someone was there hours before.

"If we're ever going to get the upper hand, we're going to need to travel through the shadows," said Arad.

"We can't use the shadows as a road unless we know exactly where we want to come out," said Jadzia, "without knowing exactly where the others are standing we would never be able to find them."

"Perhaps there's a way to find the end of the road," replied Arad before drawing his wand and pointing it at one of the nearby trees. With a series of little chirps, a small bat came flittering down from where it had been resting and landed on a rock in front of Arad. The monstrous look of hateful malevolence on Arad's face whenever he looked at another human being melted as he smiled gently at the little creature.

"*I need you to help me,*" said Arad with a strange otherworldly voice that sounded like it was being carried on the wind rather than coming from his mouth, "*We are tracking a group of people moving north out of the forest. They passed this way sometime before sunset. Go and find them for us. They are traveling with a giant. It shouldn't be too hard for you to see them. When you return, I will reward you greatly for your service to our cause.*"

The bat blinked a couple of times and then took flight, disappearing into the darkness of the night. Arad unfastened his cloak and threw it on the ground before laying down on top of it and closing his eyes. Jadzia sat down on a tree stump a few feet away and stared sadly into the southeast. It was so dark, they could see only a few feet in front of their noses so it took Arad a few minutes to realize Jadzia was crying.

"What's wrong with you?" he sneered.

"Nothing I expect you to understand," said Jadzia with a sob.

"Fine, don't tell me," replied Arad.

"My sisters and I grew up not far from here," she said suddenly, "I don't think I ever told you that. Our father bought a large farm on the southeast edge of the forest when I was nine. He retired from the Knighthood after my mother died and brought me and your aunts out here to escape the drudgeries of a life at court."

"Does this story have a point?"

Jadzia ignored Arad's rudeness and continued without pausing.

"It's sad how things don't work out the way we want them. My father wanted us to have a good life and, for a while we did. But then he got sick and everything changed. I often wonder what our lives would've been like if we'd stayed in Atlantis. Idris and Aneira would've married gentleman of the court and given birth to lots of babies. Oryne would've joined the Holy Orders as a Priestess of the Veil, or gone to live with the Queen's Guard. And I…I would've been a scholar. I loved books more than anything. Books and magic."

"You still do," remarked Arad cynically.

"Not in the same way. I was innocent once. Before we met her…"

"The Nameless Goddess," smiled Arad. He knew the story of how the four sisters had tried to save their father's life by asking the Nameless Goddess to intervene with her magic. The three older sisters didn't give the goddess what she truly wanted and so they were struck down. But Jadzia was honest and, for her honesty, she was given the gift of eternal youth. Arad didn't know how Jadzia retrieved her sisters' souls and he really didn't care. He despised Jadzia almost as much as he hated Araxim. In time, he intended to deal with both in the harshest manner. Arad and Jadzia remained by the pond for nearly two hours before they were joined by the Shadow-Weavers and Arad's slaves, Valera and Xavin. Seconds later, the bat reappeared and squeaked erratically at Arad. Arad looked from the bat to Jadzia and then back again, grinning widely like a child preparing to get onto his favorite ride at a carnival.

"There not far from here," said Arad, "they're camped next to an ancient oak tree at the base of the hills just beyond the forest. There's a little stream a few yards from them and what looks like a grouping of boulders on the opposite side. Is that enough information for you to open a pathway into the shadows, mother?"

"Oh, yes…yes it is," smirked Jadzia.

Aras and Darendon were cuddling near the fire when they heard a loud crash back in the direction of the Marshland Forest. They jumped to their feet and looked around, Aras with his hands held out in front of him, Darendon with his sword at the ready. Enaret was on the other side of the fire, staring at the tall flames vacantly like she had fallen asleep with her eyes open. Judging from the loud snores coming from behind a fallen tree at the edge of the firelight, Gyrdhan had not been disturbed by the crash. Anaximander was nowhere to be found.

"Maybe it was just a rotten old tree falling," said Darendon, "that forest was full of them."

"I don't know, Dar," replied Aras, "it didn't sound like a tree falling to me. It sounded more like a boulder smashing into a cliff. But there aren't any cliffs around here. I'm worried about Anaximander."

"Why?" grinned Darendon, "He's like a thousand years old and the most powerful wizard in the world. I think he can take care of himself. Let's go back to sleep. It'll be light soon and you need the rest. I'm sure Anaximander will be back any minute."

They were just about to lay down when there was another crash, closer than the one before. Gyrdhan snorted and sat up, rubbing his eyes groggily and snarling slightly, like a hungry dog whose been deprived of a nice, juicy bone.

"What's happenin'?" he grunted, "The hell was that?"

"That's what we're trying to figure out," said Aras, his eyes darting back and forth as he stared into the darkness.

"Anaximander's not here," said Darendon, "and Aras thinks it's because there's something evil lurking in the woods."

Just then, Enaret gasped, taking in a deep breath of air as if she'd spent the last five minutes underwater. She blinked tears from her eyes and rocked back and forth.

"Jany prychhodzia," she spat incoherently, "ciemra viadzie ich nam i dzviery zbirajecca adkryc."

Aras went to console her, kneeling before her and placing his hands on her knees. She stared at him with her wet eyes and, for a moment it seemed she would pull him into a passionate hug. Instead, she repeated the same words she had just spoken again and again, as though she expected Aras to catch one and do something.

"I don't understand," said Aras.

"D-d-door," she wheezed, "Door to open. They come. They come."

As if it had been waiting for Enaret to speak those words, the earth shook and a third loud crash sounded only a few yards behind them, just far enough into the darkness of the night for Aras or the others not to see what it had been. They didn't have to wait long. As they strained their eyes to see, five strangers appeared out of nowhere and began fighting them. There was a beautiful young woman using magic to subdue Darendon and three other women, all shrouded in crimson cloth, who attacked Gyrdhan. And there was a tall young man with a wand of the Grey Robes. He didn't wait to see Aras' face before he began firing curses towards Aras with his wand. Aras dodged the spells by diving behind the remnants of a fallen tree. Meanwhile, Jadzia fought Darendon and the Shadow-Weavers rounded on Gyrdhan. Valera and Xavin stayed back. Their shackles prevented them from fighting, something they wouldn't do anyway, even if they were free.

"Don't hide," sneered Arad as he made his way around the fallen tree but Aras was gone.

"Whose hiding?" asked Aras as he appeared from the heights of a nearby tree. He channeled all his power into his fists and drove them into Arad's back. Arad was hurtled a dozen yards and slammed into a tree, dropping his wand somewhere on the ground.

Aras wrapped himself in a sphere of *pure light* as he came to stand over Arad. Arad's hood was obscuring his face as Aras used his telekinetic abilities to lift Arad off the ground and hold him in the air, unable to move. Without his wand, Arad was powerless to stop Aras as he began telekinetically pulling Arad's hood off his head. But before Aras could succeed, Jadzia picked Arad's wand up off the ground and threw it to him. With his power returned, Arad violently disrupted Aras' telekinetic control causing a violent psionic explosion that knocked everyone off their feet. The battle ceased as each of the bewildered participants pulled themselves off the ground. They then turned on each other again, Aras facing off against Arad, but they never reengaged their fight. Arad's hood had slipped from his head and Aras was greeted by his face, as though he were gazing into the surface of a still pond at his own reflection. Arad was equally confused, but wore an expression of suspicion while pointing his wand at Aras' chest.

"What the hell is this?" sneered Arad, "some kind of trick."

"It's no trick," said Anaximander as he stepped out from the nearby bushes, "you are twins, born of the union of Elam Orthelios and the Elfin Lady Caenara…"

"If my father was a man, and my mother was an elf," said Aras, "and this is my twin brother, then…"

"You are halfelfin," said Anaximander.

Part Two
"Together"

"The Orthelios Twins"

Chapter Twelve
"Revelations"

"What do you mean by halfelfin?" asked Aras as Anaximander moved to stand between him and Arad.

"Exactly what it sounds like, you fool," spat Arad, "our father was a man and our mother is an elf…what don't you understand? It's not that difficult to comprehend."

"What do you mean our mother *is* an elf?" asked Aras.

"I mean she's an elf…clearly I inherited all the brains," sneered Arad.

"She's alive?" said Aras.

"In a manner of speaking," smiled Arad.

"You've seen her, I can tell by the look on your face," said Aras.

"She is a prisoner of the mad wizard, Araxim," interjected Anaximander, "there is nothing you can do for her now, Aras. You must focus on the task at hand. We're nearly to our destination and with Arad's help I'm sure we can find the crown."

A guttural, sinister laugh burst from Arad's mouth as he raised his wand and pointed it at Anaximander. Anaximander made no attempt to counter Arad's clearly offensive move. Instead, he smiled warmly, fueling Arad's anger to the point that he began to turn seven shades of red. He curled his lips and a twisted spell escaped from his lips. His wand suddenly came to life, generating a wide web of darkness that hurtled furlong towards Anaximander and Aras. Anaximander stomped his staff on the ground in front of him and the web of darkness dissipated in a brilliant shower of purple light, like fireworks lit to mark a great celebration. Arad narrowed his eyes in resentment before firing another hex, this one a giant ball of green fire. Meanwhile, Jadzia conjured a terrible pestilence and threw it at Anaximander and Aras, hoping that two spells coming from opposite directions would confound them. Unfortunately for her, her temporary shift of focus gave Darendon the advantage he needed as he rendered her unconscious with a well-placed hit to the back of her head with the hilt of his sword. Anaximander transmuted the green ball of fire into a spray of silver water and Aras narrowly stopped the pestilence with a telekinetic shield.

"You can't win, Arad," said Anaximander.

Arad was standing alone against Aras, Anaximander, and Darendon. Gyrdhan disappeared earlier across a nearby ridge with the Shadow-Weavers in pursuit and Enaret in chase with no sign of them since. His slaves were cowering behind a nearby tree but they would be of no practical help. Yet Arad stood his ground. His rage made his eyes bloodshot and caused the vessels on his forehead to pop out. He was looking less like Aras by the second. He started waving his wand in strange patterns around him and spoke a spell that sent chills down Aras and Darendon's spine.

"Azarag natu kar kulesh…amra akira nos vara menzahari…"

Even as Arad's spell began to unfold, an even greater voice echoed through the trees, drowning out his words with its own otherworldly magnificence. It was Anaximander speaking but the voice was greater, deeper, and more alive.

"Rhoi'r gorau iddo yn awr gyda eich gwinuidd," boomed Anaximander, *"en gwirodydd coir yn dod yn foir."*

Suddenly the trees around Arad sprang to life, their boughs descending upon him like a hammer hitting a nail. The vines and leafs of the giant tree tangled themselves around Arad so that he was forced to drop his wand and gasp to breathe. Anaximander walked over and picked up the wand, examining it closely before snapping it in two. The murky gray orb that was Arad's spirit was left floating there in the damp, warm air. With a touch of his finger, Anaximander caused the orb to fly through the air and rejoin with Arad, taking up its rightful place deep within him.

"As I said," smiled Anaximander, "you cannot win. You're powerful, I'll give you that but you're unfocused and rash. If you had been raised in the Light you would understand how to quiet your emotions and truly master the complexities of magic."

Arad replied with a heinous glare.

"If only you weren't alone in this battle," said Anaximander.

"He's not alone," came a voice from behind Anaximander and, for the first time that night, he looked afraid. The Shadow-Weavers had returned from over the ridge but they were not alone, and it was not them who had spoken. It was a massive and ghoulish daemon, with legs ending in hooves and horns like a bull. His skin was as black as tar and his eyes burned red with unholy fire. The air around him smoked and he snorted steam like a dragon. Anaximander thrust his staff out in front of him and a great sphere of *pure light* erupted from it, encapsulating Anaximander, Aras, and Darendon in its shimmering brilliance.

Darendon drew his sword and began to advance towards the Shadow-Weavers and the daemon but Anaximander used his free hand to prevent him from leaving the sphere of light.

"You can't hope to win," said Anaximander to Darendon.

"Listen to the man, boy," spat the daemon, "you wouldn't wanna end up like the giant and the old hag…or maybe you would…"

This time it was Aras that tried to leave their sphere of protection and it was Darendon that stopped him. Anaximander looked from Aras to the daemon and back again, fear and sadness seeping from every pore of his face and eyes.

"It's Arad you want," spat Anaximander, "so take him and be on your way. I won't try to stop you."

One of the Shadow-Weavers picked Jadzia up off the ground while the other two freed Arad from the vines holding him captive. The daemon advanced to the very edge of the *pure light* sphere protecting Aras and the others, its eyes alive with hatred and sycophantic desire. It snorted a monstrous laugh and narrowed its eyes.

"Someday soon, wizard," said the daemon, "I'll catch you without your staff and then…then you're mine."

"Maybe…and maybe not," replied Anaximander.

The daemon joined the Shadow-Weavers, Arad, and Jadzia near the trees holding Arad prisoner a few seconds before. With one final snort, the daemon raised its fur covered arms above its head and, with a powerful burst of darkness, it and the others disappeared, leaving Anaximander, Aras, and Darendon alone, still wrapped in the protective sphere of light. Aras took off immediately, sprinting over the nearby ridge in the direction Gyrdhan had disappeared earlier. Anaximander dropped the *pure light* shield and chased after Aras with Darendon right behind him.

It only took Aras minutes to stumble across the gruesome sight he was hoping not to discover. Near an embankment on the shores of a shallow creek, Gyrdhan was lying face down in the mud. His body was covered with terrible burns, still smoldering like crisp bacon in a hot frying pan. Enaret was beside him on her back covered in the same burns, her bloodshot eyes staring lifelessly towards the stars. Aras let out a terrible cry as he raced to Gyrdhan's side, flipping him on his back. Gyrdhan's eyes were closed and he wasn't breathing. Aras buried his head in Gyrdhan's chest and cried incoherently until Darendon pulled him into his arms. Anaximander knelt over Gyrdhan and examined him closely.

"Your tears come too soon," said Anaximander, "he has not yet left on the journey to Avalon."

Anaximander placed the tip of his staff on Gyrdhan's forehead and muttered something under his breath. A dull golden light erupted from the staff and bathed Gyrdhan in its warmth. The burns covering his body stopped smoldering and began to heal. His breath returned to him and, after a few moments, he opened his eyes. By the time Gyrdhan stood, the burns were reduced to nothing more than little purple scars blotting his skin like freckles. He seemed slightly disoriented but otherwise healthy, his strength and natural endurance returned to him.

"What happened?" asked Gyrdhan.

"You were attacked by a daemon," replied Aras, wiping the tears from his eyes and running to hug Gyrdhan, "I thought you were dead but Anaximander healed you."

"Doesn't look like he can do the same for Enaret," said Darendon.

Anaximander was kneeling over Enaret. He gently reached down and closed her eyes before moving a few feet away and pointing his staff at her. She immediately burst into flames and, seconds later, she was nothing more than pile of ashes carried away into the forest by a sudden burst of warm wind. Anaximander let out a long sigh and bowed his head, saying a prayer to Araset, God of the Dead, asking for safe passage through Avalon for Enaret's spirit. After concluding his prayer, Anaximander produced a small golden coin from his rags and tossed it into the nearby creek.

"We should get moving," said Anaximander as he walked over to join the others, "the hills are near and the sun will rise soon. If we walk without stopping, we should reach our destination in a couple hours."

"How will we find our way without Enaret?" asked Aras once they had journeyed a fair pace from the site of their encounter with Arad and the forces of darkness.

"She was leading us due north…we'll continue on that path and, hopefully, it will lead us where we need to go," replied Anaximander.

"And what about the daemon?" asked Arad.

"What about him?" said Anaximander.

"He seemed to know you…"

"He does…or at least he did. He is called Azgarog, chief servant of the evil Black Prince. I thought him dealt with but it's clear I was wrong. His presence here complicates matters."

"How?" asked Darendon, who was walking beside Arad listening contently while Gyrdhan held up the rear.

"If Azgarog is here, the Black Prince can't be far behind," replied Anaximander, "and that thought frightens me. The last time he was here, the Black Prince was nearly impossible to defeat, and in those days there were more wizards and wise men."

"I've heard tales of the Black Prince," said Darendon, "my father told me all about him. He actually tried to conquer Albion twice, didn't he?"

"Yes, he did," said Anaximander, "The first time was a very long time ago, when the Elfkind still ruled in Albion. He descended upon the living world with the powerful talisman, the Amulet of the One God, in his possession, bringing terrible war and endless death to the peoples of the Atland and Lemuria. The Elfin Empress Saavika sacrificed herself and merged her spirit with the Autumn Crown to level the playing field and give her daughter, Xanyra, the opportunity to defeat the Enemy. She forced him to relinquish the Amulet of the One God to her before transforming him into a decrepit old gnomish-man and banishing him to the deep places of the Wynterlande Forest."

"Then he somehow got the amulet back and returned to power," said Darendon.

"Exactly," continued Anaximander, "he conned an innocent Dunmor into retrieving the amulet from the Red Tower, where it was being guarded by Xanyra's daughter, Leanida. Once the amulet was back in his possession, the Black Prince killed Leanida and returned to his former body. He came forth in bloody war but he was defeated by the Wyt Robes. They took his talisman and placed in a place so hidden it could never be rightfully resurrected again. And there it stays…"

"So Arad and his friends want to get the Autumn Crown for the Black Prince, since his amulet is out of his reach," said Aras.

"But they are still faced with a serious problem," said Anaximander.

"I'd say," interjected Darendon, "since the Black Prince is supposed to be dead."

"You cannot kill the Black Prince," frowned Anaximander, "only strip him of his earthly vessel…but he can find another. When he was defeated by the Wyt Robes, they banished his spirit form into the deepest recesses of the Void. There is only one spell on this earth that can free him, hidden in the mind of a single wizard."

"You," said Aras.

"I guard that secret, along with many others. My only fear is that the Collective became privy to those secrets after they took control of my old body…if they did, they may use that knowledge to advance their own goals at the expense of Albion and all its people."

The sun rose to their right, over the eves of the few trees straggling outward from the forest. The hills had arisen to meet them almost at once and soon they were traversing a narrow ravine leading them to what sounded like a river rushing in the distance. Anaximander struck out ahead of the others to scout the path while Darendon kept his sword drawn and his senses sharp. Aras would invoke his magic if it was necessary but their surroundings were calm and peaceful. They came across a few does grazing in a patch of grass and a mountain goat climbing the side of the ravine but otherwise their path was unobstructed.

After a couple of hours, the ravine widened into a large valley hidden amidst the hills. At the edge of the valley was the source of the rushing water. It was a wide waterfall falling into the valley from the heights of the ravine to form a small pond that led off to an underground aquifer. The valley possessed a more temperate climate the Marshland Forest. The air was cool and refreshing. Apple trees were growing in abundance across the breadth of the valley, along with bushes, hedges, blackberries, and various types of beautiful flowers. It was as though they had left the summer of the south behind and entered a perpetual springtime haven. There were black swans floating around on the little pond at the base of the waterfall. A fox was drinking along the bank, and the birds were singing elegant songs that reminded Aras of life and love. The sun was shining its morning glow and the grasses were growing wild and untamed.

"This place is not what it seems," said Anaximander quickly.

"I think it's perdy," smiled Gyrdhan.

"And it's much cooler here," added Darendon.

"Precisely my point," replied Anaximander, "we have not left the south of the Atland. It should still be stifling summer here. If we go further north we will reenter the winter. There is no middle ground where it would be spring…none that I've ever encountered."

"Yet here we are," grinned Darendon before running off towards the pond to join the swans in the water, stripping his clothes off as he went. Gyrdhan moved away without speaking and started picking luscious apples from a nearby tree, laughing and smirking like a baby with a rattle. Aras was smiling intensely but he was reluctant to leave Anaximander's side. Instead, he sat down beside the wizard and started smelling the flowers growing at his feet. Anaximander looked around at his traveling companions and then the surrounding scenery before focusing on a large boulder sitting amidst the grove of apple trees where Gyrdhan was plucking away at the fresh fruit. The boulder seemed oddly out of place. It was too far away from the walls of the widening ravine to have ended up there in a rockslide and its type was unfamiliar to the region. Anaximander pointed the tip of his staff at the giant rock and called forth a powerful spell that echoed through the valley.

"Toddi gorwedd hon ac yn dangos y gwir."

With a burst of violent red light the serene valley disappeared. In its place was a barren rock pit with only a few sage bushes growing near the opposite edge of the deep hole. Aras, Darendon, and Gyrdhan snapped out of their euphoric fantasies and returned to reality, looking around in disgust at the real scene before them. It was still bitterly cold and there was no waterfall. But what drew the attention of the group was the translucent apparition of a she-elf floating above the large boulder towards which Anaximander had fired his spell. The ghost was barely more than a yellow silhouette. Her features were difficult to discern and the natural brightness emanating from her form made them shield their eyes. Only Anaximander continued to gaze in her direction, a look of recognition and surprise adorning his youthful face.

"Eanora," he exclaimed with a bow.

Chapter Thirteen
"A Face for Faceless"

Faceless, who was really the Nameless Goddess, sat in her bedchamber on her plush feather bed, running her fingers across the Amulet of the One God and staring into a mirror she held in her other hand. She wasn't wearing her usual veil and purple robes. Instead, she was adorned in a thin slip of red satin and her head was uncovered. She was noticing how worn her face had become. She was an immortal but even she was subject to the wares of stress and suffering of the body. She remembered a time when she was youthful and innocent, before her exile into the poisoned well, before she murdered the One God.

In those early days of her life she was called Tsira, meaning 'Absent Light' in the language of the Old Gods. She was the youngest of four sisters born when the light of the moon hit the waters of the sea for the first time. All four sisters sprang forth from the spray as the sea hit the shores of the isle called Mu. First came Narenna, then Selena, followed by Maru, and, finally, Tsira. They were taken in by Raanon, God of Light, who fostered them in his Golden Pyramid where the city of Lemuria would one day come to stand. Because of the nature of their birth, Raanon dubbed them the Daughters of the Moon and appointed each a place and a purpose. Narenna became the Goddess of the Waning Moon, a guardian of wisdom and the gateway to death. Selena was made the Goddess of the Full Moon, a protector of the High Secrets of Godly Magic and defender of the powers of the *pure light*. Maru became the Goddess of the Waxing Moon, a symbol of strength and vitality, of youth and innocence. Meanwhile, Tsira was begrudgingly appointed Goddess of the Dark Moon, mistress of the shadows and consort of the charioteer of death.

In time, the older three sisters came to understand their purpose and took up their duties as members of the pantheon called the Old Gods. Tsira, on the other hand, despised her position. The Old Gods worshipped the power of the *pure light* above all things, viewing Raanon as their King and Selena as their Queen. Tsira was untouched by the *pure light*, left to forever encompass the infinite darkness. This left her an outcast unloved by her peers. Her sisters were worse. She could remember the day that her three older sisters were communally given the secondary title of the Triple Goddess. Tsira was left in the vacant halls of the Palace of the Moon, on the shores of the Atland, while the other sisters went to the Golden Pyramid of Raanon to thank him for their new title. When they returned, they found Tsira seated on the edge of a fountain in the courtyard, gazing up at the moonlit sky.

"Why didn't you come and honor our King, sister?" Selena asked Tsira as she came to stand over her, "It is improper for you to ignore your duties and pine away here by the water…"

"I don't know why I should go to the Golden Pyramid," replied Tsira, "It was not me who received a new title."

"You're jealous," snapped Maru, joining them in the conversation.

"I am," admitted Tsira, "You are each given endless honors and glory while I am an outcast, shunned and mocked for something over which I have no control. Tell me, where are my titles? When will I be made royal?"

"Never," said Narenna simply, "unless you wish to call yourself the Queen of Death…"

"What is that supposed to mean?" cried Tsira, "I'm a herald of death…I do not serve him directly. Even if I did, Araset is given greater honors than even you, Selena, and he is Death Embodied."

"He is given honors because of his long service to the Cosmos," said Selena, "he has been alive for centuries, nearly as long as Raanon, and he has never once abandoned his duties."

"Neither have I," pouted Tsira.

"Lies," said Maru rudely, "You have never given yourself over to your purpose…you have always hungered for more, to become something that you are not meant to become. When are you going to learn? You are nothing and nothing you will stay."

"Well put," said Selena before she and Maru walked away.

"You must learn your place if you hope to live as we do, sister," said Narenna, "otherwise, you will always dwell in the shadows."

That particular memory faded and was replaced by another, a darker moment in the long life of the fallen goddess. It was just after she had been stripped of her name and cast into the poison well as punishment for murdering the One God. The Nameless Goddess, as she had come to be called, was sleeping in the bottom of the well when her sister Narenna appeared in the world above and summoned her. The Nameless Goddess rose as an apparition to greet her sister, the dark fire of her soul muted by the frigid chill of her watery prison.

"Why have you come here, Narenna?" asked the Nameless Goddess without veiling her contempt.

"I wished to give you the opportunity to repent," said Narenna, "you are my sister…if you tell us how to destroy the amulet you created and free the spirit of the One God, we will allow you to return home."

"Even if I knew how to destroy it, I would never tell you. Go back to your palace and your high place and forget you ever knew me. You are here because you feel sorry for your poor little sister, Tsira. I am not Tsira. I am the Nameless Goddess. I will strike fear into the hearts of all those who look upon me and, I promise you, one day I will have my revenge and destroy each and every one of you…"

"That will be hard for you to do when you can never again enter the Otherworld," said Narenna, "If you are here and we are there, how can you possibly bring us harm?"

"I will find a way," vowed the Nameless Goddess.

Faceless was abruptly revived from her daydream in the halls of her memory by a loud knock on the door of her bedchamber. She rose from her bed and rushed to the nearby bureau, slipping on her robes and pulling her veil over her face.

"Enter," she said.

The door swung open and in walked the leader of her elite soldiers, a Lemurian man of some renown by the name of Marek of Ki. He was a tall, broad-shouldered man in his early forties with a full beard and long brown hair flecked with white. His body was lean and his jaw strong, as was typical of Lemurian men. He wore the black tunic and breeches emblazoned with a yellow rose donned by all soldiers of the Army of the One God. His curved sword was sheathed at his waist and he wore a small shield tied to his back. He bowed deeply as he approached Faceless.

"Forgive the disturbance, m'Lady," he said with a thick Lemurian accent, "but there is news from the Marshland Forest. Our spy has confirmed that both twins are in the woods hunting for the Autumn Crown. They believe the Yellow Lady will give them the answers they seek and are readily searching for her in the hills north of the forest. It's just as the Collective foretold. This Yellow Lady will show them the way and then our spy will tell us and we will beat them to the prize."

"That is wonderful news, the One God be praised," said Faceless, "Tell our spy to keep us informed..."

"As you wish, m'Lady," replied Marek before retreating from the room, leaving Faceless alone with her thoughts.

Faceless had never given much thought to the prophecy made by the Wyt Robes when she burned them alive. She knew the twins had been born and did her best to track them down and destroy them but her enemies were faster. One child was taken by the followers of the Black Prince and the other by the remnants of the Wizarding Clans. For nearly two decades, they had remained hidden, beyond Faceless' reach but now they were openly traveling through the Atland. Once they served their purpose and discovered the whereabouts of the Autumn Crown, she would instruct her spy to destroy them in their sleep. The end result would be Faceless with the Amulet of the One God and the Autumn Crown, while the mighty twins of prophecy would be permanently out of the way. She was only steps away from realizing her long-plotted revenge and couldn't help but grin fanatically as she tucked the Amulet of the One God under the folds of her robes and exited her bedchamber.

Faceless made her way to the Great Hall of the Palace of Silver Light, where the other Matriarchs were already seated upon their beautiful chairs. Faceless sat on her throne at the center of the others and clapped her hands, signaling for the steward to open the doors and allow those seeking an audience to enter, one at a time. The first was a Lord of the Old Nobility, a stern elderly Atlandish merchant named Norin Falleri. Lord Falleri was a leading member of the established aristocracy subtly opposed to the rule of the Divine Matriarchs. The Matriarchs were the supreme leaders of the Tetrarchs and the Tetrarchs were engaging in a total erasure of the Old Nobility through the economic liquidation of their estates and assets. Lord Falleri was one of few who remained secure in his social position and he used that security to continually press the Matriarchs into acting on the behalf of the established aristocracy and punish the Tetrarchs accordingly.

"My Ladies," said Lord Falleri with a slight bow as he came to stand at the base of the steps leading up to where the Matriarchs were seated.

"Your Grace," replied the Matriarch called Draena.

"As you know, I have been working tirelessly on behalf of the peers of the Atland to secure their financial futures…they are being terrorized by your Tetrarchs," said Lord Falleri, "I know my Ladies would never openly endorse the actions of your subordinates but your ongoing silence in this matter has led some to question your integrity. When you came to our shores and freed us from the tyranny of the Wizarding Clans, we all pledged ourselves willingly to the service of the One God. We are congregants at the Temple and accept your divine authority over secular affairs. Still we are punished…I came here today seeking an explanation and to beg my Ladies to intervene in this matter."

"While your words are sophisticated and teem with fidelity," replied the Matriarch, Lylid, "your actions speak an entirely different story."

"You have been seen conversing with some less than savory characters as of late, my Lord," continued Draena, "and it seems some of them are now in your employ, with the express mission of assassinating not one but all five of us. I hoped these accusations were nothing more than idle gossip…until you were seen by one of our own guards."

"We are afraid," said Lylid, "We have no other recourse than to remand you into custody pending a formal trial…"

"No," interrupted Faceless, "His punishment must be more severe. Take him now to the courtyard and burn him alive…and make sure you rally a crowd to watch…"

The guards rushed forth and seized Lord Falleri, dragging him out of the Great Hall towards the front of the Palace of Silver Light. As they passed the other individuals seeking an audience, Lord Falleri screamed and violently flailed against the guards. The lead guard knocked him atop his head with the hilt of a sword and Lord Falleri stopped.

"You had no right to do that, Sister," said the Matriarch, Lylid, after the doors to the Great Hall closed, "Even we are subject to the Law of the One God…and that law states clearly, all men accused of a crime against the temple or the people governed by the Tetrarchs shall be given a fair hearing in front of a holy conclave before judgment is passed."

"Your point?" hissed Faceless.

"We are not above the law," countered the Matriarch, Draena, "You are not above the law."

"I am the law!" snapped Faceless.

"I believe Sister Faceless is overwrought," interjected Elora, "Perhaps it would be best if she retired to her chambers and let us deal with the rest of today's audiences…"

"I am not overwrought, I am thinking very clearly," said Faceless, "There can be no resistance to our authority, to the authority of the One God. The Tetrarchs are the high priests of our Holy Master and they cannot be called into question by the laity. That offense is beyond the provenance of the Judiciary…it is unforgivable."

"As Sister Elora was saying," added Anorra, "Sister Faceless needs to rest…Goran?"

Faceless' faithful manservant, Goran, appeared from the corner of the platform upon which the thrones of the Matriarchs sat. He sauntered over to Faceless and, with an exaggerated bow, extended his hand. She reluctantly took it and together they exited the Great Hall. Goran led her sweetly towards the stairs leading back to her bedchamber but, just as they were about to mount the first step, she stopped.

"I wish to go to the courtyard," said Faceless and they altered their course, walking down a set of steps to the main passage leading out of the Palace of Silver Light. Even as they arrived on the balcony overlooking the courtyard, Lord Falleri was being set afire in front of a large crowd corralled into the courtyard by the palace guards. Lord Falleri screamed in agony as the flames licked his body while the crowd booed and cried out for justice. Faceless stood there, her eyes transfixed on Lord Falleri uon his pyre until he stopped writhing and screamed no more.

"Make sure his assets and estates are transferred into the purview of our personal exchequer," Faceless said to Goran as she turned to reenter the palace by way of its central staircase.

She walked amidst the shocked audience members waiting to be shown into the Great Hall, all of whom reluctantly bowed as she passed them.

She threw open the doors to the Great Hall and waltzed in like she were an exotic princess demanding respect for her position amongst her peers. The other Matriarchs looked deeply concerned but none of them made any motion to stand or protest her outburst.

"I will make one thing painfully clear this moment," barked Faceless, "I will not be dismissed, or be made to look a fool. Without me, none of you would be here…those chairs would not sit in the Palace of Silver Light. The four of you would still be in the convent where I found you…you'd be nothing and you'd do well to remember that."

Faceless climbed the stairs and joined the other Matriarchs, taking her seat with exaggerated gestures before clapping her hands, signaling the steward to once again open the doors and show in those awaiting an audience. The scene with Lord Falleri caused the line to shrink considerably. Only four remained. The first was a young woman by the name of Thea who had come to request an extension for repayment of loans she borrowed from the Temple several weeks before. Without consulting the other Matriarchs, Faceless denied her request. The next audience was with a Tetrarch called Brother Pren. Brother Pren requested an allocation of gold to his Temple on the edge of the isle of Walweitha. Again, Faceless spoke on behalf of all the Matriarchs and his request was irrevocably denied. The third request, made by a woman called Xenia, and the final request by a woman called Imri, were both not only rejected but laughed at by an irrational Faceless.

When they were finished giving audiences, the doors of the Great Hall were closed and sealed. Faceless rushed off with Goran, returning to her bedchamber, while the other Matriarchs went to one of the small libraries in the south wing of the palace. They rang for tea and cakes and spent over an hour discussing Temple doctrine before the discussion turned to a conversation about Faceless.

"I just don't understand her behavior lately," began Lylid, "She seems not to care about anything anymore."

"She's been under a great deal of pressure lately," began Elora, in defense of Faceless' behavior, "I think it's starting to get to her, that's all...maybe she needs to take a vacation."

"A long vacation," interrupted Draena, "let's face it, she isn't the person she used to be...she's cruel and selfish, and increasingly acts without consulting us, like this afternoon."

"I agree," said Lylid, "Sister Faceless is no longer acting in the best interests of the Temple. She seems to be concerned only with her own position, her own power. I cannot stand by and watch as she smears the good name of the Temple and usurps our authority."

"You are both being ridiculous," said Elora, "Faceless is right about one thing...we wouldn't be here if she hadn't come along. We owe her everything and you two want to turn against her?"

"Three," admitted Anorra.

"Not you too," frowned Elora.

"Today was the last straw," said Anorra, "I have made excuse after excuse to try and explain Faceless' behavior but the truth is, there is no excuse. She can't keeping acting without consideration for the law. Let's get one thing clear right now, Sisters. She may have helped us get our power but it's the people who will permit us to keep it. We must adhere strictly to the law of the Temple to set an example for the people, no matter the cost, even if that cost is Faceless."

"And how would you propose we deal with her?" frowned Elora.

"Poison," replied Anorra simply.

"Are you out of your mind?" shouted Elora.

"There has to be a less severe way," added Lylid.

"I don't think anyone was suggesting we kill her," said Draena.

There came a creak from the far corner of the room, where the servant's entrance led out to a narrow passage connecting the library to the kitchens. The Matriarchs stopped talking and bent their ears towards the disturbance. When they were sure it was nothing more than the boards of the palace shifting, they resumed their discussion.

"I won't be party to murder," said Draena.

"Neither will I," said Elora.

"Nor I," added Lylid.

"Then I'll do it myself," snapped Anorra, "I don't need any of you, I just wanted to give you the courtesy of informing you of what I am planning. I would ask you to keep silent until the deed is done. At this point, the choice is simple, either Faceless lives, or I do."

What none of the Matriarchs knew was the source of the noise was not the floorboards shifting and settling. Faceless' manservant, Goran, had come to the library to invite the Matriarchs for an apologetic luncheon with Faceless but stopped when he heard the Matriarchs talking. He panicked and ran back to Faceless' bedchamber in a hurry, causing the floorboards in the narrow passageway to creak as he left. He was in such a state of panic when he arrived that Faceless had to slap him hard across the face to get him to regain his senses.

"What is happening, Goran?" she demanded.

"Oh…m'Lady," he sobbed, "M'Lady…they mean to kill you. The Matriarchs mean to poison you."

Chapter Fourteen
"The Yellow Lady"

"I have been waiting for you, old friend," said the apparition floating above the boulder at the heart of the desolate rock pit, whom Anaximander had referred to as Eanora.

"I believe you," replied Anaximander.

"You have come in search of the Autumn Crown...I can tell you where to find it. But first a warning. The enemy you face is not the one you think. The Black Prince has yet to break free from his eternal prison..."

"But it's the Prince's minions who are pursuing the Autumn Crown," said Aras, "and you tell us he is not the enemy we need to worry about?"

"Indeed, Aras Halfelfin," replied Eanora, *"The servants of the darkness seek the Crown to free their Master from captivity but, without their Master, they are unfocused and weak. There is a greater threat who still draws breath in the living world. It is she we must all fear..."*

"You don't mean?" said Anaximander with a tremor in his voice, "It can't be her."

"You see the truth clearly, old friend. The Nameless Goddess has indeed risen and she is hunting the Crown relentlessly. If she finds it, she will wreak untold havoc upon this world. Even now she believes she has won."

Anaximander looked from Aras to Darendon to Gyrdhan and back to the apparition of Eanora. He seemed confused and concerned for his companions. The youthful features of Anaximander's new body were temporarily overshadowed by the mannerisms of a fatigued old man ready to conclude his endless years of life. He leaned heavily upon his oaken staff and sighed heavily.

"My worst fears are being realized," said Anaximander sadly.

"It is far worse than you think…The Nameless Goddess already controls the power of the Amulet of the One God. She has used the amulet to gain power and authority as the saint and martyr of the New Religion. Now she is queen in all but name."

"She's posing as one of the Matriarchs," said Anaximander.

"She is the greatest of their ranks, the one they call Faceless."

Anaximander's knees nearly gave out as he tightened his grip on his staff. He looked down at the ground with his brow furrowed, overwhelmed by the terrible realization that Albion had unwittingly fallen under the rule of one of its greatest enemies.

"I'm confused," said Darendon, "If this Nameless Goddess, Faceless person already has the Amulet of the One God, why does is she seeking the Autumn Crown?"

"To bring fruition to a plan she has long been plotting, to seek her revenge upon those who have wronged her…"

"A very long time ago, before Elfkind even came to our world," continued Anaximander, "The Nameless Goddess was banished from the Otherworld for committing a terrible crime against her own people. She was cast into a poison well at the heart of the Marshland Forest, to serve as her prison for all the ages. But she escaped…she now has the most powerful godly talisman in her possession and she seeks the crown…all so she can murder the Old Gods."

"A task which is not so simple," interrupted Eanora, *"The Old Gods reside safely in the far reaches of the Otherworld, a place where the Nameless Goddess cannot go…in order to have her revenge, she must bring the Old Gods to us."*

"She intends to merge the three worlds," said Anaximander in shock.

"And she needs not only the power of the amulet, but also that of the crown to do it," added Aras, finally beginning to understand.

"Such an act would have terrible and unforeseen consequences, resulting in the destruction of everything in this life, the next life and all that rests in between."

"Then why not leave the crown where it is?" asked Aras.

"I agree," added Darendon, "It's obviously safe."

"It will never be safe…nothing will ever be safe as long as the Nameless Goddess continues to live in Albion…the power of the Crown must be used to destroy her but it can only be found by the two souls that are one, bound together by the prophecy of the burning Wyt Robes on the day the Nameless Goddess came to power…"

Aras understood immediately. Eanora, the Yellow Lady, was the one who sent Enaret's grandson to retrieve the Autumn Crown from the Elfin Lady Rheis. The crown was returned to Eanora. It was she who hid it and it would take both Aras and Arad working together to get to it. He shuddered when he thought about seeing Arad again. Anaximander took note of Aras' reaction and spoke softly to reassure him.

"It must be done, Aras," he said, "if it's the only way."

"It is," said Eanora, *"You will find your road at the footstones of the Palace of Silver Light…"*

With those final words, the apparition of Eanora vanished, returning the rock pit to silence. Aras and Anaximander looked at one another for a long time, each disbelieving all they just heard from Eanora. Then, one by one, they retreated from the pit the way they had come, back through the narrow ravines that deposited them on the south side of the rolling hills north of the Marshland Forest. They decided to stop and rest for a while before turning their path eastward along the outer groves of the swampy woods. Anaximander led them onward for hours, until the sun fell behind the distant horizon and a moonless night enveloped them in darkness. Anaximander chose a grassy knoll next to a series of jagged rocks as their campsite and lit a fire with his magic. Darendon and Gyrdhan journeyed into the nearby thickets in search of rabbits or other small game that could satisfy their hunger, leaving Anaximander and Aras to lounge by the fire.

"What are we going to do?" said Aras with concern, "We can't willingly put ourselves in the path of that daemon again."

"I'm not worried about Azgarog," said Anaximander.

"You were just hours ago. What changed?" asked Aras.

"Everything," replied Anaximander.

The return of Gyrdhan and Darendon interrupted their conversation. The pair were successful in killing a few marsh hares which they set to work skinning and cleaning for dinner. Anaximander laid down by the fire and closed his eyes, though he wasn't truly asleep. Aras watched Darendon and Gyrdhan work and thought about what their ordeal had nearly cost him. The two people Aras loved the most were being constantly put in life-threatening danger because of him. Darendon noticed Aras' change of demeanor and came over to sit beside him near the fire.

"I know what you're thinking," whispered Darendon in Aras' ear, "and none of this is your fault."

"If anything happened to you," began Aras.

"It won't," interrupted Darendon before kissing Aras gently on the neck and putting his hand on his knee.

"Anaximander thinks we can face the daemon again, that we can convince it and the others to help us," said Aras.

"And they will help us," interjected Anaximander from where he was laying, "Once Jadzia Hanara is made aware of this news, she will move heaven and earth to destroy the Nameless Goddess."

"And you know this how?" asked Aras.

"It was the Nameless Goddess who made the Shadow-Weavers what they are today," said Anaximander, "a fact that Jadzia will not have forgotten. She will help us and Azgarog will follow."

"Yer sure 'bout that?" said Gyrdhan as he placed the skinned rabbits on spits over the fire.

"Absolutely," replied Anaximander.

The four friends ate their meal in silence before Gyrdhan and Anaximander went to sleep. Aras and Darendon slipped off to bathe in the nearby river meandering slowly passed the large group of rocks. They slipped off their clothes and waded out into the deeper water, splashing at each other like playful children. They washed each other's backs and hair before making love in the shallows of the river. Aras let Darendon push his manhood into him for the first time. It was sheer pain that quickly gave way to indescribable pleasure as Darendon thrust himself back and forth with the determination of a hunter overcoming his prey.

"I love you," said Darendon after he was finished.

Aras used his tunic and breeches to make a place for him to lay down. He stared up at the stars with a warm smile. He was overwhelmed by his feelings for Darendon. He was fast becoming the most important thing in Aras' life and he cherished him, the way an old woman feels about the few fading photos that constitute her life and memories.

"You look worried," said Darendon as he cuddled up to Aras.

"I am worried," replied Aras, "I don't feel right about this whole situation. I mean, we're talking about a daemon and a bunch of dark witches. Not to mention the twin brother I never knew I had…a twin brother…it's so shocking. I used to wonder what it would be like to have a sibling. But I never imagined he would be anything like this Arad guy. I don't trust him…I won't trust him."

"I don't think Anaximander's asking you to trust him," said Darendon.

"How are we even going to find them?" asked Aras.

"Not to worry, my dear," said the cold, hollow voice of a woman, "We found you…"

It was as though an invisible curtain dropped as Jadzia, Arad, Azgarog, and the Shadow-Weavers appeared suddenly, only feet from where Aras and Darendon were laying. Arad's slaves, Valera and Xavin, were cowering behind a rock near the water, watching eagerly as their master and his comrades advanced on Aras and Darendon. Darendon jumped up and grabbed a large stick off the ground. He lunged forward and swung the stick, bringing it down as though it would hit Jadzia hard in the head. However, with a simple wave of her hand, the stick crumbled into dust and Darendon fell to the ground. He was quick to recover but before he could mount another attack, Azgarog reached out with his giant clawed hand and grabbed him by the neck, yanking him off the ground with such force it nearly caused Darendon's spine to snap.

"Let him go," screamed Aras, inadvertently manifesting a giant ball of green fire that he hurtled towards the daemon. Azgarog laughed a deep, maniacal laugh as he reached out and flicked his finger at the ball of flames, which sputtered out like a balloon losing its air. The momentary distraction provided Darendon the opportunity to land a solid and powerful kick to Azgarog's neck, causing the daemon to drop him. But, with one powerful blow with his knee, Azgarog sent Darendon flying into a tree. Darendon crumpled like a rag doll to the ground and didn't move again. Azgarog began advancing towards Aras but Arad stopped him.

"He's mine," said Arad.

Arad invoked a telepathic blow meant to knock Aras off his feet but Aras countered with his own burst of psionic energy which collided with Arad's attack with a powerful vibration. Arad called forth a powerful wind and compelled it to encircle Aras, raising the dust and small rocks to blind his brother and allow him to deal a fatal blow. Aras responded by teleporting a few feet to the left, thereby escaping the wind attack altogether. The look of rage on Arad's face was intensified as he shot a violent bolt of purple lightning from his fingertips towards Aras. The lightning hit Aras in the shoulder and knocked him to the ground but he was back on his feet before Arad could conjure another spell, sending his own blast of lightning in Arad's direction. Arad dove out of the way just long enough for Aras to see Azgarog picking Darendon up off the ground before producing a long hunting knife from a sheath at his waist.

"Noooo," yelled Aras fiercely and Arad was knocked off his feet.

Aras focused all his will into saving his lover. He reached down into the depths of his being and channeled energies he never knew he possessed. He called forth the bright and unbeatable essence of the *pure light* in the form of a celestial longsword and battle armor. Sheathed in his new protection, Aras lunged at Azgarog, driving the sword of *pure light* deep into the daemon's back. Azgarog screamed fiercely and began swatting at Aras like he was an annoying mosquito feasting on his blood. Every time the daemon's fingers came into contact with Aras' armor, they were severely burned. Azgarog dropped Darendon to the ground.

"If you want your boy lover to live, you will remove your sword," spat Azgarog.

Jadzia and the Shadow-Weavers tried to help Azgarog but they were repelled by the power of Aras' *pure light* armor. Arad was the only one with the power to get close. He came up behind Aras while he was focused on Azgarog and conjured a bolt of darkness which he threw square at Aras' back. Aras' armor rang out with a high pitched tone before cracking and crumbling like a porcelain doll left too long in a hot oven. His celestial sword remained, driven deep into Azgarog's back, but he was forced to abandon it when Arad threw another bolt of darkness at him. Azgarog's hand was scalded as he pulled the celestial sword from his beck and threw it to the ground. He then picked up Darendon and, with one swift motion, drove his hunting knife into Darendon's gut. Darendon awoke with a scream and then, clutching at the bleeding wound in his stomach, he looked sadly at Aras. Aras exploded with a rage he had never felt before. Every fiber of his being was boiling with passionate hatred. The air around him began to heat to the point that Jadzia and the Shadow-Weavers were forced to back up. Then, Aras burst into flames, hot, red flames that licked the air like the tongue of a viper. The fire didn't harm Aras, or Arad, but Azgarog began to burn like he had stepped into the heart of a bonfire. Darendon was also burning.

"Stop this," said Anaximander as he arrived on the scene.

Anaximander used a sphere of *pure light* to protect himself, Gyrdhan, and Darendon from the effects of Aras' present state. Arad was too afraid to try and stop Aras as he steadily began to burn brighter, the flames around him turning from red to blue. The water of the nearby river began to boil and the trees were set aflame. The ground turned molten and the sky itself filled with a haze induced by the heat Aras was emanating. Anaximander pointed his staff at Aras and, with a single whisper, fired a spell that cocooned Aras in a bubble of freezing water. The fires around Aras were extinguished as he fell to the ground with a splash. Arad saw it as his opportunity and began moving quickly towards Aras but, with a small shift of his staff, Anaximander knocked Arad off his feet.

"Enough," commanded Anaximander, "all this fighting is pointless."

"I agree," said Jadzia, "You can bring this all to an end if you tell us where to find the Autumn Crown."

"Speak for yourself," growled Azgarog, "I won't stop until I've made the wizard my morning meal."

Anaximander smiled at Azgarog and then looked sternly towards Jadzia. The Shadow-Weavers were standing weakly behind their sister, shrouded from head to foot in their usual crimson rags. Anaximander felt sorry for the Hanara sisters. They never really had a choice in what they became. It was either serve the Nameless Goddess or serve the Black Prince. They never had the strength or conviction to serve themselves.

Azgarog began wailing against the sphere of *pure light* with his fists but its power was too strong. Instead, he turned his attention towards Aras, still disoriented and wet. He scooped him up like a mother picking up her baby and bit into his leg with his razor sharp teeth. Aras screamed loudly as Azgarog ripped a chunk of his flesh from his leg and swallowed it.

"Tastes good," smiled Azgarog, his teeth covered with blood.

Azgarog took another bite but, even as he was tearing away Aras' flesh, Aras reached down and touched Azgarog on the forehead with his finger. Aras' finger pulsed with a single bright flash of silver. At first, there seemed to be no effect as Azgarog swallowed his second bite of Aras. Then, the daemon shuddered, like he had been hit by a terrible chill. He lurched backwards, grabbing at his left arm, coughed a couple of times, looked at Jadzia, and then burst into flames. The powerful white fire consumed Azgarog in only seconds, leaving nothing but a pile of red ash. Jadzia and the Shadow-Weavers' eyes widened as they stared towards Aras in disbelief. Arad was also shocked but he still tried to attack Aras. Anaximander again knocked him off his feet.

"I am telling you for the last time," said Anaximander, "there is no need for us to fight…I need to speak with Jadzia alone and this quarrel must cease long enough for me to do so. I promise you, if you give me a chance, it will change everything."

"Very well," replied Jadzia, "you have ten minutes."

"And you swear to me the fighting will end?" said Anaximander.

"I swear," said Jadzia before glancing sternly towards Arad. Arad grumbled something under his breath and then moved off towards the edge of the river. Anaximander dropped his sphere of *pure light* and walked off in the opposite direction with Jadzia. Aras used his magic to heal his wounds and then ran over to where Darendon was still lying motionless on the ground. Aras bathed Darendon in a soft golden light which closed his cuts and healed his bruises. After a few minutes, Darendon opened his eyes and looked lovingly at Aras.

"I told you you'd get hurt," frowned Aras.

"It wasn't that bad," replied Darendon weakly with a smirk, "What happened?"

Anaximander and Gyrdhan filled Darendon in on all that had transpired, giving special attention to Aras' defeat of Azgarog. Azgarog was not dead. He would regenerate in time and come after them but Aras' display had shown him would strike fear into his heart forever. While Aras conversed with his friends, he kept his eyes glued to Arad. Arad was also staring at Aras. They were examining each other like a metallurgist analyzing the purity of gold. They were identical in almost every way, except for their expressions. Arad was cold and callous, Aras was warm and caring. When ten minutes had passed, Jadzia and Anaximander reappeared. They were walking next to each other talking softly while the others drew closer.

"From now on, we will all be working together," said Jadzia forcefully.

"But," began Arad.

"This is something you will never truly understand but, in this matter, you'll have to trust me," said Jadzia, "everything has changed. Aras and Arad must work together to retrieve the Autumn Crown and deal with this."

"Deal with what, sister?" asked Idris.

"The Nameless Goddess," spat Jadzia, as though the name were acid burning her tongue.

The Shadow-Weavers looked at each other intently and Jadzia's lip curled in a look of pure hatred. The Nameless Goddess had brought them to the fate they endured for years on end. It was clear to all those present that the destruction of the Nameless Goddess was more important to Jadzia than anything else. She would willingly work with Anaximander and the others to ensure the defeat of her greatest enemy. Then their hostilities could resume with the murder of Aras and Anaximander.

"I won't do it," snapped Arad, "I won't work with him."

"I'm not giving you a choice," replied Jadzia harshly.

Arad shrugged his shoulders and pouted like a spoiled child being chastised by a stern parent. Anaximander, Jadzia, and the Shadow-Weavers gathered together near the embankment of rocks where Aras and his friends had been camping, leaving Gyrdhan, Aras, and Darendon near the edge of the meandering river.

"I'm hungry again," said Gyrdhan.

"There's some jerky in my traveling bag," said Darendon, "I'll go get it for you."

"Thanks," replied Gyrdhan as Darendon leaped to his feet and ran towards a small grouping of pear trees where he left his satchel earlier in the evening. He leaned over and flipped open the pocket on his pack but instead of producing jerky, he pulled out a small circular hand mirror set with a cold handle. He tapped the surface of the mirror three times and it began to churn and ripple like the water of a maelstrom. Darendon's reflection faded and was replaced by a face covered by a thick gray veil.

"What do you have to report?" asked Faceless through the mirror.

"We are headed your way," replied Darendon, "Both the twins, the wandering wizard, a giant, the Shadow-Weavers, and Jadzia Hanara. All united against a common enemy. They know about you...and they know what you're doing."

"It matters not. Do they know where to find the Autumn Crown?"

"Yes, my Lady."

"Good. Let them find it...and when they do, you will steal it and bring it to me."

"As you wish," replied Darendon.

Chapter Fifteen
"To the Eternal City"

Aras and Arad didn't speak a word to each other the whole journey from the hills north of the Marshland Forest south to the edges of the sand dunes surrounding the Eternal City. Anaximander and Jadzia led the group and spent their time conversing like old friends, while the Shadow-Weavers lingered in the back. Arad walked near his aunts, pulling Valera and Xavin along behind him. Darendon and Aras kept to themselves and Gyrdhan walked near to Anaximander and Jadzia, hoping to overhear what they planned to do as they approached the Eternal City.

The Eternal City, Atlantis, was once the jewel of Albion, boasting wealth and prestige unparalleled by Lemuria, or even the Three Cities to the west. But the many years of war and violence took their toll on the illustrious city from which Albion was governed. The golden walls had fallen in on themselves and the waterway avenues were polluted by rotting bodies and human waste. The outer districts, traditionally populated by peasants and immigrants, were nothing more than piles of rubble. The occupants were all gathered in front of dilapidated structures, cooking rats over open fires and collecting rainwater from the gutters. The Middle Districts of the city were less desolate. These were populated by merchants, lawyers, and artisans, the 'middle-class' of the Eternal City. The houses and villas remained largely intact. But they were neglected and worn, the pain chipping and the windows broken. There were some people who gathered along the waterways begging but, for the most part, the courtyards and markets were empty.

It was remarkably simple for Anaximander, Jadzia, and their respective peers to slip unnoticed through the first two sections of the city, gliding silently across the water on a tiny barge. It was not until they came to the Inner Districts that they ran into trouble. In order to pass from the Middle Districts to the Inner Districts of the city, one must travel through one of four archways, each heavily manned by Palace Guards. Since the rise of the Matriarchs to power, the guards were ordered to allow no one without Notes Pater to pass through the archways. Notes Pater was the system which distinguished the landed aristocracy, or New Nobility, from the rest of the city's occupants. Since none in Anaximander's party were members of the New Nobility, they were not likely to be allowed entrance.

"Who goes there?" shouted a guard from the narrow causeway above the arch but, before he could look down at the little barge, the Shadow-Weavers cast a spell of concealment which made them and Gyrdhan invisible to the common eye.

Jadzia, Aras, and Arad looked to Anaximander as if he had an answer that would prevent the guards from descending upon them. But it was Darendon who spoke.

"We are emissaries sent by Sir Kalendron Kyree of Walweitha," he said loudly, "My father, Sir Kalendron, is engaged in ongoing trade negotiations with the Tetrarchs…we are here as his proxies, to meet with Tetrarchs Jaeb, Caro, and Vondt at the quarter afternoon."

"Why does your companion carry a staff?" asked one of the other guards suspiciously.

"He is lame," said Darendon.

The guards looked from one to another and then signaled the little barge to pass. Darendon and Aras manned the poles and shunted them onward before the guards were given the chance to change their minds. The Inner Districts of Atlantis were virtually untouched by the dilapidation gripping the rest of the city. The districts were filled with large palaces, wide annexes, multilevel mansions, spacious gardens, and luxury markets. However, they were empty. The houses looked vacant and the businesses were closed. It was just after midday and yet it seemed like the middle of the night. Not even a guard could be seen wandering the walkways at each side of the water avenues.

"Where is everyone?" asked Aras.

"They're here," said Jadzia flatly, "they're just afraid to come out."

Aras tried to imagine what the city was like before the wars that brought Faceless to power.

"It was an amazing place, once," said Anaximander, "and it will be again…you'll see."

"Don't give the boy false hope, Anax," said Jadzia, "You don't know what the future holds for any of us. The Wyt Robes spoke of the twins with a single soul, but Aras and Arad each have their own spirit, their own nature. The future is always changing and things aren't always what they seem."

"No matter what the future holds, these boys are destined for greatness," said Anaximander.

Aras and Darendon poled the barge all the way down the waterway, to the small island at the heart of the city, where stood the Palace of Silver Light, a tall pillar shining like a lantern warding away the darkness. They moored the barge at a dock just off the gardens surrounding the palace and crept ashore silently. They expected the courtyards and gardens to be filled with guards and Tetrarchs but they encountered no one as they maneuvered towards the foundation of the palace. The footstones of the Palace of Silver Light were four specific giant marble slabs placed as markers over a thousand years ago by the Elfkind to illustrate where they would one day raise their palatial home. They were a beautiful tone of polished, smooth white but were not unordinary in any way.

Aras and Anaximander examined the footstones closely, inch by inch, while Jadzia meditated with her sisters. Arad paced, Darendon sat on a small boulder, and Gyrdhan chewed his fingernails. Valera and Xavin were left behind in the barge by Arad after expressing their fear of Atlantis.

"This is pointless," said Arad as Aras searched the footstones.

"Perhaps if you helped instead of always complaining," said Aras.

"You want me to help," snapped Arad, "Fine…I'll help."

Arad walked over the footstones and spit dramatically on the middle one before wiping his mouth, his face contorted by his devilish grin.

What no one expected was for Arad's tantrum to actually have an effect but, as his spittle ran down the stone, two identical hand imprints appeared, side by side, as though the footstone was once wet cement in which someone left their mark. The indents were exactly the same size and both required a right hand. Anaximander knew before anyone else what it meant. The Yellow Lady, Eanora, insured the twins would be the only ones capable of retrieving the Autumn Crown by creating a spell only they could break together. Jadzia also understood.

"You both need to place your right hands on the stone at the same time," said Jadzia to Aras and Arad.

The brothers moved forward and did as they were instructed, each putting their hands in the indents formed by Arad's spit. Without warning, the footstone disappeared and, as though the passage behind were a vacuum and the twins specks of dust, Aras and Arad were sucked inside. Anaximander made to follow but, before he could enter, the footstone reappeared, blocking the way and plunging the passage on the other side into total darkness. Both Aras and Arad attempted to conjure a fire spell to light the way but their magic was not responding. The Yellow Lady had invoked a dampening spell that rendered the twins powerless. The narrow passage was cold and damp. The twins clang to the walls as they moved inch by inch deeper into the hidden catacombs beneath the Palace of Silver Light. It was clear none of their companions would be joining them, leaving their fates wholly in each other's hands.

"You're moving too fast," said Aras after Arad's pace quickened.

"You sure like to whine," mocked Arad.

"And you like to complain, about everything," replied Aras.

"I tell it like it is," said Arad, "Plain and simple."

The passageway leading the twins deeper beneath the Palace of Silver Light soon split into two even more narrow tunnels that descended sharply nearly a hundred feet. Since the twins couldn't see or use their magic they had to guess which way turn, taking the tunnel to the left. After stumbling a few times down the sharp slope, they emerged on a flat smooth surface. This passage was lit by a dozen small torches hanging on the walls, casting a soft glow on the granite walls. There were nine archways leading off the main expanse, each as dark as the entrance had been. Aras and Arad stopped there for a moment to regain their senses and think.

"The Yellow Lady said we are the only ones who can find the crown," said Aras, "I think she left us clues. We should look for anything that out of the ordinary."

Arad remained silent, standing to begin examining the archways one by one. Aras joined him and, within only a few minutes, they noticed that the third passage on the right was marked by a tiny symbol etched into the stone wall, a character representing one of the Old Gods. They took it as a sign and moved quickly into the darkness of that passage which eventually emerged on a landing at the edge of a deep chasm. There were several holes in the top of the cavern through which soft golden light was trickling and the twins were met by a dead end.

"Now what do we do?" sneered Arad, "So much for that idea."

"Be quiet," snapped Aras as he stared around the cavern, taking in every minute detail. The chasm was at least thirty feet across and potentially hundreds of feet deep. There was an identical landing to the one on which they were standing on the other side, where another series of torches were burning softly, leading through an archway and out of sight. There were no other distinguishing features, except for a small square tile bolted to the floor of the cavern. The tile was marked with another symbol of the Old Gods, this one in the image of a fiery raptor. Aras stared at the tile for nearly twenty minutes while Arad complained and expressed a desire to give up. Finally, Aras realized that the raptor image was moveable. He twisted it clockwise until it clicked and the cavern began to rumble. A narrow bridge rose from the depths of the chasm, connecting the two landings and allowing the twins a safe way across.

The twins rushed over the bridge and through the lit archway, into another very narrow passage that led downward in a gentle decline. They were moving deep enough into the earth that the temperature began to spike, causing sweat and fatigue. Finally, after what seemed to be an hour, the passage emerged into not a cavern, but a perfectly square room with its walls, floor, and ceiling covered in mirrors. Everywhere the twins looked, they saw themselves staring back at them. But Aras was always met by a reflection of Arad and vice versa.

"Another riddle," said Arad harshly, "And in this one I get to stare at your ugly face."

"Our faces are the same," replied Aras, which was essentially true. They had the same fair, overly white skin, and almond-shaped eyes the color of molten silver. Their faces were narrow and perfectly symmetrical, while their ears came to a very subtle, almost unnoticeable point. But there were differences too. Arad had two scars running along his left cheek from the days when Araxim tortured him, while Aras had a beauty mark just below his left eye. Both had wild, red hair that fell loosely to the small of their back, and their eyebrows were slanted in precisely the same manner. However, Arad's expression was hard and full of hate, while Aras' was consumed by sadness and disbelief.

"I don't understand what we're supposed to do," hissed Arad, "Maybe we should just start breaking some mirrors."

"That's not the way to solve this puzzle," said Aras calmly. He noticed the angle of the mirrors made it impossible for the twins to look away from their other self. The puzzle clearly had something to do with their faces and then it dawned on Aras. The answer washed over him like water escaping from a showerhead.

Aras moved to the nearest mirror to test his hypothesis and, sure enough, he found it sat on hinges and could be moved a few degrees to the left or right. Every mirror was hinged and moved the same way, or up and down. Aras started twisting and turning the mirrors before returning to the spot where he had been standing as they entered. Arad didn't move. Finally, after two hours of careful manipulation of the mirrors, Aras returned to his spot to discover that his face and Arad's had been merged, so that they seemed to be the reflection of one person rather than two. The position of the mirrors coupled with pressure devices beneath where the twins were standing activated a pulley system that opened a large door on the opposite side of the chamber. They moved through the door to discover another large chamber similar to the mirrored one. This room had granite walls and was completely devoid of furniture aside from a tall pedestal at the center of the chamber atop which sat a thick, leather-bound book.

"Now we get to have a reading lesson," grimaced Arad.

"Look," said Aras, pointing to a shelf on the opposite wall, "It looks like there are a series of riddles written on that wall in the Old Language."

There were four phrases etched into the wall, each situated over a thin iron arrow on hinges. Below the arrows were four potential answers to the riddles. It was clear the twins needed to solve the riddles and then position each arrow towards the right answer for each question. Arad grumbled something violently under his breath and refused to cross the room.

"What's the matter, now?" asked Aras frustratingly.

"I'm going to stay here," said Arad, "I don't know how to speak the Old Language…"

"That doesn't mean you can't help. I'll translate," said Aras.

Aras looked at the runes making up the first riddle for a few seconds before turning to his brother.

"It says: In the days before, the time of yore, when the Tall Ones with milky white skin were free, and mankind could see all the wonders of nature…Who stood the tallest in pride and grace, a smile always upon her face, the fairest of the fair, dressed to impress…Tell me the name of the Last Elfin Empress…"

"I guess this is where the book comes in," said Arad.

"Probably, but we don't need it," replied Aras, "Anaximander told me last night that the Yellow Lady was the ghost of the Last Elfin Empress."

Aras moved the iron arrow to point to the name *Eanora*, represented by a rune shaped like an autumn leaf. Aras then started deciphering and translating the next riddle.

"It says: My name vanished when I fell from grace, along with my face…I drew my breath from a poison well, a narrow gateway to my private hell. To my sisters I brought nothing but shame and them I shall always blame in by subtle distress for calling me the Nameless Goddess…"

"Should we consult the book?" asked Arad.

"Yeah…the names written here are: Narenna, Audrid, Soria, Tsira, and Tsiporah. It's not Narenna or Audrid…Narenna is Goddess of the Waning Moon, and Audrid is the Goddess of Love."

The twins approached the book on the pedestal and unlatched its clasp, opening the thick jacket to reveal hundreds of weathered old pages upon which were written the annals of history, not in the Old Language but in the Dark Tongue. Arad smiled sheepishly at his brother.

"It looks like I finally have a job to do," he smirked, "unless, of course, you speak the Dark Tongue."

Aras shook his head before Arad began skimming the passages in the book, turning the pages quickly until coming to a particular set of symbols that intrigued him.

"Tsira," he said simply, "Her name was Tsira, Goddess of the Dark Moon and Herald of the God of Death."

Aras returned to the wall where the riddles were etched and pointed the second iron arrow at the name *Tsira* before moving on to the third riddle, studying it closely for only a few seconds.

"It says: When I ruled the world, it was moved by the dead, I put a price on everyone's head, filled their hearts with dread…my armies moved as if unseen…commanded by the power of the Witch Queen."

Both the twins knew the answer without consulting the book. Both heard the tales of the Witch Queen of Albion when they were children, how the Lady Nerys Sanva married and murdered the second Wyt King, declared herself the tyrant queen of the living world and raised an undead army to do her bidding before she was defeated by Anaximander. Aras quickly positioned the third iron arrow towards the name *Nerys*.

"The final riddle says," began Aras but he was interrupted by Arad.

"It doesn't matter what it says. Just move the iron arrow from one name to the next until something happens. Aras shifted the arrow from the first phrase to the next to the next and then stopped as a large door popped open in the granite wall, exposing a passageway sloping downward towards the heart of the earth.

The twins traveled along the passage for over a half an hour before it widened into a magnificent chamber with gold-plated walls and floors hewn from silver. Positioned on each side of the room were two identical podiums with a single step leading up to a flat surface. On one podium sat a wand and on the other a staff, each with a set of freshly sewn and richly embroidered robes. On the left-hand podium, the wand was forged from gold, with a strand of silver wrapping around it towards a set of brackets meant to hold a gemstone which was absent from its tip. The staff on the right-hand podium was made from silver and the serpent-like strand wrapping up it was forged from gold. The robes were in exact contrast to each other, one made of silver silk, one of golden satin, the robes of silver embroidered with golden thread, the robes of gold with silver. The twins looked at each other and then at the podiums before noticing something sitting carefully on a pedestal at the heart of the room. It was unspeakably beautiful, intricately crafted from silver so that it looked to be assembled by a series of maple and juniper leaves, intermittently weaved together with holly. At the heart of the tiara was set a large yellow diamond with a smaller white diamond set to each side. It was large enough to be set upon a woman's head and would make even a lowly beggar dressed in rags look like a queen.

Aras looked at Arad and they shared the same thought, each setting out at a sprint, hoping to beat the other to the pedestal and lay their hands on the Autumn Crown. However, before either of them were within reach the chamber shook violently and the large yellow diamond at the heart of the crown fell out of its setting, hitting the floor with a crack.

Chapter Sixteen
"The Autumn Crown"

As the yellow diamond hit the ground and cracked the shaking stopped, returning the chamber to a calm, eerie silence. Then, the remnants of the gemstone crumbled to dust in a shower of blinding silver light. When the twins' eyes acclimated to the dull glow of the torches, they were met by a tall, apparition similar to the Yellow Lady, only glowing with a radiant silver light. She was clearly elfin, or had been in life, and taller than the Yellow Lady, with a more regal presence. Her features were completely alien, like those Arad had observed the day Araxim took him to meet their birth mother, but her eyes were caring and calm. She floated there in silence as the twins registered the awesomeness of the moment.

"You're the spirit from within the crown," said Aras, "The one who created it…to defeat the Black Prince."

"In life, I was called Saavika Thirdborn," said the apparition, *"Though more frequently I bore the title of Elfin Empress. But those days are long since gone…I have dwelt within the Autumn Crown for centuries, waiting for the day of my release, when a greater power would come to tip the scales back towards the Old Ways."*

"Is there such a power?" asked Arad cynically, "Saavika or Elfin Empress or whatever I'm supposed to call you."

"Had I lived to abdicate my throne to my daughter, Xanyra, then I would have borne the title of Duchess…and since my home has long been the crown…you may call me the Autumn Duchess."

"Well, Autumn Duchess, where is this great power?" replied Arad sarcastically.

"There were six powers greater than myself," continued the Autumn Duchess, *"The Nameless Goddess standing alone, with no talisman to help her, is still a*

power greater than most, as is the Black Prince, but he is secure in his prison...for now. The Ring of a Hundred Souls bore a greater power than even the talismans of godly origin but, as you are aware, it has long since been broken. The Amulet of the One God, which hangs even now around the Nameless Goddess' neck, has a power equal to that of its mistress, doubling her strength and making her untouchable by even the greatest wizards. Anaximander himself would not dare to approach her directly. And then there are the powers of the prophecy..."

"You mean us," said Aras.

"Yes, sons of my daughter's daughter. From the moment of your birth it has been your destiny to arrive here, at this very hour, in this very cavern. You are the only Halfelfin children ever to be born in the living world, because your mother chose to ignore an ancient law decreed by my mother's mother, Saavika Firstborn, forbidding any of Elfkind, be they male or female, from rutting with man or woman."

"My mother understood what it would mean for the two races to mix their bloodlines," continued the Autumn Duchess, as if she and the twins were gathered around a table listening to an after dinner story, *"She spent many days in the company of the Old Gods before the road between the worlds was shut to us. The souls of Elfkind are filled with a cool, silver radiance that matches our bonds to the living world and the universe beyond. The souls of mankind burn with a passionate, golden fire that often makes them a slave to their emotions and clouds their judgment but provides them what we of the elfin line have never truly experienced..."*

"The ability to love, or to hate," said Aras, as though he had read the Autumn Duchess' mind.

"Elfin folk feel emotions, but we are tempered and detached. The Light in the Art is our only true nature, its practice, its personification...to us nothing else truly matters. Men are free to feel, to follow their passions to glory. To die with the knowledge they truly experienced everything that life has to offer."

"Get back to the point," hissed Arad.

"Now, in power and prestige, the gods are of greater stock than either elf or man, because their spirits are a blending of both the Silver Light and the Golden Fire. Their

power goes beyond the measure of our own to a place we cannot fathom. When my mother's mother stood before Raanon, the Light Bringer, he told her that a soul confined to mortal flesh could never survive the blending of the powers and that it must never be attempted. Yet here you stand, twins of the prophecy, with strength that matches that of the gods. Take to the podiums set before you so that I may show you something…"

The Autumn Duchess pointed at Aras and directed him towards the pedestal will the silver staff sat, while Arad went to stand at the podium with the golden wand. The Autumn Duchess picked up her crown and placed it upon her transparent head so that it too took on a ghostly quality, as though it were not truly there.

"Dod allan eu hysbryd fel y gellir eu gweld," she said in the Old Language, *"Aras yn gyntaf…"*

Aras was suddenly overcome with the urge to vomit. He lurched over as pain curled his stomach and drove his muscles into uncontrollable spasms. He started to sweat and his body was wrought with fever while his nose bled and his eyes watered ceaselessly. With a series of violent seizures during which Aras was fully conscious, a bright orb began to materialize in the air before him. It was glowing with a bright silver light, like the apparition of the Autumn Duchess, but at its heart there burned a golden fire mixing its own radiance with that of the silver surrounding it. As Aras gazed at his soul floating in front of him, Arad succumbed to the same series of pains that Aras had just endured before his soul also materialized. Unlike Aras', it was glowing intensely with a golden fire and, only after straining the eyes, the core of silver light was barely noticeable.

"That's not my soul," sneered Arad angrily, "I've seen my soul before, and that's not it."

"It is your spirit, Arad Orthelios," replied the Autumn Duchess, *"Do you remember the day you were left alone in the company of the Shadow-Weavers? When they whisked you away to the heart of the ring where their souls are being held prisoner by Jadzia Hanara?"*

"I do," frowned Arad, "What about it?"

"The spell they cast upon you insured that no matter what damage Araxim wreaked upon your flesh, your spirit would recover. It was gray and tarnished last time you saw it but, as it has laid to rest deep inside you, it has been wiped clean, washed in the power of the Shadow-Weaver's spell. If you convince your mind to forget all the terrible things you have had to endure, you will find your spirit ready to embrace you."

Arad ignored her as he stared at his fiery spirit. It was only when the Autumn Duchess plucked the two remaining diamonds from her crown that he again took notice of her presence. She floated over to the podium on which Aras was standing and picked up the silver staff with the strand of gold wrapping around it and placed one of the diamonds in its top. The moment the gemstone was joined to the staff, Aras' spirit was drawn into it, so that the diamond began to glow with silver light with a hint of golden fire at its heart. She repeated the process with the golden wand sitting in front of Arad and Arad's spirit was drawn into it, burning with a bright golden light almost blinding to look upon.

"These are your talismans, Orthelios Twins. Let them guide you to victory and rest assured in the knowledge that within them rests the power to face the Nameless Goddess. Stop her before it's too late."

"What about you?" said Aras.

"I go now to my eternal rest in the Silver City beyond the River," she said, *"My work here is done. Wear these robes as a symbol of your unity with the world of Man and that of Elfkind, resting now in the infinite twilight. Never doubt your power and try to remember your bond...you are twins, and you are Halfelfin. The only of your kind."*

The Autumn Duchess smiled a bright, warm grin before fading away, taking her crown with her on her journey to the Otherworld. The chamber returned to its natural state, with the gentle glow of the torches providing the only source of light. The twins' talismans had also gone dark, though a slight glimmer reassured them they were still housing their souls. Aras remained in his green tunic and black leather breeches and put the silver robes embroidered with gold in his pack. Arad also stayed in his gray robes, tucking the golden robes stitched with silver inside his own traveling bag. They each gripped their talismans tightly and then retreated from the chamber back the way they came but, after an hour of backtracking up the cold, dark passages, Arad stopped dead in his tracks.

"We've still got a long way to go," said Aras.

"I think I might know of a faster road," replied Arad, looking down at his golden wand, "She did say we're the most powerful of them all."

Arad focused on the garden near the footstones where they left the others, concentrating on being there with every corner of his mind, before he waved his wand. He and Aras vanished in a flash of silver light, reappearing seconds later near the footstones but the others were gone. They spread out and searched the surrounding gardens and teahouses. In one of the smaller gardens, they found Darendon bound and gagged. Arad used his magic to free Darendon while Aras ran over to help him to his feet.

"Are you alright?" said Aras empathetically.

"Yeah, I think so," replied Darendon shakily, "But they took the others. Jumped out of the bushes and ambushed us when we weren't expecting them. At least nine guards…"

"Jadzia could take down nine guards by herself," sneered Arad.

"Probably…but these guards didn't give any of us a chance to fight. They tossed a gas bomb. Took us all down in seconds," said Darendon.

"Even Gyrdhan?" asked Aras.

"I don't know," said Darendon, "He was still standing when I blacked out. I woke up briefly when they were tying me up…they said they were leaving me behind to deliver a message: your friends are the guests of the Matriarchs and, if you want to see them again, you'll seek out Faceless immediately. We better hurry…"

"You'll be going by yourselves," said Arad.

"What do you mean?" asked Aras, "You're not going to help?"

"Neither are you," said Arad forcefully.

"Excuse me," said Aras defiantly.

"Think about it," replied Arad, "Faceless is using your friends and my mother as bait. If we go charging in without thinking, she'll have us trapped. And then what?"

As difficult as it was for Aras to think about Gyrdhan being held prisoner by Faceless, he understood what Arad was saying. Faceless would be waiting for them and, with the Amulet of the One God in her possession, she would be evenly matched to, if not slightly stronger than the twins.

"What do you suggest?" Aras asked Arad.

"It's late," replied Arad, "I'm guessing the sun went down at least two hours ago. We need to find a place to spend the night and get some food. Then we can sit down and plan out how we're going to rescue my mother…and your father."

"And Anaximander," added Aras.

"Yes, who could forget Anaximander?" grimaced Arad.

"But Faceless' message said we need to go now," said Darendon, "If we wait, what's to stop her from killing them?"

"We'll just have to take that chance," said Arad.

"I don't think we should split up," replied Aras, "Come with us, Dar. I'm just as worried about Gyrd as you are, if not more, but if we just go charging in there, Faceless will have us right where she wants us."

"I don't know," said Darendon.

"I do," countered Arad before walking off towards the little barge which carried them to the Palace of the Silver Light. Aras looked lovingly at Darendon. Then, with a wink, he followed his brother. Darendon stayed there for a moment, staring off towards the nearby bushes, before traipsing off to join the others.

Arad and Aras poled the barge back through the archway connecting the Inner and Middle Districts of the city. The guards didn't give them any trouble. They seldom bothered the travelers exiting the heart of the Eternal City. Once safely in the Middle District, the twins turned the barge up one of the smaller avenues connected to the main waterway, leading towards a large market with rows of public houses on the other side.

They docked in front of the pubs and disembarked. Arad chose *The Rose Cottage* as their temporary home, an inn at the end of the row. It was a quaint little stucco building surrounded by gardens filled with exotic flowers and little fountains gently gurgling with water. The interior of the cottage was furnished with antique furniture upholstered in shades of pink, purple, and blue. There was a fire burning in the large hearth on the far wall of the common room with a series of small tables positioned around it. An elderly, overweight woman rushed over to meet them. She was cheerful enough and wore a purple apron that matched the surrounding furniture.

"Goodness me," she said with a plucky voice, "we don't get very many guests these days…how may I help you gentlemen?"

"We need a room and a good meal," said Arad simply.

"Only one room?" asked the woman.

"One," echoed Arad.

The old woman bustled away and then returned a few moments later with a small iron key in her hand.

"Room Two," she said, "It's at the top of the stairs…second door on the right. Dinner service is over but I'm sure I can find something that'll resemble a meal…there's hot water in the bathhouse out back. Feel free to wash up…I'll bring the food to your room when it's ready."

The twins and Darendon mounted the small staircase in the corner of the room, leading them up to a narrow hallway with doors to the left and right. Arad slipped the key into the lock on the second door to the right and it swung gently open. The room on the other side was small but comfortable. There was an extra-large feather bed covered with quilts and pillows, a small sofa upholstered with black leather, and a washbasin with a mirror. A tiny hearth sat, sunk into the wall, a few feet from the bed, with a small pile of wood and kindling stacked beside it.

Arad left immediately to go wash up. Aras and Darendon made love quickly before joining him in the spacious barrel tub. The warm water was wonderfully relaxing and all three found themselves nodding off after scouring their skin with soap.

"Hello," said the old innkeeper, rousing the boys from their sleep, "Sorry to disturb but you boys'll drown in there. The food is ready. Would you like me to take it to your room or, perhaps you'd like to dine in the common room with me and the mister."

"We'll eat in the room," commanded Arad.

"Very well," said the innkeeper meekly.

The boys leapt out of the tub, their stomachs growling uncontrollably. They each pulled on a white linen bathrobe left by the innkeeper for their comfort before returning to their room where a small but satisfying meal was waiting on a dinner tray. The boys ate quickly, finishing every morsel on their plates, before nestling down into the feather bed, Arad nearest the fire, Darendon in the middle, and Aras closest to the door. Darendon got up and left the room to relieve himself and change into something more comfortable while Arad drifted off into a deep sleep. Aras stared at the ceiling and thought about Gyrdhan. He could barely stomach the idea of his foster-father being tortured or killed. It wasn't until Darendon returned that he relaxed. They made love again quietly so as not to wake Arad. Aras was filled with a sense of security and peace as he laid in the arms of his lover, hearing the gentle thump of his heartbeat.

"So, tell me…what happened down there, under the palace?" asked Darendon curiously.

"It was like a series of puzzles that had to be completed by me and Arad together," replied Aras, "The Yellow Lady made sure only we would be able to get to the crown."

"And did you?" asked Darendon, "Get to the crown."

"Sort of," said Aras.

"What do you mean?"

"We found the Autumn Crown but before we could take it, it broke. The spirit inside was released. She told us a bunch of stuff about our lineage and then used the diamonds from the crown to create talismans for me and for Arad."

Aras pointed to the silver staff leaning against the wall with its snake-like band of gold wrapping up its shaft.

"She removed my soul and placed it in that," continued Aras, "she said it would make me as powerful as the Nameless Goddess."

"So, the Autumn Crown is gone?" said Darendon confusedly.

"Yeah," replied Aras, "The spirit from inside it put it on and, when she disappeared, it vanished with her."

"That changes things," said Darendon with a tone Aras had never heard before as he stood and walked over to the door, flipping the latch and allowing the door to swing open, revealing a tall woman dressed in purple robes, her face obscured by a veil, standing silently on the other side. She swept into the room, the door closing magically behind her, and stood over the twins as they laid in the bed. Arad woke up and Aras was dumbfounded as Darendon came to stand beside the woman.

"These are the great Halfelfin Twins," said Faceless with a sneer.

"Did you hear?" asked Darendon.

"I heard everything," replied Faceless, "and you boys have some explaining to do."

Chapter Seventeen
"Sister"

"I don't understand," exclaimed Aras, looking from Faceless to Darendon with a face of absolute shock.

"What's not to understand," yelled Arad, "Your boyfriend is working for the enemy. And you were just stupid enough to fall for him. How long has he been barking up your tree? Long enough to get the job done."

"He's been my best friend my whole life," said Aras.

Darendon looked sinisterly at Aras, as though he were something revolting to behold. Aras had never seen such a look on Darendon's face, not in all the years they'd known one another. Aras turned to Arad in shame and, for the first time since their reunion, it seemed like Arad actually felt sorry for his brother. He jumped up off the bed, compelling Aras to do the same, and together they began conjuring a spell of *pure light* but, before they could even mutter a word, Faceless called forth a hex with the Amulet of the One God which imprisoned the twins inside invisible forcefields. Faceless removed her veil, to expose her thin, gaunt face, and smiled wickedly.

"The all-powerful twins of the prophecy," she sneered, "the ones who bear the strength to destroy me…pitiful."

Arad struggled relentlessly against his bonds but Faceless' spell was impeding his ability to use magic. Aras remained still and calm, staring intently at Darendon with a look of disgust and abhorrence. He couldn't believe he'd been sharing his body and his life with a traitor.

"Hard to believe isn't it?" snickered Darendon, "If it makes you feel any better, the real Darendon would pluck out his own eyes with a wooden spoon before hurting you…"

"The real Darendon," said Aras with his brow furrowed.

"This one's a succubus," sneered Arad, "You can tell by the way it keeps licking its lips."

Darendon laughed before starting to shake uncontrollably, as though he were standing atop an idling engine. Then his skin began to flake off, shedding like a snake in the desert heat. His hair fell out and his eyes bulged. In only a few seconds, the gorgeous, athletic Darendon had shed his entire outer shell, revealing a hideous worm-like creature underneath. The monstrous worm was as slimy as a slug crawling out from underneath a fern, with two beady little black eyes and an enormous circular mouth filled with rows of razor sharp teeth. The room was filled with a smell that resembled a gangrenous limb as the succubus wheezed and gurgled. Faceless put her arm around the nasty thing and kissed it gently near its mouth.

"The Black Prince isn't the only one with servants," grinned Faceless, "Yes, I know about the daemon, Azgarog, and how you dealt with him, Aras. I know everything about both of you…where you were raised, who you spent your time with. I've known where to find each of you for years. My little succubus minions have been with you from the start. First as adults you could trust and then people close to you in age and interests."

"Where is the real Darendon?" said Aras in a rage, "The imposter talked about him in the present tense, meaning he's still alive so, I'll ask you again, where is he?"

"I wanted to kill him when we abducted him a week before my soldiers showed up at your cottage on Walweitha Isle," said Faceless like she was conversing with an old girlfriend over coffee, "but Valgra here insisted your little friend remain alive so he could study his mannerisms and his behaviorisms. Valgra is a master of his art…he had you convinced."

"You didn't answer my question," said Aras angrily, "Where is Darendon?"

"You'll see him soon enough," smiled Faceless before replacing her veil and tucking the Amulet of the One God beneath her robes. She snapped her fingers and both twins were rendered unconscious as though they'd been hit in the head with a hammer at the same time. Meanwhile, the succubus transformed back into his Darendon form.

"Bring them," said Faceless sternly. Succubus Darendon picked up Aras and Arad, one slung over each shoulder and followed Faceless out of the room, down the stairs, passed the bloody corpses of the innkeeper and her husband, and into the street beyond.

The twins awoke to find their hands bounded and their ankles shackled. They had been stripped naked and their talismans were missing. The Succubus Darendon was leading them down a dank stone passage with a series of circular iron doors in the floor. The succubus used a set of keys to unlock one of the heavy doors and swung it open before pushing Aras, then Arad, inside. They fell about eight feet and landed in a thick layer of dirt which broke their fall. The succubus grinned and blew Aras a kiss before slamming the door, plunging the underground cell into total darkness. Aras and Arad huddled together for warmth. Aras was scared and Arad was angry. They thought they were alone until they heard a cough from the corner.

"Who's there?" barked Aras weakly.

"Ari?" came a familiar voice that warmed Aras' heart.

"Gyrd," exclaimed Aras as his giant foster-father felt his way over to where the twins were sitting and pulled Aras into a hug. He then pulled the large wool blanket off his shoulders and threw it over both the twins. Aras felt nauseous and weak, like he'd been put through the ringer, kicked in the gut, chewed up by a giant, and then spit out on the cold, dirty floor. It was the absence of his talisman. Without the energy of his soul near him, he was weakened and frail.

"Is my mother here?" said Arad sternly.

"She was," replied Gyrdhan, "They came for her a while ago and I haven't seen her since. Your slaves are here…they're sleeping on a feather mattress they found under the dirt. And Darendon's here…"

"Where?" said Aras with a burst of energy that made him momentarily forget about all that had happened.

"Come on," said Gyrdhan, taking Aras by his shackled wrist and leading him slowly away from the center of the room until they were met by a wall. They followed the wall to a little pile of hay from which Gyrdhan produced a makeshift torch. Aras focused with all his might and conjured enough of a spark to light the torch, revealing a pale, emaciated man with a long, disheveled beard and ratty hair laying naked at the heart of the haystack. He had numerous scars running up and down his back and one of his eyes was swollen shut. He was biting at his thumb and muttering incoherently about his father and their market on Walweitha. Aras sat down and pulled Darendon towards him so Darendon's head was resting in Aras' lap. Aras stroked his best friend's grimy hair and cooed at him the way a mother does to quiet a screaming baby.

"What are we going to do, Gyrd?" asked Aras, "And where's Anaximander?"

"Haven't seen him since we was captured," said Gyrdhan.

"I'm sure he's dead," said Arad, "My mother's dead, the Shadow-Weavers are dead, Darendon might as well be dead…and then there's us. We're going to rot in this cell…"

"You don't know that," said somebody from the shadows and it took a moment for everyone to realize it was Valera, Arad's slave girl. She'd never spoken before.

"The little bird starts chirping," mocked Arad, "Shut your mouth and remember your place. If I say there's no hope, who are you to contradict me? You're nothing but a useless easterling whore."

"You shut yer mouth 'fore I rip out yer tongue and use it as a snack," bellowed Gyrdhan at Arad, I don't think any 'a them is dead. If this Faceless was in the habit 'a killin' folks we'd all be on the funeral pyre by now. She wants us alive fer some reason…Can you two think 'a any reason she might wanna keep us here? Do ya think she might wanna sacrifice us or somethin' crazy like that?"

"She already got what she wants from us," answered Arad, "whatever else happens is just for her enjoyment."

"She got the Autumn Crown," said Gyrdhan as more of a statement than question.

"In a manner of speaking," replied Aras before recounting for Gyrdhan all that transpired in the chamber beneath the Palace of Silver Light with the Elfin Empress Saavika Thirdborn. Gyrdhan watched in amazement as their tale unfolded and then hung his head when they got to the part about the Succubus Darendon and Faceless stealing their talismans. It was hard to tell in the darkness but Aras thought Gyrdhan might be crying softly into his giant hands.

Anaximander was hanging from a cross in a large room in the east wing of the Palace of Silver Light. He had nails piercing his wrists, holding him loosely to the wood and causing him a great deal of pain. His staff was laying on the ground near the door but, no matter how hard he tried to compel it into his grip, the staff did not move. Various bladed and blunt torture devices were strewn around the room, one of which was already painfully jammed into Anaximander's rectum. He tried to force it out but, the more he pushed, the greater the agony.

"I wouldn't do that if I were you," said a voice from the corner of the room. It was Faceless' manservant, the hideous Goran, looking as gleeful as a child in a candy shop, "That particular instrument is a nasty little device the easterlings call a *Prykladam Rychlilnikau*. It doesn't really translate but I think you get the gist of how it works. If you keep pushing, the razors on each edge will tear you apart from the inside out."

"What do you want?" said Anaximander weakly, "No doubt it's information you're after…"

"What makes you think I want something?" laughed Goran, "I'm just having a little fun while we wait for my mistress."

"Are you aware of whom it is you serve?" asked Anaximander.

"I serve the highest religious authority in Albion," replied Goran proudly, "The Voice of the One God on earth. I can think of no greater honor than serving my God dutifully and with faith."

"You're so blind," mocked Anaximander, "You think you're serving God but really it is the devil who is your mistress...she calls herself Faceless but her true name is the Nameless Goddess, The Great Deceiver, and the Poisoner of the Well of Shadows."

"You lie," said Goran nonchalantly.

"Oh, my dear, faithful Goran," said Faceless as she entered the room, "You have always been so good to me and I have repaid you with deception. The wizard speaks the truth...I am as he says."

Goran came completely unhinged, backing away from Faceless like a frightened child facing their worst fears. Faceless removed her veil to reveal a wicked smile on her callow face. Her eyes gleamed red like rubies catching the light of the midday sun as she approached Goran and pulled him into a firm embrace.

"You have been my greatest friend," said Faceless, "Thank you."

Faceless released Goran and, with a flick of her wrist, caused his neck to snap like an overextended clothes line. Goran sputtered as he fell to the ground, his open, lifeless eyes fixed on the woman who had been his mistress and companion for ten years.

"What a shame," exclaimed Faceless as she maneuvered behind Anaximander to remove the torture device buried deep inside him, "We have no more need of such barbaric devices. So uncivilized."

Faceless walked over to where Anaximander's staff was laying on the floor and tried to pick it up but, as her fingers approached it, the staff shot furlong across the room, landing on the floor near the window. Faceless' eyes narrowed into a malevolent glare as she stared at the staff. Then she shifted her blood-curdling eyes towards Anaximander.

"I have felt that power before," she hissed, "Whose spirit resides in that staff? It's not yours…"

Anaximander took note that Faceless had a staff and a wand clasped tightly in her left hand. The staff was silver with a strand of gold, the wand gold with a strand of silver but it was the diamonds which caught Anaximander's attention. He could feel the familiar vibration of Aras' soul resonating from inside one of them and surmised the other contained the soul of Arad.

"They're beautiful, aren't they?" said Faceless.

"And they're not yours," replied Anaximander.

"They are now. When I put their strength to use they will grant me a power unlike any that has ever existed. Enough strength to call the Otherworld here, to bring the Gods to me so I can make them pay."

"What is it you want from me?"

"Tell me whose spirit resides in your staff."

"Even if I knew I wouldn't tell you," spat Anaximander.

Faceless walked over to the staff again and this time used the power of the Amulet of the One God to amplify her own magic, enveloping the oaken staff in an eerie purplish glow. The staff fought her but ultimately began to vibrate at a high speed. Then, with a wisp of red light an apparition appeared in the air in front of Faceless. It wasn't an elfin ghost like the Yellow Lady or Saavika Thirdborn. It was greater than that, an omnipresent female form which radiated a heavenly glow like it had captured millions of stars in its aura. Faceless looked like she had eaten some bad food as her face turned green with revolt.

"Hello, Tsira," said the ghostly figure, "It's been a long time. You look well…"

"Selena," spat Faceless.

The ghostly figure smiled gently as she floated over and came to rest before her sister. Selena was the Goddess of the Full Moon, the most powerful of the four sisters representing the culmination of *pure light* in the living world. The more Faceless scowled at Selena, the gentler Selena's smile became. It was clear that whatever ill will Selena felt towards her little sister vanished long ago.

"Why are you here?" seethed Faceless.

"To beg you to end this foolishness," replied Selena, "When the wizard's spirit passed into his new body, it took a detour on its journey. It came to me in our palace on the edge of the Otherworld. Anaximander told me all that had come to pass in the living world. Even though he was still ignorant to your identity, I knew this new ruler was you. So I cast my spirit into his staff, to provide him with great power, because I knew we would come to this moment."

"So now you are a prophetess come to divine my future," sneered Faceless mockingly.

"What I am is your sister and I care about you. Do you remember the prophecy of the mad god destroying everything by trying to merge the three worlds into one? The one we ourselves saw all those years ago? It is plain to see that you are that mad god and I will do everything in my power to bring about a peaceful resolution to this matter. It is time for you to come home, Tsira."

Faceless replied by conjuring a bolt of absolute darkness, hurtling it at the apparition of her sister like a javelin. Selena's ghostly form evaporated only to reappear on the opposite side of the room. She warmly smiled at her sister again. Faceless glowered at Selena, trying to think of a spell or hex that would deal with Selena once and for all.

"There is no magic in the living world that can do be harm," said Selena warmly, "The only outcome would be the return of my spirit to my body, waiting peacefully in the Otherworld. Give in, Tsira, and come home.

Our sisters are waiting. I promise there will be no consequences, no punishments…not this time."

Faceless responded by calling forth the most powerful spell she could muster. The walls and ceiling began to quake as a mighty cyclone of wind whipped up around them. The light emanating from the torches on the walls was muted by a dark shadow descending from above and several bolts of lightning shot out from Faceless' hands towards Selena's apparition. Selena simply evaporated and then reappeared.

"I see you're not ready," said Selena sadly, "I hope one day you will be…until then know this: you cannot win."

The room continued to shake and the shadow to grow as Faceless muttered words in the Dark Tongue, words meant to curse and kill. She focused all her power towards her sister, conjuring a great sphere of crimson fire and flinging it like a spit ball hitting the ceiling. The fireball flew furlong at Selena but, with a blinding eruption of silver and golden sparks, she, Anaximander, and the oaken staff vanished.

Chapter Eighteen
"Empress of Albion"

Anaximander crept down the corridor without making a sound. The spirit of Selena, Goddess of the Full Moon, had returned to her resting place deep within Anaximander's oaken staff, lending him her power to amplify his magic, though not enough for him to match off against the fallen goddess, Faceless. He moved slowly with large strides while generating a concealment spell that hid him from the eyes of most, though such an incantation would not work against Faceless or her magic-wielding minions. The passages were barely lit with an occasional guard posted at various entrances and archways. Anaximander knew where he wanted to go and exactly how to get there. It was not his first time inside the halls of the Palace of Silver Light. In the hundreds of years he'd been alive, Anaximander had been in every nook and cranny of the palace at least a thousand times. He moved down three sets of stairs that were used only by servants, until he emerged on the main floor of the palace near the kitchens. It was early in the morning, before sunrise, but the kitchens were bustling with servants preparing the morning meal. Anaximander strengthened his concealment spell and then crept down three more passages, arriving at a guarded staircase leading to the dungeon.

With a subtle shift of his staff, Anaximander caused the two guards at the top of the stairs to fall gently to the floor in a deep sleep. He stepped over them and descended into the darkness, to the passage above the cells. He could feel the twins' energy as he drew closer. He broke the lock on their iron door and jumped into the cell, causing it to light up with the brightness of his spirit. Aras looked at Anaximander and nearly cried while Arad's features didn't change. Gyrdhan ran over and clapped the wizard on the back and pulled him into a bear hug.

"We must go," said Anaximander, "Faceless will assume I'd come here to free you..."

"And go where?" asked Aras, "She has our souls...and I know enough about magic to know what will happen to us the further we get from them...we'll die, Anax. And I don't want to die."

"I wasn't suggesting we leave the palace...but moving away from the dungeons is probably a very good idea," said Anaximander before leading them back the way he had come, to the main floor of the palace, and out into the gardens. They found a small teahouse near a pond to hide in and talk. Darendon was in bad shape, emaciated and catatonic. Gyrdhan decided he would remain behind in the teahouse and care for him with the slaves, Valera and Xavin, while Aras, Arad, and Anaximander would go back into the palace and confront Faceless.

"I ain't gonna be no help in a wizardin' fight," said Gyrdhan, "And Dar needs to be nursed...he ain't doin' too well."

"I don't see why any of us should go back in there," said Arad harshly, "Faceless is more powerful now than ever. She'll crush us in seconds...we haven't got any weapons to match her strength."

"No, but I have a plan," said Anaximander, "She fooled us with an imposter...I wonder if we could do the same."

"Is there anyone she trusts who could get close enough to do her harm?" asked Aras, "I was under the impression she didn't have a lot of friends...she did murder her manservant and try to kill her sister."

"I believe there is one individual she might let get close to her," said Anaximander.

Faceless appeared in the great hall the following morning dressed in her usual attire. Since her recent outburst, the other Matriarchs took great care to avoid her but their duties to the people of Atlantis forced them to mingle. Lylid and Draena had stopped wearing their ceremonial robes, choosing instead to wear plain purple slips as a statement of their unwavering devotion to the One God, a gesture which made Faceless laugh. Elora and Anorra were not quite as brazen but they did nothing to hide their contempt as Faceless took her seat. She clapped her hands in the usual manner and the stewards threw open the main doors but there was no one outside seeking an audience, no one besides Marek of Ki. Marek moved swiftly into the room and honored the Matriarchs with a military salute before placing his helmet and gauntlets on the floor at his feet.

"What is it we can do for you, Sir Marek?" said Lylid with a nod.

"I come bearing news for my Lady Faceless," he replied, "We have not yet located the twins and there is no sign of the others."

"Don't worry about them," said Faceless from beneath her veil, "They're nothing anymore. We have more pressing matters…the time for the Unveiling has come at last."

Marek of Ki saluted again, turned on his heel, and swept out of the room. The stewards slammed the doors shut and then walked away towards the servants' entrance after Faceless waved them away, leaving her alone in the massive room with the Matriarchs.

"What's this about an Unveiling?" asked Elora.

"We didn't hear about this," continued Anorra.

"It has nothing to do with any of you," hissed Faceless, "Your parts in this game have unfortunately come to an end."

Faceless clapped her hands again and a dozen armed palace guards marched into the room through all its entrances. They pulled each of the Matriarchs, except Faceless, from their chairs and dragged them down the stairs to the main floor of the Great Hall. The guards stripped them and kicked them and spit in their faces. The Matriarchs screamed for mercy but were met only by the cold and callous smile of Faceless as she pulled her veil over her head. The guards took their turns raping the Matriarchs before binding them in chains and leading them out of the room. Faceless laughed loudly, a shrill sound that echoed through the empty room, before pointing at each of the Matriarchs' chairs, which took their turn bursting into flames. She was just about to do the same to her own seat when the doors flew open and Marek of Ki returned.

"You told me they wouldn't be harmed," he said angrily, "The Matriarchs are women of the cloth."

"But you know the truth about the One God," replied Faceless.

"I know that you murdered him long ago," replied Marek, "I'm not so naïve to believe in him but I believe in the symbol of power he represents…without the Matriarchs, the Tetrarchs will turn against us, they will take with them the power of the Temple and all their new, highly influential, Atlandish converts. How will you maintain your hold on Albion if your allies turn against you?"

"With these," smirked Faceless before stripping off her purple robes to reveal the Amulet of the One God sitting atop an exquisitely stitched, tightly fitting red gown. Faceless produced the silver staff containing Aras' soul from behind her seat the gold wand with Arad's soul from inside the folds of her purple robes lying nearby. She was at once overwhelmed by the raw power coursing through her veins. She glowed with a bright orange light and everything in close proximity to her combusted into bright red flames. Marek of Ki took a few steps back as she completely took on another look, an alien, otherworldly visage that chilled his blood and made his stomach curl into knots.

Faceless glided across the room, as though her feet weren't touching the floor, and stared into Marek's eyes with her strangely opalescent gaze. She pulled his face to hers and kissed him violently, shoving her serpentine tongue so far down his throat he choked. Her mutated hands with their thin, overly long fingers and unnaturally sharp fingernails, grabbed at Marek's chest before Faceless reached down at grabbed his manhood, squeezing it tightly in her powerful grip. Marek grunted from the pain but tried desperately to show no emotion as Faceless ripped off his clothes like a ravenous wolf tearing into the skin of its freshly caught prey. She threw Marek to the ground and mounted him, slipping him inside her with such force that he again let out a loud grunt. Her skin had gone pale and wrinkled, while her breasts were strangely shaped and hairy. She no longer even resembled a woman. She looked like a cross between an old hag, a wolf, and a daemon as she bucked and wailed like a pig begging for food. Marek was revolted but kept a straight face as Faceless climaxed. She ran her talons down Marek's chest, producing several deep lacerations that bled steadily.

"Get dressed…there's a great deal of work to be done," she hissed, replacing her purple robes and veil so that she again looked like a woman of piety and faith, hiding the monster she had become.

Anaximander led the twins back into the Palace of Silver Light by way of the supply corridor, the one used primarily by merchants and traders delivering food and other wares to the palace kitchens. It was early morning and the servants were busy preparing meals and lighting fires. They didn't notice as Anaximander and the twins slipped passed them into the storerooms behind the larder. Anaximander found a place amidst a series of large crates for them to sit down and drink some water.

"I don't understand what we're doing here," said Arad.

"You and Aras are going to search out something we need," replied Anaximander, "I just hope it's still here…"

"And what about you?" asked Aras.

"I need to send a message to what's left of the Wizarding Clans and the Knights of the Old Guard," said Anaximander, "We need their help."

"Then I'm going to find a way to get close to Faceless," said Anaximander, "and you're going to find the means to defeat her. In a chamber deep beneath the palace his hidden a book called *The Wytrannikon*. Inside *The Wytrannikon* is a spell known as *The Supreme Conjuring*. You two must find the book and commit the incantation to memory. *The Supreme Conjuring* won't defeat Faceless but it'll keep her from hurting anyone with her newfound powers. It might be all we can do. The stairs leading down into the lower chambers are in the hallway adjacent to the bathing rooms at the end of the corridor just outside this storeroom. Once you reach the lower levels, follow the right hand passages. You will see a large mirror with two candleholders on each side. Step through the mirror...the book should be there...find it, then return to the Teahouse. I'll send a message to Gyrdhan with the location where the Clans are going to gather. It shouldn't take them long to arrive in the city."

Anaximander didn't wait for the twins to respond, standing and sweeping out of the storeroom as fast as his legs could carry him.

"I guess we're on our own," said Aras.

"You mean you're on your own," replied Arad, "I've got something else I need to do..."

"I need your help," said Aras sadly, "Please."

Arad grunted with a nod before leading the way out of the room and down the corridor towards the secret stairs Anaximander told them about. The stairs were easy to find but descending them was a bit more difficult. The stone steps were in a severe state of disrepair and, more than once, the twins nearly slipped and toppled down the stairs on their necks. A journey that should've taken fifteen minutes took them nearly an hour. At last they emerged on a narrow landing with a low ceiling. It was damp and dark. The twins each carried a torch as they wound their way down an endless series of passages, mindful to always choose the right-hand turn when presented with the decision. They walked and walked for more than three hours and were about to give up when they finally stumbled across the giant mirror with two large candles burning on each side.

"Wait," said Arad before Aras stepped through the glass.

"What?" replied Aras.

"Faceless has lived in the palace for years and it was home to the Black Prince for years before that," said Arad, "Don't you think one of them would've already found this place?"

"There's only one way to find out," said Aras, "I'll go through…If I don't pop back out in thirty seconds, it was a trap."

Aras took a deep breath and then leaped towards the mirror. Under normal circumstances, the glass would've shattered into a thousand pieces but, as Aras made impact, he was absorbed into its depths, as though it were a pool of water. Arad stared towards the mirror as it returned to its normal consistency. Thirty seconds passed, then sixty, and then ninety without Aras reemerging. Arad turned to walk away but hesitated. With an exaggerated sigh he followed his brother's lead and jumped into the mirror.

Arad felt he knew what it was like to be a fish swallowed by a whale as the mirror squeezed him and sucked him downward. He was surrounded by a strange, wet substance but he could breathe. It was extremely sticky, like the strands of a spider web, and Arad was completely unable to move. It wasn't until he bumped into something solid that Arad realized it was Aras. He seemed to be stuck. Arad struggled with all his might to raise his leg and plant his foot in Aras' butt, causing Aras to emerge from the mirror into a small circular room with a large book sitting on a pedestal at its heart.

"Hey," shouted Arad.

Aras turned around to face the mirror and reached inside it with his arm, grabbing Arad by the foot and yanking him out.

"That must be *The Wytrannikon*," said Aras.

"Obviously," replied Arad, "Let's find this conjuring spell and get out of here…"

As the sun reached its apex in the sky, Faceless dressed herself in an exquisitely stitched green gown embroidered with tiny pearls. She placed an ornate silver tiara over her perfectly styled black hair with matching earrings.

The Amulet of the One God was resting comfortably over her breasts and the twins' talismans were gripped in her left hand. The monstrous visage she manifested the night before was gone but she still looked unfeeling and fake, like a woman made from plastic. When she was satisfied with her gown and jewelry she hid them beneath her traditional purple robes and thick veil.

Jadzia was chained to the right, front bedpost of Faceless' luxurious featherbed. She had been beaten, maimed, raped, and tortured. Her usually cynical, powerfully apathetic face had given way to fear and loathing. She looked weak and wary, dressed in the tattered remains of her traveling clothes. One of her eyes was swollen shut but the other was wide open and staring malevolently at Faceless. She coughed a raspy wad of phlegm as she began to speak in almost a whisper.

"Don't you look pretty," said Jadzia weakly, "Like the belle of the ball…much better than the last time I saw you."

"Ah…finally it speaks," replied Faceless from beneath her veil, "Thank you for the compliment, darling. I wouldn't be here today if it weren't for you and your sisters…"

"Where are my sisters?" coughed Jadzia.

"Resting, as they should be," said Faceless before producing a small black box containing the souls of the Shadow-Weavers. Jadzia's personage was contorted by rage as she tried desperately to break the chains holding her to the bed with magic but nothing happened.

"Really," exclaimed Faceless, "Your magic was nothing more than fraction of my own when I was trapped in the poison well. Now that I bear the power of four gods, you are akin to a tick trying to burrow into my skin. You're an irritation…and I intend to squish you."

"You should know better than anyone," said Jadzia mockingly, "I can't die…not by any hand on this earth."

"Correction. There are one pair of hands that can force the life from you, the same hands that gave you the gift of immortality…mine."

"Then kill me and be done with it," snapped Jadzia.

"All in good time, my darling," smiled Faceless, "First you will be my honored guest at the Great Unveiling…it's time for the people of Albion to know the truth…to know whom they really serve."

Faceless clapped her hands and the Darendon doppelganger entered the room with another succubus, this one in the form of a tall, voluptuous woman with tawny blonde hair and vibrant green eyes. Doppelganger Darendon unchained Jadzia from the bedpost and led her out of Faceless' bedchamber, the other succubus on their heels. They took her down a set of spiraling stairs, through two passages, and out onto a balcony overlooking the large and extravagantly designed Royal Courtyard. Directly below them, tied to four separate stakes piled high with freshly cut kindling, were the four Matriarchs: Lylid, Draena, Elora, and Anorra. There was a large unruly crowd gathered just beyond the Matriarchs, being contained by nearly all the palace guards. The people were shouting in protest at the sight of their beloved Matriarchs being prepared to burn at the stake and many wondered where Faceless was and why she didn't also stand accused. In response to the cries of the crowd, Faceless waltzed out onto the balcony in her easily recognizable attire and raised her arms into the air. The noise in the courtyard faded and all eyes were fixed on Faceless.

"My dear friends and loyal subjects," said Faceless loudly, "I have heard your cries and your desperate prayers and come now to you with much deserved answers. Since our rise to power nearly twenty years ago, we have kept the statues of our great One God covered in reverence with thick white shrouds. We have done this for two reasons…The face of your beloved and holy leader was concealed while the Atlandish people were converted to our faith…second, the time to show you everything needed to coincide with other, more personal matters. I am elated to announce that today, finally, the statues, and I shall be unveiled."

"You can't be serious," muttered Jadzia.

The shrouded statue in the center of the courtyard was approached by two guards. They pulled the white tapestry away from the stone effigy with a single powerful thrust, exposing not the form of the One God, but that of the Nameless Goddess underneath. The crowds in the courtyard once again erupted into violent cries and chaotic uproars until the palace guards fired a volley of arrows into their midst, striking down at least a dozen innocent peasants. The crowds quieted and reluctantly redirected their attention to the balcony as Faceless removed her veil and robes, standing there in full regal attire, the perfect likeness of the statue below.

As the attention of the guards and people of Atlantis was focused on the dramatics of Faceless on her balcony, it went completely unnoticed when mysteriously cloaked figures began appearing in the city, teleporting from parts unknown by the dozens and converging on an old storehouse near the line demarking the Middle and Outer Districts of the city. Anaximander had sent word to Gyrdhan on the wings of an eagle telling him to take Darendon, Valera, and Xavin and rendezvous with their newly arriving allies at the storehouse, but not before leaving the message in the teahouse for Aras and Arad. Gyrdhan stared out one of the dusty, clouded windows towards the nearby waterway, nervousness overpowering his rational mind.

"I'm getting' worried," he said, "They should 'a been here by now."

"Perhaps they ran into unforeseen complications," said a Blue Robe by the name of Mauren. He was one of fifteen wizards who had answered Anaximander's call for aid, most coming from the Blue and Green Order, though there were two Greys and a Red also present. The rest of the three dozen individuals gathered in the storehouse were former Knights of the Old Guard, middle-aged men in rusting armor armed with claymore swords they could barely lift anymore. The lackluster quality of their army did nothing to alleviate Gyrdhan's fears. It wasn't until he saw a small raft carrying two hooded figures dock near the storehouse that he took a breath of relief. Aras and Arad crept quietly down the stone walkway connecting the storehouse to the canal but were stopped at the heavy doors leading inside by a group of Knights questioning their identities. Gyrdhan rushed over and forced himself through their ranks.

"That's enough 'a that," barked Gyrdhan, "these here are our boys."

The twins dropped their hoods to reveal their nearly identical faces to those gathered behind the doors of the storehouse. Aras looked like he had aged ten years in the course of two short weeks, while the reverse effect was happening to Arad. The wrinkles caused by his near endless scowling were lightening some and his eyes had taken on a slight twinkle. Aras took the time to hug Gyrdhan and Darendon before turning to Mauren.

"Where is Anaximander?" asked Aras urgently.

"No one's seen him," replied Mauren.

"Damn," muttered Arad, "I really thought he'd be here."

"We thought he was with you," said Gyrdhan.

"No," replied Arad, "he had another errand to attend to."

"What are we supposed to do now?" said Aras.

"Anax left us with instructions and we have spies out in the courtyard watching the Nameless Goddess," said Mauren, "Here comes one of them…look over there."

With a sound like the snap of a rubber band and a faint flash of blue light, a young man with shoulder-length blonde hair, carrying a mahogany staff, appeared near the doors of the storehouse. He rushed passed the Knights positioned at the front of the large room and came over to speak with Mauren and Gyrdhan. His face was twisted with a look of horror the likes of which Aras had never seen and he trembled as he opened his mouth to speak about what he had observed.

"I've never seen such an atrocity," said the young wizard, "Never in my life. It was horrible."

"What was horrible?" said Mauren, "Speak boy!"

The young wizard hesitated. It was like he lacked the courage to speak about what he'd seen, as though the Nameless Goddess had robbed him of his tongue and deprived him of his will to resist. He stared vacantly at the floor like a dog cowering away from a cruel master using violence to intimidate his faithful pet.

"I said *speak*," said Mauren forcefully, placing a magical emphasis on the last word so that it carried the energy to compel the young wizard to end his silence and overcome his fears.

"She killed them, burned them alive," said the young wizard, "the four lesser Matriarchs are nothing but ashes and Faceless...Faceless has declared herself Empress. She said she is Faceless and Nameless no longer...She is the One Goddess."

Chapter Nineteen
"One World"

"You're insane," snapped Jadzia at Faceless.

"You have no idea," said Faceless as she gazed down at the remains of the lesser Matriarchs smoldering to ash upon their pyres. The palace guards were forced to use violence against the crowd to keep them from saving the Matriarchs and many were lying dead in the blood-strewn courtyard. Even as the guards cut down the protesting onlookers, more peasants and merchants and members of the Old Nobility began flooding into the courtyard, armed with blunt instruments, kitchen knives, ceremonial daggers, and other makeshift daggers. Then, Faceless noticed wizards appearing in mass towards the back the crowd. They began conjuring various spells and incantations against the palace guards, slowly turning the tide against Faceless' forces. Gyrdhan led the Knights of the Old Guard against a contingent of guards near the front of the column, armed with his giant double-bladed axe and a look of uninhibited rage. As fireballs, powerful gusts of wind, tiny earthquakes, and other elemental spells rocked the courtyard, the doors to the balcony flew open and Marek of Ki walked out to speak with his mistress.

"We need to get you out of here," said Marek, "My Lady, the enemy is winning. My guards are proving useless against their magic. They'll soon have the means to storm the palace…"

"They're not the only ones with magic," hissed Faceless who began to once again transform into her terrifying, monstrous form with her forked tongue and opalescent eyes, *"It's time for me to fulfill my destiny…and bring the three worlds together forever…"*

"Noooo," screamed Jadzia from where she was chained.

Faceless began to levitate several feet above the balcony as the Amulet of the One God, and the Twin Talismans began to glow with a fiery mixture of gold and silver light. Faceless' looks were further contorted as she took on a purely daemonic look, complete with horns and a tail. She opened her mouth to speak and out flowed a spell unlike any heard for ages in the living world. It was neither the Old Language nor the Dark Tongue. It wasn't Atlandish or the language of the Easterlings. It was something far more ancient, a secret speech reserved for the highest of celestial beings.

> *"Glaoch mé chun tú sa chéad teanga*
> *Fórsaí thar na déithe.*
> *Cinn d'aois a rugadh I dtús*
> *Scaoilfeadh glas ar na slabhraí de spás*
> *Atú Albion agus Avalon leis*
> *An domhan thar…"*

As Faceless' spell created violent shockwaves that rocked the Palace of the Silver Light and the Royal Courtyard, the forces of light succeeded in routing the majority of the palace guards and began flooding through the palace gates. Marek of Ki left the balcony to join what remained of his guards in their struggle against the oncoming wizards and Knights of the Old Guard. Faceless continued to remain suspended in air repeating her spell.

> *"Glaoch mé chun tú sa chéad teanga*
> *Fórsaí thar na déithe.*
> *Cinn d'aois a rugadh I dtús*
> *Scaoilfeadh glas ar na slabhraí de spás*
> *Atú Albion agus Avalon leis*
> *An domhan thar…"*

The shockwaves emanating from Faceless were intensified and their effect on the environment began to become apparent. The nearby sea rose up in violent waves and the wind howled uncontrollably. Violent crimson clouds formed heavy in the sky, blocking out the natural light of the sun and casting an eerie, soft glow on the living world.   Green bolts of lightning sparked in the heavens and the earth lurched under the raw power of the ancient words being spoken like a song filling every corner of the world.

"Glaoch mé chun tú sa chéad teanga

Fórsaí thar na déithe.

Cinn d'aois a rugadh I dtús

Scaoilfeadh glas ar na slabhraí de spás

Atú Albion agus Avalon leis

An domhan thar…"

As a final, devastating shockwave burst forth from Faceless, the living world began to flicker and fade like a weak signal disrupting a television program.   Each time it reappeared, the world was different.   There were parts that remained the devastated Eternal City but there were other parts that became entirely different.   Entire districts of the city became sprawling fields filled with apple groves.   Where the ocean had been before, great mountains appeared.   And a part of the courtyard had been swallowed by a wide river filled with what looked like thousands of corpses staring hauntingly up from beneath the surface of the glassy water.   Faceless landed gently on the balcony and returned to her humanlike visage.   She stared out at the chaos with a joyous smile adorning her glowing face while Jadzia trembled in fear.

"You have no idea what you've done," said Jadzia.

"I know precisely what I have accomplished here," smiled Faceless, "And soon, the three worlds will become one and I will finally have the opportunity to seek my revenge.   I will draw the Old Gods to me like flies drawn to honey and, with my newfound power, I will bring each and every one to an end once and for all."

The earth shook and the sky darkened as more of the Eternal City vanished, replaced by foreign landscapes that were both beautiful and terrifying to behold.   The entire fabric of space and time was beginning to unravel and the costs were irreparably detrimental to the natural balance of the living world. An entire quarter of the Atland was lost to the sea, so that all the tropical and warm parts of the vast continent were lost forever, except for the small southeastern strip where the Eternal City stood. The Sylveroad Woods and the Marshland Forest vanished. The One Mountain at the heart of Lemuria erupted with molten lava that consumed the island in only seconds, while the Forgotten Lands beyond, traditionally wasteland deserts, sprouted lush hills and valleys, rivers and rainforests. But the more the world changed, the greater the tumults grew, threatening to undo the bonds of reality and cause all existence to fly apart.

The forces of light rushed up the stairs within the palace and began fighting through the last remnants of Faceless' guard. Marek of Ki again appeared through the doors. He bore a long gash on his cheek and was nurturing a severe wound to his left shoulder.

"My Lady," he said quickly, "I am begging you…we must leave. Our enemy is on our very doorstep and my guards are gone. All of them."

"We will stand our ground," said Faceless before muttering a quiet spell under her breath, *"Yn ein gwyneud yn diogel."*

There was a sound like the loud ringing of bells and what felt like a gentle wind whisked passed Faceless, Jadzia, and Marek of Ki, encompassing the whole balcony in its strange warmth. Jadzia knew what Faceless had just done but Marek of Ki looked wholly confused.

"No matter how hard they try," said Faceless, "The forces of light cannot breech my enchantment. We are completely safe here."

They could hear their enemies banging against the doors of the balcony with weapons and spells but they were unable to pass the border of Faceless' spell. She laughed maniacally as the world continued to morph and shift, to shake and darken. Jadzia screamed obscenities at Faceless as Marek of Ki came to stand beside her.

"You won't succeed," said Jadzia loudly, "By the Old Gods…you cannot win…"

Faceless ignored Jadzia's continued complaints as she ripped at her gown and removed her tiara so she stood there completely naked, aside from the powerful talismans which continued to glow brightly. Faceless tore at Marek's clothes and soon he too was nude. She threw him to the ground and mounted him like a lioness in heat, bucking and thrusting wildly and howling like a wolf baying at the full moon. The world shook and shattered as Faceless forced Marek to fuck again and again. When at last she was bored, she allowed him to stand and replace his clothes but she remained wild and naked, looking like a barbarian princess leading her tribe into war.

"Now that you've seen the wonders of my power," said Faceless, turning to speak to Jadzia, "I have no more use for you."

Faceless produced the small box containing the souls of the Shadow-Weavers from the pocket of her purple robes lying nearby in a pile. She spoke some words in the Dark Tongue and the Shadow-Weavers appeared out of the darkness, rising from their slumber and bearing down on Jadzia like coyotes stumbling across a healthy deer carcass. They each bit into their sister, tearing chunks of her flesh down to the bone, devouring her bite by bite with ravenous hunger. Jadzia screamed for them to stop, imploring them to remember who she was but no matter how much she writhed in agony, the Shadow-Weavers continued to consume her.

"Stop, sisters, I'm begging you," screamed Jadzia as something unexpected began to occur. The black box containing the souls of the Shadow-Weavers began to shake violently in Faceless' hands, so much that she was forced to drop it. It broke against the hard stones of the balcony and the three spirits rose into the air in a shower of golden sparks. The Shadow-Weavers stopped tearing away at their sister and turned vacantly towards the lights hovering above them. One by one, the Shadow-Weavers fell to the ground and did not move again. Meanwhile, Jadzia's gift of immortality caused her wounds to heal almost instantly but not before she was able to slip out of her chains and stand to face Faceless.

The spirits of the Shadow-Weavers began to transform, taking on human silhouette in the form of ghostly apparitions. Idris, Aneira, and Oryne hovered next to Jadzia with the looks they had before being killed by the Nameless Goddess, beautiful young maidens, both innocent and kind. They looked lovingly at their sister, as if speaking to her without words, and then they rushed Faceless as though they were a stampede of elephants trampling a bed of peanuts. Faceless was temporarily overwhelmed by their untainted brilliance as they circled around her repeatedly, blinding her with their light and confusing her with spells spoken in the Old Language. This gave Jadzia the opportunity to grab Marek's longsword, drawing it quickly from its leather scabbard before jumping towards Faceless to join her sisters. Marek of Ki remained frozen in astonishment near the edge of the balcony.

Unfortunately, just before Jadzia could land a fatal blow to the back of Faceless' head with the sword, Faceless invoked a terrible spell which caused the spirits of the Shadow-Weavers to instantly evaporate, giving Faceless the time to turn around and grab Jadzia by the throat. Jadzia dropped the sword as she gasped for air. Faceless smiled at her malevolently and then tossed her against the railing of the balcony so hard that her spine cracked violently. Jadzia crumpled into a ball on the floor, unable to stand.

"You've won," conceded Jadzia, "Damn it, you've won…it's over. Let me die…let me join my sisters…"

"I changed my mind," said Faceless, "I think I'm going to let you live. Your back is broken and your legs are dead…an injury I infused with magic so that your gift of immortality cannot heal it. Without the ability to walk, you're going to be powerless, and you're going to be my pet. Now, cower, dog, as I invoke the final part of my spell."

Faceless was again lifted into the air, taking on her monstrous, daemonic form. Jadzia tried to raise herself up using the rails of the balcony for support but she couldn't. Faceless spoke the truth. Her legs were dead and gone. She cowered as Marek of Ki came to stand over her. He picked up his sword and replaced it in his sheath before kneeling beside Jadzia and gently straightening her hair.

"Don't worry," he said with a voice that was not his own, "You're going to be fine...we're all going to make it through this. We just need to wait until she's weakened...then we'll strike."

"Who are you?" asked Jadzia in a whisper.

"You'll find out very soon," replied Marek with a wink.

Meanwhile, Faceless invoked the final part of her terrible incantation with a ferocity that brought the survivors in the city below to kneel in submission out of fear as her voice echoed through every corner of the materializing conglomeration of the three worlds.

"A tharraingt anuas na déithe óna caisleán I bhfolach,
Iad a thabhairt chun seasamh anseo ar mo chosa.
Slabhra iad le rópaí déanta as an dorchadas,
Leagan orthu utu anseo í nysbryd..."

The earth quaked with terrible tremors that caused parts of the Palace of Silver Light to break off and plummet to the ground. The balcony on which they were standing buckled and swayed slightly but remained steadfastly anchored to the rest of the palace. Faceless fell back to the balcony and hit the floor hard before pulling herself warily to her feet. She glared and Jadzia with an eerie look of satisfaction before, one by one, twenty individuals began to appear around the edge of the balcony, ten males and ten females. They were slightly larger in height and build than other men but possessed the same general features. But they were pale and weak and their eyes were absent life. They looked like peasants who'd contracted some incurable disease, like the Red Sweats. If it hadn't been for their regal, otherworldly attire, it would've been easy to make that mistake.

"At last," sneered Faceless, staring towards the two beleaguered females standing closest to her, "It's been a long time sisters."

"Not long enough," said the younger of the two females.

"You don't look well, Tsira," said the older of the two.

"Neither do you," replied Faceless coldly, "but you don't have to worry about me. I'll be feeling better very soon."

"Oh, yes," said the tallest of the males, "your revenge…well it should be easy for you to accomplish. The laws of nature have been turned upside down and you've torn a gaping hole in the heart of the cosmos. Any power we had to resist you is gone…"

"Wonderful," laughed Faceless, "than you can face your deaths slowly and with unimaginable pain."

"Not so fast," shouted Marek of Ki and Faceless turned around to see him transform from her loyal bodyguard into the wizard, Anaximander, standing proudly with his oaken staff in hand.

"Now boys," continued the wizard. Suddenly, Aras and Arad leaped out of the shadows where they'd been hiding, each dressed in the robes given to them by the Autumn Duchess. Without looking at Faceless, they began to recite *The Supreme Conjuration* which they'd memorized from the pages of *The Wytrannikon*. Their voices filled the air like a choir singing an angelic hymn and Faceless stepped back in fear, covering her ears in pain.

"Ag an codlata cumhachta ag cróílár an spéir,
Caitheadh balla thart ar an diabhal.
Cealaigh h damáiste
Impigh againn."

With a loud boom, the damage being inflicted to the world stopped. Then a great dome descended from the heavens to encapsulate the balcony where Anaximander and the twins stood facing off against Faceless. The Old Gods recognized the words of the spell and smiled at the twins of the prophecy, as though they were their own children. Faceless watched the dome as it made contact with the ground, quarantining the Palace of Silver Light from the rest of the Eternal City. The parts of the landscape that were foreign to Albion began to fade. The sprawling fields and crystalline mountains, the strange river flowing through the heart of the city, all vanished in a wisp of smoke. The seas stopped churning and the sky cleared, returning the light of the sun to the devastated remains of the living world. The Atland did not recover its southern half and Lemuria remained buried in mountains of ash. Entire districts remained missing from the Eternal City and the palace was damaged beyond repair.

"Thank you," said the tallest of the Old Gods to Aras and Arad before he faded away, followed by the nineteen others, fading one by one. Faceless boiled over with rage as she watched her long-awaited opportunity to enact her revenge disappear forever.

"What have you done?" she screamed, turning on Anaximander and the twins with fiery rage boiling in her crimson eyes.

Chapter Twenty
"Last Stand"

Faceless fired off a few sloppy hexes which Anaximander easily dodged. She was overwrought with anger, clouding her judgment and making her magic unfocused. The loss of her opportunity to kill the Old Gods, as punishment for their mistreatment of her, caused Faceless to become maddened with grief and she inadvertently transformed into her monstrous, daemonic alter ego.

"I hope destroying my dreams was worth it," growled Faceless, "Because it was the last thing you will ever do in this world."

"I don't think so," said Anaximander warmly, "I think you've forgotten the tale of the day Lady Rheis came here to retrieve her mother's crown from the Wyt King."

"Speak plainly wizard," spat Faceless in annoyance.

"You have forgotten…well I'll remind you," said Anaximander, "Rheis went amongst all the ranks of the Wyt King's forces and demanded he relinquish the Autumn Crown to her. When he refused, she faced off against him and, in the height of their battle, the crown abandoned him for Rheis. Do remember why?"

"Enough of this," spat Faceless, "I am not a schoolchild in need of a nursery lesson…"

"It was because the crown recognized Rheis. The soul within, being Rheis' grandmother, compelled it into her hands," said Anaximander, "now imagine what a talisman would do if the spirit within encountered its own body…its own other half."

Arad and Aras stepped forward and put out their hands like they were going to pull an invisible rope in a game of tug-of-war. Their talismans abandoned Faceless and flew through the air, despite her best effort to catch them. The silver staff landed in Aras' waiting grip, while the gold wand went to Arad. They grasped them tightly and were at once rejuvenated, made powerful by the presence of their mighty souls.

"It makes no difference whether the whelps have their toys or not," spat Faceless, "I am still more powerful…I possess my own godly spirit and the power of the One God…"

Faceless summoned a terrible unspoken spell in an attempt to break through the mystical barrier sequestering her from the rest of the living world. But even as her presence grew fearsome and a deep shadow grew in the air around her, the twins moved simultaneously, Aras casting a ray of *pure light* and Arad a wave of absolute darkness, both hitting Faceless square in the chest and causing her to recoil. Meanwhile, while the boys engaged in battle with Faceless, Anaximander ran to Jadzia and healed her wounds so that she could stand again on her own two feet. Then they joined the twins in facing off against Faceless. From afar, the brilliant bursts of black, red, green, and white light looked like celebratory fireworks. Many of the survivors within the city were drawn to the palace out of curiosity but could not cross through the barrier drawn by the power of *The Supreme Conjuration*.

Faceless used the powers at her disposal to manifest two giant hands of fire that reached out and wrenched the twins from the ground in their searing grip. Fortunately the twins were impervious to the effects of fire, a side effect of being born the sons of the Firebrand. They countered with a spell that brought the waters of the only canal within the barrier to rise up and douse Faceless with its cool spray, causing her to release the twins. They scurried back to where Anaximander and Jadzia were standing and all four put forth a spell of forgetting that hit Faceless hard in the face. She was forced dangerously near the edge of the balcony by the weight of the spell and, for a moment it seemed the enchantment would work. Then Faceless put out her hands and the spell dispersed, like a glass hitting the pavement after a four-story drop. The force of her rebuttal was such that Anaximander was forced to envelop the twins, himself, and Jadzia in a powerful psychokinetic shield to avoid being killed by the strength of Faceless' terrifying onslaught.

"There's only one way for this to end, Faceless," said Anaximander.

"With your death," spat Faceless.

"That barrier won't come down until you've been defeated or surrendered...I would prefer the latter."

"The day I surrender will be the day the daemons of hell are unleashed in mass upon the living world," sneered Faceless before throwing another powerful spell in their direction. This one meant to rip their souls violently from their talismans and induce a quick death. Anaximander's psychokinetic shield began to crack from its repeated exposure to Faceless' attacks so he compelled himself to teleport away from the others, coming to stand only feet in front of their enemy.

"I can feel your sister's power flowing through me," he said to Faceless, "And I can hear her thoughts. She wants very much for you to forgive her...she was foolish in her abuses. She says they all were. If you give her a second chance, she'll make it up to you..."

For a split second Faceless let down her guard. The monstrosity of her daemonic visage gave way to one of a frightened child looking frantically for her parents in a crowd. Then she was once again hardened by her own hatred, driven back into the depths of the darkness, and away from any chance of reconciliation with her sister and the others. She flung a powerful curse directly into Anaximander's face, causing him to double over and scream out in agony. When he again stood, the flesh on half his face had dissolved, exposing his musculature and jaw bone. Even in terrible pain, Anaximander found the strength to send a nearly identical curse back at his unsuspecting enemy.

"You have called yourself Faceless for so long," said Anaximander, "It's only fitting that is what you become."

The curse caused Faceless' face to melt, as though it were the wax of a candle left burning overnight. She wailed as her flesh oozed off her bones and her muscles burned away, exposing her skull, absent eyes, attached weakly to the top of her spine. She was unable to speak but telepathically manifested a spell of such magnanimity that it caused the rail of the balcony to crumble and produced a blinding flash of black light. Anaximander was thrown against the wall of the palace with such ferocity that he fell broken to the floor and did not stand again. It was Jadzia who stepped forward to take her turn facing off against her greatest enemy.

"You failed to kill me, mistress," said Jadzia mockingly, "That was a big mistake…"

Jadzia flung a series of large fireballs at Faceless who conjured shields to deflect them, despite her disorientation. The flesh began to regrow on her face as she returned the onslaught with a barrage of lightning bolts, two of which made contact with Jadzia, piercing her flesh and producing festering burns on her shoulder and her lower abdomen.

"Enough of this," spat Faceless as her face finished repairing itself.

She sent a mixture of hexes and curses which telekinetically causing Jadzia to freeze in midstride. Faceless walked over to face her as the twins advanced in defiance.

"I'm not ready for you," sneered Faceless and, with a simple wave of her hand, she send the twins flying off their feet.

Faceless used her powers to cause Jadzia to lurch towards her, hovering just inches off the ground. Jadzia's face was fixed in an apathetic look of revulsion as Faceless reached out and stretched her hands around Jadzia's neck.

"What were you saying, my darling?" asked Faceless, "Something about failing to kill you."

In one swift motion, Faceless squeezed Jadzia's throat so hard that it caused her head to become severed from the rest of her body. Blood spilled relentlessly from the open cavity in Jadzia's neck as the majority of her fell lifeless to the floor. Faceless kept her grip on Jadzia's head, which despite the laws of nature, was still living.

"Any last words?" asked Faceless coldly.

Jadzia turned her eyes towards Arad and, with great labor, sputtered an almost imperceptible phrase.

"I did love you," she wheezed.

Faceless laughed viciously before dropping Jadzia's head to the ground. With a faint smile, the light left Jadzia's eyes and it was apparent it would not return. After 200 years of life, she finally received her long-awaited release, to join her sisters and father in the Otherworld.

Aras looked down at his foster-mother with tears briefly welling up in his eyes before turning towards Faceless with pure, unbridled rage. The air around him ignited into a fiery raptor that grew to engulf the balcony, incinerating the bodies of Jadzia and the Shadow-Weavers in seconds with its immeasurable heat. Aras joined his brother and, taking his hand, caused the bright red fire of the raptor to turn bluish white, while a golden aura emanated from the heart of the creature where the twins stood.

Anaximander awoke soon enough to protect himself with a psychokinetic shield but even he began to experience burns on his arms and his legs. Faceless stood her ground, using the Amulet of the One God to keep the onslaught of heat from piercing her flesh. The twins took on a different look as they advanced towards her. Their skin went milky white and their ears grew long and pointed. Their molten silver eyes glowed with the spark of creation and their hair became one with the flaming raptor reaching outward around them.

"We grow tired of this fight," said the twins in unison with an otherworldly voice that made them seem alien. Faceless laughed as she hurtled a series of curses towards the raptor protecting Aras and Arad. None of her attacks succeeded in penetrating the fires of the celestial creature. The

twins responded with their own spell. In a feat never before achieved by any wizard, they called a meteor shower from the stars to change its course and bear down on Faceless one at a time. The tiny rocks pierced Faceless like bullets, each one tearing a piece of her body away. Ten and then twenty, finally thirty meteors punctured Faceless before she finally fell to her knees and, coughing blood, fell dead to the floor. But the fight was not over.

As her body twitched and wheezed its last breath, Faceless' spirit rose from her corpse in the manner that she used to appear from the poisonous well when it served as her prison. She swooped down to grab the Amulet of the One God from her dead body but the twins used their powers to compel the necklace into Anaximander's care. Anaximander didn't put the amulet around his neck. Instead, he pointed his staff at it and, with an echoing voice, he spoke a spell in the Old Language.

"Rwy'n rhyddhau chi Theis duw y byr..."

There came a sound like the shattering of a thousand plates as the crimson ruby of the amulet cracked. A bright orange light spilled out of the fissure and took on the form of a man of average height with a balding head and long gray beard. He locked his translucent brown eyes on the apparition of Faceless with a grimace.

"Hello, Tsira," he said with a soft, warm voice.

"Theis," replied Faceless and, for the first time that day, she looked genuinely frightened. The ghostly One God floated over to her and she recoiled from his presence like a rat turning tail and running from an ensuing feline. The One God reached out and grabbed her shoulder, forcing her to turn and face him.

"I am not angry with you," he said, "You did as you felt you must to heal the hurts inflicted upon you by our kin. It's the same reason I remained behind when the rest of you moved on to the Otherworld. I see the folly in my choices now, just as I see yours. It's time for us to move on, Tsira. It's time to go home."

Faceless looked at the One God with narrowed eyes, judging each of his words with cynicism and suspicion. He left her there to ponder her choices and floated over to Anaximander.

"I am going to need that," said the One God, pointing at Anaximander's staff.

Anaximander stared at his oaken staff for a few moments before handing it to the One God. The instant it touched the One God's ghostly hand, it burst into ash and the apparition of Faceless' sister, Selena, appeared next to the One God. She looked back at Anaximander with gentle eyes as if to say thank you. Then she and the One God returned to where Faceless was floating, pondering her choices.

"What of it, sister?" said Selena, "Are you ready?"

Faceless nodded meekly in submission.

Selena nodded compassionately at her sister and then turned to face Anaximander.

"I must warn you, old friend," she said, "I feel something is not right. The damage brought by my sister's spell was not wholly undone."

"Do you know what it is we should fear?" asked Anaximander.

"No," replied Selena, "But whatever it is, it's dangerous."

Anaximander pondered Selena's warning as she floated over and took her sister's hand. Faceless then took the One God's hand and, in a shower of pure white light, they vanished, returning to the palace on the distant shores of the Otherworld to rejoin the other gods and goddesses. Anaximander dropped the broken Amulet of the One God on the ground while the twins allowed the fiery raptor to extinguish. They released each other and joined Anaximander. Without the threat of Faceless, *The Supreme Conjuration* was broken and the giant shimmering dome surrounding the Palace of Silver Light dissolved. The surviving citizens of the Eternal City crossed the gates of the palace and soon were overwhelming Anaximander and the twins.

Aras went at once to find Gyrdhan and Darendon while Aras stayed close to Anaximander. The devastation done by the battle with Faceless was beyond horrific. The walls of the Eternal City were completely gone. The canals were filled with the blood of palace guards, the wizards, and the Knight of the Old Guard, as well as scores of peasants. The paved streets of the city looked more like a battlefield than the center of the greatest metropolis in the history of the living world.

Aras searched the courtyard like an inspector checking picture frames for dust. He grew more concerned with each passing moment as he failed to find either his foster-father or his best friend. He did find Xavin, kneeling over the bloated corpse of Valera, who'd been run through by a long spear. Aras didn't stop to speak to Xavin. He was on a mission and wouldn't be deterred. He finally found Gyrdhan near the walls separating the courtyard from the small market avenue beyond. He had a large gash on his forehead and was severely bruised. But he was alive. Aras jumped into his arms and hugged him tightly.

"I'm so glad you're alright," said Aras with a smile.

"Is it over?" asked Gyrdhan.

"It's over," replied Aras.

"Thank the Gods," exclaimed Gyrdhan, "I was 'fraid it was never gonna end…are ya alright?"

"I will be. Have you seen Darendon?"

"I'm so sorry, Ari, he didn'a make it," said Gyrdhan sadly.

"No…you're lying," said Aras, "What happened to him? Where is he, Gyrd?"

"His father took his body on 'a cart outta the city 'bout ten minutes ago," said Gyrdhan, "He's takin' him home to be buried. He was struck down by 'a stray arrow."

Aras ran away from Gyrdhan and back towards the palace, unable to think straight. He had lost the person he loved the most in the living world.

He didn't know how or if he wanted to continue. Then, he saw his brother and Anaximander walking towards him, a mob of peasants at their back. When he looked at Arad, Aras remembered that Arad lost his foster-mother. He had the same look of sadness and, in some strange way, it brought Aras some relief as he went to join them in their triumphant march through the remaining districts of the city, calling its inhabitants to come forth in jubilation and rejoice that Faceless and her Matriarchs were gone forever.

Chapter Twenty-One
"Divergence"

Anaximander, Gyrdhan, and the twins remained in Atlantis for a fortnight, residing in the Palace of Silver Light and spearheading the efforts to restore some semblance of order and beauty to the once fair city. The New Nobility consecrated under the rule of Faceless and the Matriarchs fled the city while the statues of the Nameless Goddess were torn down. The Temple of the One God in the Fifth District remained open to those who chose to continue his worship but all other laws and locations associated with the religious tetrarchy were dismantled. The Old Nobility, the few remaining members of the Wizarding Clans, and the followers of the Old Religion were welcomed back into the city and, with their efforts, the bodies were removed from the streets and the waterways were washed clean. A council came together daily in the palace to discuss the future of Atlantis and Albion but a consensus on any one plan was difficult to reach.

"We have had many forms of government in the Eternal City," said an old man known as Lord Oredd Anrikou, "and none have yet been free from tyranny."

"Wrong," said a Green Robe named Eadren, "The Wyt Robes were not tyrants…"

"Neither were the Wyt Kings for that matter," interjected a nobleman called Sir Regan of Tec.

"Some would disagree," countered Eadren, "and besides…the line of House Kalenti is extinct. Who is it you propose be named King?"

"It was the wandering wizard who saved us…I say Anaximander should be our king," said a noblewoman named Lady Teana, "If he would be willing to accept such an honor."

"I would not," said Anaximander from the head of the table, "and it was not me who saved Albion…it was the twins, Aras and Arad."

Aras and Arad were sitting uncomfortably at the back of the room. Neither one had participated in the daily debates, nor had they taken any interest in the establishment of a new government. They were present only at Anaximander's insistence. The council turned to look at the twins, who in turn stared at the floor.

"I don't believe it is the destiny of the twins to become kings," said Anaximander, drawing the attention of the council back to him.

"Besides, there are many of us here who would rather die than see a return of the monarchy," said a nobleman named Lord Drax, "I say it's time for Atlantis to become a Republic."

"I agree," said another nobleman.

"As do I," said Eadren.

"Then it seems we may have stumbled upon a solution," replied Anaximander to the outcry of the council, "It may be in the best interest of the people for this very council to rule on their behalf. Take up these chairs daily and bring all to hear your words under the roof of the palace. Encourage the people, give them rights through decrees, and always hold true to justice. There can be no greater law."

Anaximander rose from his chair and left the room with the twins on his heels. They were all sharing the largest of the royal suites in the palace with Gyrdhan, who was busy preparing an evening meal when they returned. Anaximander sat down by the fire and lit his pipe, while Aras and Arad joined Gyrdhan at the little nook serving as his kitchen. They hadn't talked about all their losses. The deaths of Jadzia and Darendon were wounds best left untouched until better healed.

The small company ate their meal in silence before deciding it was time to retire for the evening. Anaximander slept in the main bed, while Gyrdhan slept on a fluffy bearskin carpet near the fire. The twins shared the featherbed positioned at the back of the large room, near to a set of small windows. Aras fell into the bed and was asleep in no time, while Arad sat there staring out the windows at the moonless sky.

When he was confident that everyone was fast asleep, Arad rose from the bed and grabbed his robes, pulling them silently over his head and fastening a traveling cloak over them. He produced a small rucksack from its hiding spot behind the dresser and slung it over his back before tiptoeing out of the suite and down the adjacent passage. He was just about to reach the stairs leading down and out of the palace when Aras caught up.

"Where are you going?" said Aras drowsily.

"I'm going back to the Red Tower," answered Arad coldly, "to Araxim and the other Grey Robes."

"But…"

"But nothing," snapped Arad, "I don't belong here. I never did. The Autumn Duchess may claim the Shadow-Weavers washed my soul clean but I don't feel it. All I feel is hate. I hate this place, I hate that wizard, and I hate you. I can't be here. You're not going to stop me."

"I wasn't going to try," replied Aras.

Arad didn't respond. He just walked off and disappeared down the stairs. Aras watched out the window as Arad emerged on the grounds a few minutes later, walking towards the perimeter marked by a small wall. When he was on the other side, he vanished with a burst of black light. Aras sighed gently and then returned to his bed.

The following morning, Aras rose before everyone else and went to the balcony overlooking the courtyard where their battle took place with Faceless. He cried endless tears as he remembered his best friend and companion. Darendon was with him for years. They grew up together. Now he was dead and Aras was alone.

"This will be a sad place for years to come," said Anaximander as he emerged on the balcony.

"Arad is gone," said Aras simply.

"I know," replied Anaximander, "I heard him leave."

Aras used the sleeve of his silver robes to dry his eyes and turned to face Anaximander.

"Are we going to stay here?" asked Aras, "Are you going to stay?"

"I wasn't planning on it," replied Anaximander.

"Well, wherever you're going, I'm going with you."

"I don't know, Aras…you should return home with Gyrdhan. Make a peaceful, quiet life for yourself in the mountains."

"I think we both know that isn't my future," said Aras.

Anaximander nodded at Aras in recognition of his words. The wizard knew the truth about the twins: even though they fulfilled the prophecy and brought temporary peace to the living world, the ominous words of Selena were hanging over their head. Something wasn't right in Albion. Anaximander could feel it and he meant to seek it out.

"We leave tomorrow," said Anaximander.

Aras didn't tell Gyrdhan anything. Just before sunrise the next morning, just like Arad, he slipped out of the suite with Anaximander at his side. By the time the sun rose over the eastern horizon, Aras and Anaximander were already out to sea. They procured a small longboat with sails from a local merchant and set a course towards open water. Once they were out of sight of the Atland shore, Anaximander turned the boat south and fixed the helm so they wouldn't waver from their course.

"Do you know where we're going?" asked Aras after eating a dinner of fresh fish and boiled rice.

"Not really," smiled Anaximander.

"That's reassuring," said Aras mockingly..

"I can feel something, like a discordant vibration," said Anaximander, looking out over the water, "the closer we get the stronger the feeling. We'll let that be our compass."

"What's it feel like to not have your staff anymore?" asked Aras while looking at the staff resting in his lap.

"I've lived much of my life without a staff," replied Anaximander.

"Aren't you afraid you won't be powerful enough to face what comes next?" asked Aras.

"Not in the least. What about you?"

"I have my staff."

"Yes," said Anaximander, "but you don't have Arad."

"I don't need Arad."

Aras turned away from the wizard and glared out over the water, unwilling to admit the truth. He missed his brother. Arad was never warm or loving but he was Aras' blood. They were identical in nearly every way and their powers worked in harmony, complimenting one another to create their celestial creature: The Fire Raptor. Without Arad, Aras would not be able to reach his maximum potential and that thought scared him.

They continued on their southern journey for nearly a week before they came to the Isle of Walweitha, the very place where Aras was raised. The villages on the island were wholly unaffected by Faceless' spell to merge the three worlds into one. They stayed at Gyrdhan's inn, though Gyrdhan wasn't there, before setting out again on the sea. Anaximander positioned the boat towards the east and a powerful wind carried them across the calm water like a dolphin swimming through the waves.

"I hope you're not headed to Lemuria," said Aras, "Word in Atlantis is that it's gone."

"We're not going to Lemuria," replied Anaximander, "We are making our way to the Easterling Isles. A man in Walweitha told me a story about strange winged creatures flying through the air at twilight, terrorizing passersby and being all around mischievous. It's worth investigating."

Aras accepted Anaximander's answer and laid down at the bough of the boat. He fell into a light sleep despite it being midday but he was awakened only moments later by the sound of wood grinding on rock. He sat bolt upright and looked towards Anaximander. The boat was caught on a small outcropping of rocks, while three creatures hovered above the boat snickering. They looked like a cross between a human and a moth, with arms and legs and large, colorless wings. However, before Anaximander or Aras could conjure a spell against the creatures, they shapeshifted into sea lions and swam away.

"What in the name of the Old Gods was that?" asked Aras.

"Faeries," replied Anaximander.

"I thought faeries were a myth," said Aras.

"In this world they are. They live in Avalon, the world between Albion and the Otherworld. But they've been extinct for years."

"Clearly they're not."

Anaximander used his magic to lift the boat out of the water. It took to the air like an eagle soaring through the heavens, traveling hundreds of times faster than when it was ocean bound. In only a few hours, they reached the shores of the Easterling Isles. Anaximander set the boat down near the largest of the islands, called Utukari, and they quietly disembarked. Causing the boat to fly through the air was extremely hard on Anaximander, leaving him fatigued and slow. He decided it was unwise for them to go any further until he created a new talisman for himself.

"Now's not the time," demanded Aras.

"It's the perfect time," said Anaximander, "I know a place nearby where we can rest, replenish our supplies, and prepare for what comes next. If the faeries are here, they can pose a very serious risk to the world. There normally fairly harmless, mostly just mischief makers, but they can be angered and then they are fearsome."

Anaximander led Aras inland to a small range of mountains called the Douhija Rohi in the easterling language, to a village called Horadvoblaka. Anaximander knew a young merchant named Piory Jarkija. Piory provided them with food, water, and wool to make clothes. He also gave Anaximander a long piece of white birch that Anaximander carried on his back as they left the village and entered the Douhija Rohi. They walked for a day before arriving at a small cavern, its entrance hidden by a series of thorny brambles. Anaximander led Aras inside and started a small fire. Anaximander laid out the provisions before turning his attention towards the long piece of white birch. He spent a day sculpting the birch with his knife and inscribing it with a series of runes written in the Old Language. Then he fell into a deep meditative state from which Aras couldn't revive him. For three days and three nights, Anaximander remained in his state of nonbeing, focusing the will of his spirit into his newly crafted birch staff. It had been many years since he'd attempted to invoke the powers of spirit-magic and, though he'd taken up residence in a new, young and athletic body, his soul was very old and the process could prove fatal.

While Anaximander meditated, Aras was faced with problems of his own. He'd never learned how to properly cook a meal over an open fire, nor was he accustomed to gathering fruits and herbs in their foreign surroundings. The water tasted bitter with minerals and the air was extremely humid, so that he couldn't stop sweating. The first night of Anaximander's nonbeing was fairly uneventful. Aras ate a small meal of overcooked pork and undercooked beans before nestling into his blankets near the fire. Strange howls and the sound of crickets filled the night but nothing came close enough to the cavern to cause Aras any alarm.

The second night was somewhat more disturbing. As Aras reheated leftover pork and beans, three small foxes appeared in the opening of the cavern. They blinked knowingly at Aras and then took note of Anaximander's strange meditative position, the white birch staff in his lap. With a few grunts to each other, the foxes turned around and disappeared through the thorny brambles. The second night, they returned and entered the cavern, coming within arm's length of Aras before scurrying away. Aras found it strange that a bunch of foxes would take such interest in him. He ignored the peculiarity of the moment and returned to his chores. He was getting the hang of providing for himself. After a sound sleep, he took a long walk through the mountain passes and foraged for wild berries. He ate some pork jerky he smoked himself before returning to the cavern in time for the sun to set. He expected his fox friends to return again but instead was greeted by something entirely different.

A tall woman with a taut body wearing a thin slip of white silk appeared in the entrance to the cavern, her platinum blonde hair pulled into a ponytail behind her back. She was wearing a necklace with a strange blue stone dangling from it and she stared at Aras with fierce green eyes as the three foxes scurried into the cavern and came to stand behind her, only they weren't really foxes. With a slight shiver, they shapeshifted into the same faeries Aras and Anaximander saw while in their boat. The woman smiled warmly at Aras just as Anaximander awoke from his long trance, successful in transferring his soul into the white birch staff. He stood and straightened his robes before realizing he and Aras were not alone in the cavern. He stared intently at the intruder in recognition.

"I know your face," he said.

To Be Continued in...

$\mathcal{F}ae$

Book Two of *"The Tales of Albion Trilogy"*

Epilogue
"From the Queen of Fae"

"I was once the most powerful woman in the living world. The mere mention of my name caused even the stoutest warrior to cringe. I came to my throne through deceit and death but I held onto it with my own fortitude and cunning. I fought against wizards, fallen goddesses, and otherworldly minions. I transformed the colloquial hamlet Atlantis into a world power, into the Eternal City. I commanded undead armies and brought the darkest bastions of the Art to realization. I rose high and I fell low, but my life was mine to live. I was the mistress of my own destiny and none bore the power to hold me down. Then I died."

"I was led by the mortal road into the heart of the Otherworld, to take up residence in the Golden City as all men and women must after they have drawn their last breath. Yet, even as I moved towards that glorious city, I knew it was not my fate to dwell within its walls. I was still meant for greatness. There was something more for me to accomplish. I didn't know what it was but I knew if I entered Elnurea that future would be closed to me forever. I did the only thing I knew how to do. I made war against the old friend guiding me towards the city, despite his warnings of dire consequences for any who dare break the law of the Old Gods and bring violence to the Otherworld. I did not care. Not until I was being lifted off the ground by a mighty elemental and deposited beneath the waters of the River Lethe, where all lost souls dwell in the deeps. The river was said to be inescapable and I fought against it for an unknown span of years. Finally, with the ferocity of my spirit, I broke free and rose to the surface."

"It was not the shores of the Otherworld onto which I washed up but the banks of that place between places known in the living world as

Avalon. It was rumored there were inhabitants of Avalon but they long ago disappeared, leaving the network of islands and hillocks void of life, a haunting place where I encountered only the occasional spirit moving from Albion to the Otherworld. I know not how many long years I wandered those hills and valleys alone. Until the destiny I knew I was meant to fulfill finally came to call on me."

"As I traveled through one of the many narrow gullies on the outskirts of Avalon, I stumbled upon a decaying monolith with runes from the Ancient Tongue inscribing it. I moved closer and, when I did, a doorway of brilliant white light opened and the most beautiful creature I have ever seen emerged through it. He called himself Cyndriel, King of the Fae, and bid me step through into his palace. Since I was already dead, any fear I might have felt was nonexistent. I eagerly entered his domain because one of the many things I knew about faeries was they possessed the power to grant immortal life, to return the spirits of the dead wholly to their flesh forever."

"I grew very close to Cyndriel during my stay in the Palace Beyond and he told me all the stories of the Fae. They used to live freely in the fields of Avalon but, after the loss of their queen and her enchanted artifact, the Summerstone, they were forced into the Palace Beyond, imprisoned within its walls until such a time that the Summerstone could be recovered. They still bore the power to change their shape but their magic was severely limited. What I desired would not be found in the Palace Beyond. It was housed inside the Callim Lamp it was pulled into years ago but, a serious problem arose immediately. The Callim Lamp was also home to Cyndriel's mother, the former Queen of Fae."

"I had to choose my path wisely. I knew the secrets of Callim Lamps but I also knew if I opened it, the queen would emerge, in possession of the Summerstone. I had to find a way to ensure the Summerstone would end up in my hands. It took me an untold span of time to figure out the answer was surprisingly simple. I would release the queen from one Callim Lamp and then activate another. As she was pulled from one lamp to the next I would grab the Summerstone and claim it as my own. It was a risky attempt but I succeeded. I became the new Queen of Fae. With the Summerstone around my ghostly neck, I set to work casting the mighty spell that would return me to my flesh forever."

"The spell was slow and painful. I had to rebuild myself piece by piece, bone by bone, muscle by muscle, like a sculptor crafting a statue out of clay with their bare hands. I wanted to look exactly as I did when I walked in the living world, with my platinum locks and my piercingly green eyes, my taut and olive complexion. When at last I finished, I laid down in my creation and became fused with vitality, opening my eyes again as a living, breathing woman. The faeries were amazed by my abilities, a feat never displayed in their long lifetimes. They fell to their knees in supplication and unyielding fidelity, prizing me even above their king. As my gift to them, I opened the doors of the Palace Beyond. The faeries were free to roam the wide ranges of Avalon again, to rebuild all they lost. The faeries took on different forms and hues to amuse me. They raised a grand house amidst a meadow of poppies to serve as my abode and brought me exotic foods that put even the most decadent earthly foods to shame. I had it all: loyal subjects, riches and prestige, a wide land to claim as my kingdom. And I was happy. But all good things must come to an end."

"One morning in the endless summer of Avalon, a daemonic voice rose from the waters of the Deep Lake. It spoke words in the Ancient Tongue and called for the unification of the three worlds. I rose from my throne and peered out the window to see my kingdom unfolding. Reality was being unraveled and I did not possess a single power strong enough to counteract the effects. The wind howled and the sky crackled as my house fell in on itself. The frightened faeries gathered around me and begged for answers. I had none to give them. It was magic I had never seen before, a power beyond my reckoning and my understanding. I was helpless as I watched the waters of the lake boil like they were in a cauldron set atop a fire. The flowers wilted, the grass turned brown, and the mountains collapsed in on themselves. Then, with a bright flash of opalescent light, we were pulled away from Avalon altogether. Or I should say we, and parts of Avalon, were transported and integrated into the living world."

"We emerged on the distant easterling islands, a place I never visited in my former life and, just as the tumults began in violence, they ended in violence. With a powerful earthquake, the parts of Avalon that had come to Albion disappeared. But we remained. The faeries turned again to me for answers and I was about to give up when, as fate would have it, an old friend happened upon my path. Now, I find myself reinvigorated, reminded of the life I once knew, and I know now why we remained in the living world. So that I may rewrite the annals of my life and introduce the world to the power of the Queen of Fae…"

Appendix

- Albion – *The Living World.*
- Anaximander – *The Wandering Wizard and emissary to the Old Gods.*
- Araxim – *Grey Robe Wizard and chief acolyte of the Black Prince.*
- Atlandish – *The language of the Atlandish Men.*
- Atlandish Men – *Men indigenous to the Atland.*
- Atlantis – *The Eternal City raised by the hands of the Elfin Empresses.*
- Avalon – *The Place between Places, indigenous home of the faeries, and crossroads of mortal spirits.*
- Azgarog – *Daemon prince and greatest servant of the Black Prince.*
- Daemons – *Monstrous life forms indigenous to the Void sworn to the service of the Black Prince.*
- Darthonia – *Largest of the Three Cities.*
- Easterling – *Language of the Easterling tribes.*
- Easterling Men – *Tribes indigenous to the Easterling Islands.*
- Faceless – *Leader of the Divine Matriarchs and theocratic ruler of Albion.*
- Faeries – *Changelings indigenous to Avalon.*
- Gnomish-Men – *Miniature versions of men.*

- Knights of the Old Guard – *Elite warriors serving Albion from the time of the Elfin Empresses until the murder of the Wyt Robes.*
- Lemuria – *The Ancient City on the Isle of Mu.*
- Lemurianese – *Language of the Lemurians.*
- Lemurians – *Tribes indigenous to the Isle of Mu.*
- New Nobility – *Aristocracy elevated to nobility under the authority of the Divine Matriarchs.*
- Norn Giants – *Giant versions of men living in the Cradle of the Norn Mountains.*
- Old Nobility – *Aristocracy elevated to nobility in the days of the Wyt Kings.*
- Sarmar – *Oldest of the Three Cities.*
- Sir Elam Orthelios – *Former Knight of the Old Guard and father of the Twins of Prophecy.*
- Spirit-Magic – *The act of removing the spirit and placing it in a talisman to enhance magical potency.*
- Succubuses – *Shapeshifting monsters serving the Matriarch called Faceless.*
- Tansapar – *Once the riches city in the Atland, it was destroyed by the Black Prince, known forever after as the Ruined City.*
- The Absolute Darkness – *Powerful magical essence representing unbridled chaos.*
- The Amulet of the One God – *Godly talisman containing within it the spirit of the deity called the One God.*
- The Ancient Tongue – *Language of Elfkind.*
- The Art – *The refined practice of magic.*

- The Atland – *Continent at the heart of Albion.*
- The Autumn Crown – *Powerful talisman containing within it the spirit of the Elfin Empress Saavika Thirdborn.*
- The Black Prince – *The fallen god, Ragnar.*
- The Black Speech – *Language of the Grey Robes.*
- The Collective – *A collection of spirits residing in the body of Anaximander.*
- The Distant Shore – *Home of the Old Gods on the far side of the Otherworld.*
- The Divine Matriarchs – *Theocratic rulers of Albion.*
- The Dreamland – *Small continent in the far east of Albion.*
- The Easterling Islands – *Island chain near the coast of the Wasteland.*
- The Eastward Ocean – *Ocean to the east of the Atland.*
- The Elfin Lady Rheis – *Lady of the Green City and guardian of the Autumn Crown.*
- The Firebrand – *The Elfin Lady Caenara, mother of the Twins of Prophecy.*
- The Frozenland – *Barren continent to the north of the Atland.*
- The Great Pyramid – *Home of the One God on earth at the heart of Lemuria.*
- The Hordaland – *Continent to the east of the Atland.*
- The Isle of Ikaria – *home of the Green City.*
- The Isle of Mu – *Home of the Ancient City.*
- The Isle of Walweitha – *A small island west of the Atland.*
- The Isles of Tin – *Islands off the coast of the Hordaland.*

- The Marshland Forest – *Swampy forest near the heart of the Atland.*
- The Old Gods – *The pantheon of gods and goddesses who dwelt in Albion before the Elfkind.*
- The Old Language – *Language of the Wyt Robes.*
- The One God – *The god, Theis, who split from the Old Gods when they left for the Otherworld.*
- The Otherworld – *The wide land of the dead beyond the River Lethe and Avalon.*
- The Palace Guards – *Elite soldiers who serve as bodyguards to the Divine Matriarchs.*
- The Palace of Silver Light – *Ancient castle at the center of the Eternal City.*
- The Pure Light – *powerful magical essence representing cosmic perfection.*
- The Red Tower – *Mystical tower at the edge of the Wynterlande Forest. Former home of the elf-sorceress called the Red Witch.*
- The Ring of a Hundred Souls – *Broken talisman that once contained more than a hundred souls, forged by the first Wyt King, Theron Kalenti.*
- The Sea of the Sun – *Ocean west of the Atland known for nearly always being calm.*
- The Shadow-Weavers – *Undead sisters with powerful magic in the service of their only surviving sister, the witch called Jadzia.*
- The Southern Sea – *Ocean to the south of the Atland known for nearly always being turbulent.*

- The Sunland – *Continent to the southwest of the Atland.*
- The Sylveroad Woods – *Forest in the southwest of the Atland. Home to the Uiwen tribes.*
- The Temple Army – *Army of the Tetrarchs, priests of the Temple of the One God.*
- The Twin Rings – *Talismans forged to serve the Twins of Prophecy.*
- The Twins of Prophecy – *Sons of Sir Elam Orthelios and the Firebrand destined to save the world from the forces of darkness.*
- The Wasteland – *Continent to the southeast of the Atland.*
- The Westland – *Continent to the west of the Atland.*
- The Wizarding Clans – *the Wyt Robes, Grey Robes, Red Robes, Green Robes, and Blue Robes.*
- The Wynterlande Forest – *Forest in the northwest of the Atland. Home to the Gnomish-Men and the Wynter Tribes.*
- Vanamar – *Smallest of the Three Cities.*
- Wildermen – *Tribes of the Frozenland.*
- Xani Barbarians – *Tribes of the Hordaland.*

The Old Gods

Ahtarrah, Goddess of the Groves.

Amhir, God of the Winds.

Anara, Goddess of the Mountains.

Annatar, God of Fire.

Araset, God of the Dead.

Audrid, Goddess of Love.

Danu, Goddess of Storms.

Eathir, God of Youths.

Galos, God of the Sea.

Karenthir, God of the Harvest.

Loryn, God of the Frosts.

Lyra, Goddess of Beauty.

Maru, Goddess of the Waxing Moon.

Narenna, Goddess of the Waning Moon.

Nerwyn, God of the Dark Waters.

Nora, Goddess of the Hearth.

Ortheon, God of the Forge.

Raanon, God of Light.

Ragnar, God of Twilight.

Selena, Goddess of the Full Moon.

Tsira, Goddess of the Dark Moon.

Tyrena, Goddess of Elders.

Varos, God of Wisdom.

Yana, Goddess of Virgins.

R.J. Pommarane is proud to have been born and raised in Oregon, discovering the wondrous mysteries of nature at an early age by exploring the woods with his father's family. R.J. graduated from Portland State University in 2008 with a BA in English before going on to attain a MA in Education in 2011. Since then, he has devoted his time to the contemplation of his own resolute spirituality, particularly through the expression of the written word. The author of <u>The Body Chaotic</u>, R.J. currently resides in Portland, OR, with his life-partner, Kevin, and their two cats: Kritty and Shadow-Weaver.

The art of Heather Lewis is developed entirely from her years of creative pursuits and the depths of her imagination. She currently resides in the Pacific Northwest with her husband, Nathan, and three children. She is primarily a stay-at-home mother and wife but dedicates much of her time to her creative endeavors. Her art is inspired mostly by the people in her life and the magic to be found in the serenity of nature.